Hot Alaska Nights

The Northern Fire Series
Book Two

Lucy Monroe

© Lucy Monroe 2019

http://lucymonroe.com

DEDICATION

For my baby sister and BFF, Mona, who wanted to be an actor when she was a teenager and was brilliant on stage. Your dreams have always been glorious and the fact you've gone back to school to pursue new ones makes me so proud! Love you to bits and beyond! And for her wonderful husband, Jason, who has supported and loved my sister like no one else could have. You two ARE a great romance!

CHAPTER ONE

"Incoming!"

The warning came a second before Deborah Banes' seat companion plopped a half-full plastic cup on her small food tray.

Right next to where she'd been tapping away on her tablet.

The strong scent of spirits hit her nostrils as the amber liquid sloshed over the sides, barely missing the minicomputer she'd given up movie nights and her favorite herbal tea at Starbucks for six months to afford.

"Cool it, Carey!" Three hours into the five-hour flight, Deborah's patience with the younger actor was wearing thin.

She couldn't decide if her co-star for the indie film she'd landed her first starring role in at the ripe age of twenty-nine was nervous, excited, or both. She sincerely hoped this was not his natural state. As they travelled together, he had annoyed with enough persistence to give her some serious concerns about the next ten weeks. Regardless of how talented his screen test had shown him to be.

"Lighten up, Debs." His affected English accent slipping, he gave her the winning smile that made the director's second assistant giggle like the school girl she'd left behind decades before.

Deborah gave a mental eye-roll. The man was from Alaska, not the UK. And apparently had the perfect location for filming, which he'd offered the producers in exchange for his role.

Not that it had been put that way to Deborah, but secrets were hard to keep in Hollywood. Talent wasn't everything in this business. Considering what starring opposite Carey James would mean for her career, she was just grateful he had his fair share of it.

She'd made her own deal with the devil to make this film and it wasn't for her credit as primary female lead.

"My name is Deborah," she told him for something like the tenth time.

Carey nodded sagely, alcohol turning his bright eyes hazy. "I know."

"So, maybe, I don't know...could you try and *use* it?"

He laughed like she'd made a joke. "Sure, Debs."

Oh, sheesh. "Carey?"

"Uh huh?"

"Don't you think you should take a nap before we land?" she hinted.

"Plenty of time to sleep later tonight." He winked. "Much later."

She could do without the heavy-handed flirting. If she thought for a second he was really hitting on her, she'd shut him down fast. But he wasn't giving off that vibe. He was what Deborah's first college roommate had called *harmlessly tipsy*.

"Or, you know, right now." She tried appealing to his ego. "You don't want poufy eyes on the first day of filming."

For a brief moment, she thought it was going to work as his expression turned horrified, but it smoothed out a second later. "The camera crew doesn't arrive with the equipment until tomorrow. They'll take at least a day to set up."

"Did you even look at the schedule?" Because the one she'd been emailed indicated preliminary takes were happening the next afternoon.

At least one cameraman with basic equipment had to have flown in with the primary film crew that arrived into Anchorage a couple of days before. The director, Art Gamble, and his assistants were supposed to visit the Cailkirn location today in order to determine initial settings.

Independent films ran on a tighter schedule as well as a *much* tighter budget. Not to mention about a tenth of the crew associated with a blockbuster production. Even so, she thought it was an ambitious schedule. Deborah might have negotiated her way into a tiny production credit and the chance to direct two scenes, but in Art's eyes she was still the actor, not an official part of his team.

According to Carey, who was never loathe to talk about himself, he had given some very detailed specs on the property outside Cailkirn, Alaska. Presumably, Art and his crew were not going in blind. Deborah still wished she was with them.

She'd never expected to go all the way to Alaska for her first break onto the big screen, or for that break to be her way to the other side of the camera.

After another jostle at her elbow that sent more of her untouched drink splashing dangerously close to her tablet, she gave up any hope of adding to her notes on her character. She put the computer safely away.

Deborah tried for a genuine smile for Carey. "Is your family still in Alaska?" It wasn't his fault he was young for his age and she was old for hers.

At least on the inside.

Her skin? Was flawless. Some things were more important than running the dilapidated AC unit in her apartment.

Carey grimaced, his expression turning almost furtive, before it smoothed into his usual smile. "Just my older brother. My sister is going to the San Francisco School of Fine Arts."

"Acting is in the blood, huh?"

"You bet. You've heard of my parents, Georgia Howell and Errol Jepsom."

Okay, so the hokey old stage names ran in the family. "Um, I..." She hated to admit she *didn't* know the pair, but she'd never heard of either actor.

"I guess they were a little older than you."

Ouch. "If they were your parents, that's a good guess."

He smiled, like he hadn't just insulted her. "They made mostly low budget films. Classics really. Mom was like Jamie Lee Curtis."

"She got her start as a scream queen?" Deborah wasn't sure the comparison was an accurate one, even if both women had gotten their start in the industry doing horror films.

Georgia Howell had clearly not parlayed that beginning to major stardom. *Unlike* Jamie Lee Curtis.

"Yeah, but she and dad fell in love, had us kids and well, they died tragically before they got their big break." Carey looked almost defensive. "They did all right though."

"So, is your brother an actor too?"

"No chance. He's got the looks. The name. Rock Jepsom, right? But he's got *no* sense of drama."

Deborah had a feeling Carey had enough dramatic sense for both brothers.

Rock yanked the fifty-pound hay bale down from the stack and carried it to Orion's stall. The large, black Percheron stallion was in the paddock with Rock's gray mare of the same breed, Amanda. He'd planned to ride this morning, but he was too pissed.

He needed to work off some of his anger before mounting a horse, even a calm-tempered one like Orion.

Damn Carey.

It wasn't enough Rock's baby brother had gone to the Lower 48 to follow the same dreams that had killed their parents. No, the idiot had to spend the entire inheritance Rock had built him out of the money their parents left chasing the fantasy.

He probably thought Rock didn't know the money was gone, but seriously? Like he wouldn't have left himself a backdoor to his brother's accounts when he turned over his inheritance. It was because of that backdoor that Carey still had money to go back to university if he wanted to.

Not that Rock would tell the twenty-two-year-old that.

Not after Carey had signed away the use of *Rock's* land as a movie location.

In exchange for a damn *lead* role.

Not that the suits who'd shown up at Rock's gates had said that exactly, but he wasn't an idiot.

And neither was his brother, really, all evidence to the contrary. Carey knew how pissed Rock would be when he found out what his little brother had done.

The boy wouldn't have risked Rock's wrath for anything less than a shot at his big break. The same big break their parents had still been chasing when their plane crashed ten years ago.

Damn it. Rock flaked the hay into Orion's stall with vicious movements.

Just damn it all to hell and back.

He could hear Carey now. *"Please, Rock. You know how important this is to me."*

The little shit was going to be shocked when he realized Rock wasn't falling for it this time.

The execs had been surprised enough when Rock refused them entry to Jepsom Acres. Both times. The director had arrived with his assistant first. When Rock refused to open the gate, he'd left, only to return an hour later with the executive producer. They'd had a hard time believing Carey hadn't told Rock about the deal. Rock wasn't.

It was typical Carey *James* move.

If he'd thought Rock would be too embarrassed or loyal to tell the execs the papers giving them access to his land weren't worth the pulp used to make them, then Carey must have suffered brain damage down there in LA.

Carey and his twin Marilyn's names might still be on the deed, but their combined ownership only totaled twenty percent. Both had opted to accept more money from Rock in exchange for most of their inherited interest in the house and land when they turned twenty-one.

At least Carey hadn't run through that as fast as he had the half-a-million Rock had been forced to turn over to his brother on his eighteenth birthday.

He hadn't wanted to buy his sister and brother out completely. They were family and should know they still had a home, no matter where their wanderlust might take them. Even if their only parent was an older brother.

But he'd needed to know his home was safe from the obsession with *stardom*. Rock had put too much into building a life completely unimpeded by show business. It was a damn good thing he'd done things the way he had.

If he hadn't, he'd have an entire film crew and cast camping out on his front lawn. Now, wouldn't he?

Excitement fizzing like champagne through her, Deborah rolled her suitcase toward the airport exit, her matching (if slightly beat up) carryon stacked on top. It wasn't Carey's full set of London Fog luggage, but she was here for the same chance he was. To star in a film that had all the right elements to launch them both a huge leap forward.

Besides, her battered bags bought at a discount outlet held what she needed and that's all that mattered. At least they did if she'd packed right.

After checking the projected weather reports, Deborah had brought clothes she usually reserved for winter in LA. Still, she wasn't sure the light sweaters meant to be layered over tank tops and T-shirts would be warm enough. Summer came to the Kenai Peninsula, but with the exception of a few days of unpredictable highs, it was nothing like summer in Southern Cali, that was for sure.

Bright neon proclaimed the *Mooselaneous* souvenir shop to her left, saying better than the *Welcome Alaska* sign that she wasn't in LA anymore. The airport's interior renovations were smooth and sleek, but the river stone columns and quirky storefronts fit her image of Alaska to a *T*.

Deborah was smiling, allowing her innate sense of adventure to surface after the long plane ride, as the sound of raised voices drew her attention from her first impression of the state with more landmass than Pluto.

Shocked by the faces that went with the voices, Deborah stopped in the middle of the concourse.

Gesticulating wildly, Carey was talking to the head producer and director.

Deborah couldn't make sense of the two major power people on the film being at the airport right now. Carey, Deborah and the other actors were supposed to take a hired shuttle to Cailkirn.

She knew they were. She even had the driver's name and number to call in case he wasn't waiting for them outside baggage claim.

Art Gamble and Elaine Morganstein were supposed to be on location already. Neither had struck her as the type to come to the airport just to welcome the cast and escort them to the location.

Sure, they might have sent an assistant to do it, but not Art and Ms. Morganstein.

They didn't look happy either.

Ms. Morganstein, a woman in her mid-fifties who'd had undisputed success as a producer in the independent film industry, had her arms crossed and her face set in severe lines. Art, the film's director and another indie film success story, was doing all the yelling.

Carey just looked like he was doing some really fast talking.

None of this spelled a relaxing drive to Cailkirn spent taking in the beauty of the Kenai Peninsula, not if they were all in the same car and Deborah had a sinking feeling that would indeed be the case. She was pretty sure she could write off the evening she'd had planned for settling in with some time to go over the script again too.

Suddenly chilled, she pulled her gray cardigan close. She should be used to this kind of drama (whatever had inspired it) in her volatile industry, but she had to admit it was one of her least favorite aspects to the career she'd chosen.

Other passengers moved around her, reminding Deborah that she was stopped in the direct line of foot traffic. Wishing she could simply pretend she hadn't seen, she forced herself back into movement, but changed her direction toward the little scene playing itself out.

She'd never found avoidance an effective course of action and this? Was too important. She wasn't young and rich like Carey. Deborah's entire future hinged on this role and the success of the movie.

The producer noticed Deborah before the others, a small, but imperious jerk of Ms. Morganstein's head indicating she wanted her female lead front and center.

As she arrived, Deborah heard, "My name is on the deed." Carey's tone implied it wasn't the first time he'd made the claim.

"It better be, Mr. James, or you are done in LA." The director's voice could have crushed rock.

Or a new actor's career.

Deborah found herself shivering again. And *she* wasn't the recipient of Art's stony gaze.

"Is there a problem?" she asked, not sure she wanted an answer, but nevertheless *needing* to know.

"Apparently there is some disagreement as to who is actually the property holder for our location." Ms. Morganstein's voice dripped acid.

Deborah winced with reluctant sympathy for Carey. If he'd screwed this film over, she'd want to kill him, sure. But the person who would come out the worse from this would be Carey James. No question.

"I don't think I understand," Deborah said carefully. "I thought Carey owned the location property."

"I do," Carey said with enough earnestness, she almost believed him.

He was an actor after all.

Ms. Morganstein's eyes narrowed, but she nodded. "Then you'll have no trouble coming with us and reminding your caretaker of that fact."

"He's um not exactly the caretaker," Carey said.

Deborah's stomach clenched with tension. This was not going to be good.

"What exactly is he?" the producer asked icily.

"My brother."

Art snorted with impatience, his brows beetling in his trademark expression. "We gathered that."

"Um, we both own the land. Along with my sister." Carey spoke with clear reluctance.

Deborah was surprised when both the director and producer relaxed. She wasn't feeling relaxed. At all. Carey seemed pleased though, his own shoulders sagging in obvious relief.

"We'll have to remind him of *that* fact then," Art said with palpable satisfaction.

Carey nodded like a bobble head. "You bet, that's what we'll do."

"So long as your name is on the deed, the contract you signed giving us permission to shoot on the property is still valid." Ms. Morganstein's tone had warmed a degree, or two.

"Are you sure about that?" Deborah asked, wishing for just this once she could ignore the practical side of her nature.

But seriously? Property law wasn't universal and it sounded like a legal mess to her.

Ms. Morganstein flicked her hand dismissively. "We'll get the lawyers on it. We may not be a big studio, but I'm sure our legal team will run rings around a provincial Alaskan man from the barely-there town of Cailkirn."

Deborah didn't mention that her research on the town had revealed that Alistair Banning, the reclusive billionaire, was also a citizen of Cailkirn and that while the town was small, it was a significant tourist stop on the cruise routes. She *wasn't* sure small town equaled provincial and Deborah *was* fairly confident provincial *didn't* mean ignorant or easily intimidated.

"Um, yeah." Carey didn't sound too sure either, but neither their head director nor their top producer seemed to notice.

"Okay, change in plan." Ms. Morganstein uncrossed her arms and started walking, talking as she covered the distance to the exit swiftly. "We go directly to the location and get this matter cleared up. Every hour it remains unresolved is costing us money."

"All of us?" Deborah asked.

"I don't think the entire cast and crew needs to descend on the poor man. I'm sure having the two primaries, the director, producer and our assistants will be enough."

Deborah felt like she was supposed to pity *the poor man*, but something in Carey's expression said he didn't think the six of them were a match for his brother.

Well, wasn't that just lovely?

Her first big role and it was in jeopardy before they'd even started rehearsals.

CHAPTER TWO

Rock wasn't surprised by the buzzing at the gate. He'd been more surprised by the fact the movie suits hadn't come back before now. Besides, he'd been expecting Carey.

The younger man had called last week to say he was coming for a visit. The fact he hadn't mentioned that the visit included using Rock's land as a film location was beside the point.

Carey might only own ten percent of it, but Jepsom Acres was still his home and as much as Rock might be tempted to tell his little brother to get lost right now, he wasn't going to. If those movie people were with him, they were fair game though. The video camera at the gate only showed Carey standing beside a large dark SUV. The tinted windows didn't reveal who was driving, or if there were others in the truck.

Rock pressed the intercom. "Yeah?"

"You know it's me, Rock." His brother glared up at the camera. "Open the gate."

"You forget your remote access?"

"It's in the bottom of my suitcase."

"Maybe you should dig it out then." Oh, yeah. He was pissed and if Carey didn't realize it, that ought to do it.

"Rock, I've got people here with me. Stop being a dick and open the gate." Carey's frustration came through the intercom loud and clear.

Rock bit back a suggestion about what Carey could do with his attitude. He was thirty-two, not twelve. No matter how mad he was at his brother. It was his job to set the example. It always had been, for all the good it had done him.

He pressed the button to release the gate.

A minute later, Rock watched from the wraparound porch as the large black rental SUV came to a halt in front of his home. The doors opened and the two suits who had tried to gain entrance to his land before stepped out from the front. Carey climbed out of the back, his hair dyed black, his clothes trendy and his smile nervous as hell.

Rock rejected his initial instinct to protect his baby brother like he'd been doing his whole life and didn't let any of his own emotions show on his face. No matter what, he was happy to see his brother, but he was pissed too. Both emotions were for private consumption only.

Unless things got out of hand and then well, the pissed was going to show in a way that wasn't going to make any of these *cheechakos* comfortable.

He frowned to himself. The term for newcomers to Alaska fit these people, though tourist might be better. They didn't plan on staying, now did they?

His muscles tight with tension he would not reveal, Rock leaned with deceptive negligence against the square verandah pillar nearest the top of the steps. He waited in silence for Carey and his posse to come to him.

Movement on the other side of the SUV caught Rock's gaze, though. The beautiful dark-haired woman stepping down had a face as smooth as porcelain, but eyes the exact shade of his favorite dark chocolate reflected fatigue and worry. Nothing in the perfect oval of her features said she was happy, or wanted to be there.

Dammit to hell. Carey hadn't just screwed Rock over with this stunt.

She came around the car, her body moving with elegant grace that made Rock hard just watching. Shock coursed through him at his instant reaction to the woman.

She wore an open gray sweater over a white top, a gray, white and pink print scarf settled stylishly around her neck and snug pink jeans tucked into brown riding boots. The outfit was not overtly sexual, but on her, it was hot as hell and gave him all sorts of ideas about peeling back her layers.

Her boot heels weren't as high as the other woman's power stilettos, but the beauty stood at least an inch taller, making her maybe eight to nine inches shorter than Rock's own six-foot-four.

His favorite height difference for his bed partners.

He couldn't even pretend not to know where that thought had come from. Despite his simmering anger, Rock's libido had woken with the first glimpse of her espresso brown hair.

Well, shit.

He did not date women in the business.

Not that sex always meant dating.

"Rock!" Carey's insistent tone and volume was impossible to ignore.

Dragging his gaze back to his brother, if not his full attention, Rock asked, "What?"

"Aren't you going to invite us in?"

"You don't need an invitation."

Carey nodded and led his little group up the stairs and past Rock. The middle-aged woman and young man who had been in the far back seats of the SUV followed last.

Rock didn't hesitate to break in between them and the beauty, walking beside her across the porch and then allowing her inside his home ahead of him.

He inhaled her scent as she walked by, his dick responding instantly to the subtle musk mixed with a wisp of spring flowers. He had always appreciated a woman who didn't drench herself in perfume, but none had ever caught his senses in a vice like this one.

He wanted to press her up against the entry wall and bury his nose in that sexy place where a woman's neck met her shoulder and just inhale. What he wanted to do after was a lot earthier.

Carey had gone directly into the living room, he and the two suits already seated by the time Rock walked in behind the woman wreaking havoc with his focus and libido.

"Rock, this is Elaine Morganstein, executive producer and Art Gamble." Carey indicated the two suits with his hand. "The director on my current film."

Rock nodded his acknowledgement but wasn't about to lie and say he was pleased to meet the two.

When Gamble didn't bother to stand up to shake Rock's hand and Ms. Morganstein merely gave him half a smile, he didn't regret that lack either.

Momentarily dismissing them, he turned to the beauty who had yet to sit down. "And you are?"

"Deborah Banes, your brother's co-star." She put her hand out.

He took it without hesitation. "Pleased to meet you, Deborah."

Her almost grimace said she very much doubted that and he appreciated the honesty of her reaction enough to grace her with a rare smile. "What do you think of Alaska?"

"What I've seen so far is beautiful, fascinating...I hope I'll get to stay long enough to get a real impression."

He inclined his head, surprised by his instant mental agreement with that hope. After a lifetime's habit, he managed to keep his thoughts to himself, though.

He hadn't let go of her hand and she hadn't tried to pull away. He liked that. Using that connection, he led her to the matching distressed leather sofa facing the one on which Carey sat.

Deborah perched on the edge of the cushion and Rock took the other end, leaving the two seats beside Carey for the as-yet unnamed guests in his home.

Rock gave Carey a pointed look. He'd taught his brother better manners.

Carey managed to look abashed and breezy at the same time, while introducing the director's assistants. He remembered the twenty-something man from the director's initial visit. The older woman was new, though.

"Carey, are you going to offer your guests refreshments?" Rock asked in the awkward silence that had fallen after the overlooked introductions.

"Is Mrs. Painter still here?"

"Why wouldn't she be?"

"I don't know. I just..."

"It's not the weekend. She's here."

"Great." Carey jumped up. "I'll ask her to make coffee."

"You do that."

Ms. Morganstein watched the interaction between Rock and his brother with narrow-eyed interest. The director was too busy looking around the living room with unmistakable avarice to notice anything else but the space.

Rock wasn't worried the man was planning to rob him. No, he was seeing location, location, location.

Shit.

"I hope this indicates you are in a more reasonable frame of mind today." Ms. Morganstein swept her hand out, indicating them all sitting civilly in his home.

"My brother brought guests to my home. That got you in the door, it didn't guarantee you access to my property or my home."

"His home too."

"Yes."

She smiled, her eyes flashing with definite triumph. "He said his name is on the deed."

"It is."

"So, our contract stands."

"What contract might that be?"

"The one we told you about yesterday," she said with some asperity. "When you refused us entrance to the property."

"Did you send a copy of that contract to my lawyer for my signature and I don't know about it?"

"What? No. We were unaware that Carey James wasn't the only owner of the property." Her tone said she didn't like admitting that little fact.

"Carey *James* doesn't own shit. Carey Jepsom's name is on the deed to my land."

"You are playing with semantics. Your brother is co-owner of this land and as such, legally able to enter into contractual obligations relating to it."

Deborah made a soft sound beside him and he guessed she wasn't as sure as her boss.

Carey walked back into the room right then, so Rock directed his comments to the younger man. "Tell your producer what percentage of Jepsom Acres you *own*, Carey."

"You said it would always be my home."

"Did you want to move back in?"

"Of course not!"

"Then that point is moot."

"Not exactly, Mr. Jepsom. Your brother's claim to this home is exactly what we are discussing."

"My brother accepted a significant amount of money from me when he turned twenty-one, in exchange, he relinquished everything but a ten percent interest in the property. I own eighty percent of Jepsom acres and that number increases while Carey's decreases with every improvement I make that increases the value of the property which he does not participate in materially."

He watched calmly as the arrogant satisfaction faded just a bit in both the director (who was now paying his undivided attention to the discussion) and the producer's expressions.

"I knew it," Deborah said under her breath.

Rock shifted his gaze to her. "Knew what, Miss Banes?"

"Deborah, please."

He nodded and waited for her to answer.

She flicked a gaze to Carey and then her producer and director. Rock wasn't surprised when she shook her head instead of answering.

"Percentages aren't the only important element in a contract like this," the director said with the authority of a man used to talking out of his ass and expecting others not to notice.

"I promise you, it's all that matters with this one."

"I'm not sure a judge would see it that way."

Carey made a familiar sound. He wasn't happy, but he didn't know how to fix something when smothering it with charm didn't work.

Rock fixed his little brother with a look he'd had to develop raising two younger siblings after their parents died. "You plan to try to sue me for use of my property, Carey?"

"I don't think it needs to come to that," Carey said weakly.

"Oh, it most certainly will if you don't find your way toward some semblance of reason," Ms. Morganstein said, like she thought the threat would intimidate him.

Rock didn't intimidate easily. "You are welcome to take this to court, ma'am, but I guarantee you'll be wasting both time and money best spent on finding another location for your movie."

"You're prepared for an expensive legal battle?" she asked in a tone that said she was sure he wasn't.

He looked around his own living room and out the large picture window at the manicured landscaping and well-maintained drive beyond. "What about my home gives you the impression I do not have the resources to grind your fancy LA lawyers into the Alaskan dirt?"

She jerked back in her chair, her mouth falling open.

"Have you even looked into Alaska real estate values, ma'am?"

He wasn't above enjoying the way she winced every time he used the word ma'am. She didn't like being referred to by a word that implied she was older than him. His mother had always hated it.

"I assure you being a big man in a small town doesn't buy you much when our so-called fancy lawyers come to town."

Irritated and done with the conversation, Rock stood up. "How about this, *ma'am*? I'll give you my lawyer's card. You have your people contact him and then you decide if *you* think it's worth pursuing this."

He crossed the room, intending to go to his office and get the card.

"Go with him," he heard the director hiss from behind Rock.

He was shocked when the person who caught up with him in the hall was Deborah, not Carey. "What they hell? Why did they send you with me?"

"I don't know."

Rock automatically adjusted his stride to accommodate the woman who'd sent his libido into overdrive. "Your bosses made a mistake signing that contract with Carey and not bothering to check the title before bringing everyone up here."

"I know."

"They don't seem like idiots."

Deborah made a sound between laughter and impatience. "Your brother can be very convincing."

"He gets that charm from our father."

"What about you?"

"What?"

"Where did you get your stubbornness from?"

He turned to face her as they came into his office. "According to my mother, it was her dad. He still runs a ranch in Texas."

He'd never met his grandparents until after his parents died. The Jepsoms had passed on by then, but his mother's people still lived in Texas.

He liked to tease his granddad about their baby-sized state claiming a couple, three of them would fit in Alaska's borders. While the truth was that Alaska covered two-point-three times the square miles of Texas, his granddad always argued. The old man swore better than lifelong Cailkirn resident Norris MacKinnon when Maisie wasn't around to hear.

"Why do you live in Alaska then?"

"It's home." And he'd had enough never knowing where that was in his younger years.

She ran her hand along the solid bookshelf he'd commissioned from Natural Furnishings. "Carey's home too."

Norris MacKinnon had built the office suite himself and Rock was proud of the solid furniture. It wasn't anything like the pressboard crap his parents usually bought because they never planned to stay in any one place very long.

"When it's convenient for him to think so, yeah."

"He loves Jepsom Acres with a sincerity he doesn't show everything else." *Even acting*, her words implied.

Rock wouldn't say how much he liked hearing that.

The woman turned him on unexpectedly and completely, but she wasn't his confessor. Or a friend.

Rock grabbed the law firm's business card and turned to face Deborah. "I'm still not sure what you're doing here."

"I'm in Cailkirn to make a movie." Her smile was soft, but her tone held a certain level of hardness he respected.

"I get that, but why did your director send you with me right now? To babysit me?"

A cynical look came over Deborah's features, making him wonder if she was older than the very early twenties that she looked. "I'm pretty sure babysitting wasn't what they had in mind."

"They noticed how I reacted to you." And weren't above using whatever or *whom*ever they needed to get what they wanted.

The question was: Was Deborah amenable to being used?

Her laugh was laced with genuine humor. "I'm pretty sure a blind man would have and those two are sharks in the water."

Carey was the only one who might begin to realize how unexpected that was, but Rock doubted his baby brother paid enough attention to have connected those particular dots.

"You don't look offended."

"I'm not."

He narrowed his eyes. "You looking back?"

"You're pretty direct."

"Subterfuge is not my thing." He stepped closer to her, the electricity arcing between them.

Her breath caught. "Not like your brother."

"Carey will work any angle to catch his big break." Though out-and-out lying? That was something new.

Had his baby brother changed so much in the four years since he left Cailkirn?

Deborah looked up at Rock, her voice coming out soft and shivering along his nerve endings. "He says your parents were in the business."

"They were." The ability to be single-minded was a family trait and right now, Rock's was set on the woman in front of him.

"Then he comes by it naturally."

Deborah couldn't have said anything more effective to throw a wash of cold water over his sexual desire.

Rock stepped back. "He could have followed my example."

"You don't like the fact he's an actor." She studied him, like she was trying to understand.

He didn't figure she'd be in Alaska long enough.

He turned toward the door. "No."

It was time to get back to the others and end this farce. No matter how he reacted to this woman, he couldn't afford to forget that she was from Carey's world, not Rock's.

Deborah laid her hand on his arm, stopping him from walking out of the office. "He's still welcome in your home."

And just like that, from a single, small connection, reason flew out the window and desire wreaked havoc with Rock's heart rate and breathing.

Doing his best not to let her see the effects such a simple touch had on him, he faced her again. "I've been taking care of Carey and Marilyn since Mom brought them home from the hospital."

"You couldn't have been that old." A gaze as warm and delicious as chocolate sauce asked him the question her words hadn't.

Rock shrugged. "I was the *oops* baby. Marilyn was planned ten years later. Her twin, Carey, was the surprise that time."

His parents had wanted a daughter. They'd gotten another son too, but one who fit their version of a family better than Rock ever had. And they'd had ten-year-old Rock to help take up the slack with his younger siblings.

"Still, ten is pretty young to be taking care of a baby." Her tone said she thought he might be exaggerating things a little.

He wished, and not for the first time, that he was. "My parents put their careers first, last and always. You know the hours your industry demands."

"I do. You had to have had a nanny."

"Sometimes." And that was all he was going to say about that. "Did you do it on purpose?"

"What?"

He backed her toward the wall, stopping only when their bodies were separated by less than a breath. "Avoid answering my question."

"I *was* looking back." Her voice was laced with the same desire heating his blood, but her expression reflected uncertainty.

Rock nodded. "Good to know."

"Is it?" she asked.

"Definitely."

"You don't mind I'm supposed to be your incentive to fall into line?"

"I'm more interested in knowing if it bothers you to *be* the incentive?"

"Who said I was?" She slid away from him and stopped at the door. "I'm an actor, not an escort."

With that, she turned smartly on her heel and left his office.

Damn, he enjoyed her spirit and he liked even more that she didn't automatically fall in with her bosses' evident plans to entice Rock into cooperation.

Rock couldn't deny enjoying the way Ms. Morganstein's mouth

pinched in consternation as she took his lawyer's card.

She silently handed it to the director, who cursed. "*These* are your lawyers?"

"Yes."

The director's expression turned crafty. "What, they file your business paperwork with the state?"

"Among other things."

"Is it your company's name on the deed, or your own?" Ms. Morganstein asked.

"Mine."

She smiled. "I think you'll find putting them on personal retainer is a bit more than you expect it will be."

"They already are." Exasperated by their ignorance, he stared at Carey. "What have you told them about me?"

"Nothing."

"I can tell."

"Why don't you tell us what your brother hasn't?" Gamble invited, all jovial.

"I already did." But the film people hadn't been listening. Typical. His parents had been damn good at only hearing what they wanted too. "He doesn't have enough vestment to make any kind of legally binding agreement regarding Jepsom Acres without my approval."

"What's the name of your company?" the producer asked crisply.

"Does it matter? I told you it's not on the deed to my land."

Mrs. Painter arrived with the coffee tray.

"Denali Venture Capital & Investments," Carey said on a huff. He glared at Rock. "It's not like it is a big secret."

"No. Just not relevant."

Apparently, the director didn't agree. He was typing something into his phone. "How do you spell that?"

Carey told him. "It's the Athabascan word for Mt. McKinley. Rock likes to think of himself as that big and that solid."

Rock ignored his brother's sarcasm and stood to help Mrs. Painter with the coffee. He wasn't surprised the rail-thin producer took hers black. Deborah refused any at all.

"Would you care for something else?" he asked her.

"Filtered water if you have it."

"This isn't LA, miss," Mrs. Painter said. "Rock's well provides some of the sweetest and freshest water you'll find, even in Alaska."

Deborah gave his housekeeper a smile Rock wouldn't mind having turned on himself. It was so genuine and sweet. "I'd love a glass, if you don't mind."

Mrs. Painter left to get it and Rock got pulled back into the conversation.

"You must realize we've got too much money invested in this location already to simply walk away," Ms. Morganstein said with firm resolve.

Gamble nodded. "We've flown in the cast and part of the crew. The rest will be here by the end of the week. Our schedule would be delayed in a way we cannot afford if we have to find another location locally, much less attempt to find one so perfect somewhere else altogether."

Ms. Morganstein set her coffee down and leaned forward. "Our investors would expect reparations. Your brother would be on the line for that as well as all the other costs incurred, not to mention criminal charges for signing a contract fraudulently."

Carey squawked in denial.

Rock just shook his head. "I'm guessing LA prosecutors have enough to do without pressing charges against my brother for criminal stupidity."

"I'm not stupid!" Carey jumped up and glared at Rock.

Rock raised a single brow. "You signed that contract without the legal right to do so."

"You always said this would be my home no matter what." Carey had the impudence to look hurt.

"To live in, to bring a guest or two to visit...not to turn into bed and breakfast for a film crew, or into a damned movie set."

"We aren't staying here. We've got rooms at the lodge," Carey said fast and loudly, like that made it all better.

"That's not the damn point." Though he privately appreciated that Carey hadn't intended Rock suffer the indignity of having his inner sanctum turned into a public hostel.

Carey's increasingly wounded expression just made Rock mad. He wasn't having a family argument in front of strangers.

"I think you underestimate how seriously Hollywood takes contracts," Ms. Morganstein said.

Rock surged to his feet and scowled pointedly at his brother until Carey returned to his seat. Then Rock turned the full force of his angry will on the two suits. "And you have overestimated my patience."

"Now, just hold on." Gamble put his hands up in a calming gesture. "There must be some kind of arrangement we can come to."

Rock shook his head. "I don't need your money." And if they

had enough to pay what the use of his land was worth, or any land like it close by, Carey couldn't have used the offer of it to finagle a starring role in the film. "I don't care for your good will."

Ms. Morganstein's looked at him coolly. "But you're brother? You aren't going to claim you don't care about him?"

Rock wasn't about to deny that truth. "You think threatening him is going to make me sign your contract?"

The producer and director's identical expression of smug certainty said they did.

"Let's get something clear, here." He let his expression settle into something only his worst business rivals ever saw. "You come for my brother and I will come for you."

"Is that supposed to intimidate me?" the producer demanded, but Ms. Morganstein's tone wasn't nearly as full-throttle as her words.

She didn't look intimidated exactly, but she did look thoughtful.

"I think, if you were independently wealthy, you wouldn't be here in Alaska, looking for a free location," he answered with characteristic honesty.

Gamble swallowed his coffee wrong and then started sputtering, "Jepsom Acres happens to be perfect for the storyline which plays out almost entirely in the country. I assure you, we do have the funds necessary for this production."

"Right now, you do. How much you have tomorrow, or next week will be in direct correlation to how far you take this thing with my brother. You want to blackball him, you go right ahead. You try putting him in jail, good damn luck funding another movie in the next decade."

CHAPTER THREE

"Rock, you can't say that," Carey cried.

Rock knew his brother wasn't protesting him threatening the producer, he was upset big brother had said to go ahead and black ball him.

"I think it would be a good idea to go to the hotel, before tempers prevail." Ms. Morganstein stood and put her hand out. "Thank you for the coffee."

Alaskan rules of hospitality, much less common courtesy, demanded he take the woman's hand and acknowledge her thanks with a nod.

The others stood as well, the two assistants heading for the door like they had a bear on their tails. Pale and tugging at the collar of his trendy shirt, Carey looked like he'd like very much to join them, but he didn't.

As angry as Rock was at little brother, he felt a twinge of compassion and respect.

The director frowned at Carey and shook his head, but he offered Rock his hand. "I can appreciate your frustration right now, but I hope as a fellow businessman you have some sympathy for our point of view."

Rock didn't say he never would have signed a contract, much less transported an entire film cast and crew before being absolutely sure of the rights of use on a location property. No need to rub the other man's nose in it.

He did appreciate that Carey had put the film makers between a rock and a glacier, but sympathy might be stretching things a little.

Rock shook the director's hand, surprised at the firm grip. "Don't be too hard on Carey. He's got his reasons for doing what he does, and I expect you sympathize with them better than I do."

Gamble's jaw tightened, but he nodded. "I suppose I do."

Carey stopped in front of Rock, his shoulders slumped, his eyes downcast and his mouth turned down at the edges. "I'm sorry, Rock. I thought you'd understand. That you'd want to support me reaching the dream Mom and Dad never managed."

"Damn it, Carey. You know I wanted something else for you."

"So, you're going to undermine my big chance?" Carey looked up at him, but his brother's expression didn't have the petulance his words implied.

"None of this is on me, kid."

Carey sighed. "I know."

"Oh, hell." Rock grabbed his brother and pulled him into a hug. "I'm still here for you, Carey."

Carey hugged him back, tight. "I know. I just wanted..."

His brother let his voice trail off and they both were probably better off for it. Carey stepped back. "I better get out there. Mr. Gamble and Ms. Morganstein are probably pretty mad at me right now."

"You think?"

Carey grimaced. "Yeah, well..."

"Come back for dinner later."

"You mean that? You want to see me later?"

Rock rolled his eyes. "You're my kid brother. I love you. Yes, I want to see you."

"Okay. Well, I'll see if it's okay with um, Mr. Gamble, I guess."

Rock nodded. His brother had a lot of explaining to do and as much as Rock might wish otherwise, he didn't think his own involvement in this fiasco was at an end.

Carey left and Rock was surprised a second later when a small, feminine hand landed on his arm. Deborah.

Every zing of sexual current humming through his body earlier came back in full force as he turned to face her, careful not to dislodge her hand from his arm.

"It was nice meeting you, though I can say with absolute sincerity I wish it had been under different circumstances." She smiled ruefully.

Rock's hatred for the industry fought with an unexpected desire to make things better for her. "Me too."

Her pretty lips settled into a wry line, but the smile remained in her eyes. "You know the old saying. If wishes were horses..."

"All beggars would ride." He'd like to ride her into tomorrow.

Hell, into next week.

Something must have shown on his face because her nostrils flared and her dark gaze heated. "I know what you're thinking."

"You think so?"

"I'm sure of it." Her voice came out low and sultry.

Not the time or the place, but he sure enjoyed the affect it had on his body.

She sighed, letting her hand slide along his arm before falling away. "And I really shouldn't be wanting the same thing."

"But you do."

The shake of her head was less a denial than clear confusion.

He had no way of knowing if she had a string of lovers back in Hollywood, or not, but something told Rock this woman didn't give into her sensual instincts all that often.

The urge to reach out and touch rode Rock hard.

This was so unlike him.

He didn't *have* irresistible urges. Yes, he was a man who knew what he wanted and went after it. But, he was a businessman with a reputation for emotionless rationality.

To be turned on to a woman so deep and so fast just wasn't in him.

Or so he'd thought.

Reaching out, he gave into the need. His hands settled on her shoulders, seeming to fit there just right. "You're a beautiful woman."

"I pay a lot to keep these flawless looks." Her honesty surprised him.

But he liked it. "Is it worth it?"

"I used to think so."

"Not anymore?"

"I don't know."

He didn't press for more. Somewhere in the back of his head was the knowledge people were waiting on her, people he *didn't* want back in his house right now.

He leaned down, stopping with his lips almost brushing hers. "I don't kiss women I just met."

"I don't either."

"I figured."

"Men *or* women."

He smiled. "I figured that too."

And then he let their lips connect. Hot lava erupted and rushed through his bloodstream, telling him how stupid this move really was.

He wanted to carry her back up to his bed, but now was not the time. *Could not be the time.*

She made a small sound of shock and then just melted into him. Damn it.

She was definitely feeling it, too.

It took all his control to keep his hands where they were and the kiss to lips only; he knew if he got tongues involved he would be lost. Even so, his cock went harder than frozen titanium, pressing against his jeans and aching for her sweet depths.

Deborah's lips moved against his with equal urgency, but she kept her hands to herself.

The sound of a car honking outside came right before Deborah's phone started playing a full orchestra version of the William Tell Overture.

Their lips clung even as he stepped back.

He dry-washed his face with his hand. "You have to go."

"I do."

"Maybe I'll see you before you leave Alaska."

She jerked like something in his words had brought her back to earth with a thump. "Maybe. You sure you won't honor that contract Carey signed?"

"Yes." But damned if something inside him didn't warn him he was a liar.

"You can't be serious." Deborah stared at the three people who had crowded into her rustic room at the Northern Lights Lodge.

Her producer, her director and that darn Carey James.

He and his brother were lethal to her equilibrium, if for entirely different reasons. She had not even the tiniest desire to kiss the younger man giving her his most winning look.

Carey's smile turned up another hundred watts. "He's into you. I'm sure he'll listen to reason if you talk to him."

She couldn't deny the attraction, but somehow, she didn't think Rock Jepsom was a man who let himself be led around by his dick.

She crossed to the window, putting as much distance between herself and the others in the room as she could. "You're his brother. You talk to him."

"I tried. We all saw how well that went." Carey rubbed the back of his neck. "It didn't get any better when I went back there for dinner."

She bet that was an *interesting* conversation. Rock had been pretty restrained in front of everyone. She would like to have seen him showing some real emotion.

And not just the need to have sex.

Though she'd enjoyed that kiss more than she wanted to admit, even in the deepest recesses of her own mind. She touched her lips in memory and then dropped her hand fast when she realized what she was doing.

Carey's expression turned genuinely sad, if Deborah could believe her eyes and not his acting ability. "Rock refused to let me even mention *anything* to do with Hollywood at dinner."

There was something in Carey's demeanor that said he'd wanted to talk to his brother about his life in Las Angeles maybe even more than the movie. He looked vulnerable and possibly a little desperate.

However, Deborah couldn't forget the younger man had brought this on himself and he'd put her career at risk as well. "Maybe you should have tried it *first* without the whole movie entourage, you think?"

"Hey, Ms. Morganstein thought it was a good idea."

"Did *you*?" Deborah asked, not willing to let the younger actor off the hook so easily.

Carey's gaze shifted to the side and he shrugged.

"You know your brother better than any of us." With great effort, Deborah refrained from rolling her eyes. The truth was that obvious. "You knew he wasn't the kind of man who was going to bend to pressure."

"He's stubborn at the best of times, but you get his back up and he gets as immovable as his namesake," Carey admitted.

That's what she thought. "You had to know bringing us all in to his home was going to do just that."

"I suppose. Just this once, he could have seen reason, though. People change."

Deborah didn't agree. Not men like that. "If you say so."

"Look, he's pissed at me about this right now," Carey said. "He's not going to listen to anything I say, no matter how much sense it makes. You were the only one he was nice to."

That wasn't precisely true. Rock hadn't been mean to Carey. In fact, he'd repeatedly made it clear he considered his home as Carey's and hugged his brother good-bye.

Her parents would have thrown everyone out on their ears, including Deborah. "He was polite to all of us, considering the circumstances."

"But he wants you," Carey wheedled. "He doesn't just go for women like that."

"He didn't go for me." Which was an outright lie, but one she felt she had a right to.

Carey didn't look convinced. Neither did the other two.

"You were in there quite a while after we left," Ms. Morganstein observed.

Art Gamble had that calculating gleam in his eyes that never boded well between an actor and a director. "And you looked like you'd been kissing."

"I was thanking him for his hospitality."

Carey made no effort to hold back his own snort of disbelief.

Deborah rounded on him. "And you think I should do what? Offer him my body in exchange for use of his land?"

Carey and the director both looked hopeful, which probably should have made her angrier than it did. She'd been on her own in the world too long to be entirely surprised by their reactions.

Ms. Morganstein had enough sense to shake her head. "No, of course not. But you can talk to him. You're invested in this working too. Need I remind you that you exchanged part of your own salary for a production credit on this film?"

"No, or course not."

Art rubbed his chin. "You aren't going to direct one scene, much less two if this film doesn't get made."

"You're directing two of our scenes?" Carey demanded.

"Not *our* scenes--" Deborah started to say.

"That's not important right now. What *is* important is that Deborah has as much invested in this film going forward as any of us, maybe more than some of us." Ms. Morganstein's subtle reminder that Deborah's career wasn't setting the world on fire and this chance to move behind the camera didn't come along every day wasn't needed.

Deborah was aware. She stifled a sigh and refused to let the frown that wanted form on her face surface. "I know."

"You're not getting any younger," Ms. Morganstein pressed.

"I *know*." And Deborah really didn't appreciate having those facts rubbed in her carefully preserved face.

She'd managed to avoid plastic surgery and the use of Botox to this point, but she wouldn't be considered for anything but *character* roles pretty soon. No matter how good her skin regime and how careful she was about the nutrients she put into her body.

Ms. Morganstein's knowing eyes said Deborah's thoughts were

transparent to her. "This is your chance to make a name for yourself, especially if you're hoping to make the shift to behind the camera. Art and I could do things for you beyond this film. Open doors."

The classic stick with a carrot at the end. Deborah felt manipulated, just like Rock no doubt did. She'd spent enough years in the business to know the studio execs didn't just take off the kid gloves, they'd never worn any. But that didn't mean she had to like it.

"All I have to do is convince one very stubborn and obviously extremely private man, who wants nothing to do with us, to change his mind about allowing us to use his home for a movie shoot." Piece of cake. Right.

Completely ignoring the thick sarcasm in her tone, Art clapped his hands together and smiled a shark's grin. "Exactly."

"I was being satirical."

"I'm not. You need to do this, Deborah." There was no question the producer was extremely serious. As in *make or break your career* serious.

"You can do it," Carey said persuasively. "My sister always has better luck with Rock than I do."

And the obvious reason for that had never occurred to Carey? "Maybe because what she asks for isn't so far from something he wants to do."

"He'll love having a movie made that saves the beauty of Jepsom Acres for posterity. It'll be great." Carey's eyes wide with sincerity and the enthusiasm in his tone said he really believed that.

"Are you on something?" she demanded.

Carey blushed and ducked his head. "No. Of course not. Rock might not know it yet, but he really will love the movie. It's in his blood as much as mine."

"I think he wishes it wasn't in yours."

"Nah. He says stuff, but that's just Rock. He was proud of Mom and Dad too. He's got a whole gallery wall dedicated to their achievements."

"Does he really?" That was unexpected.

"Yes."

Maybe it wasn't as hopeless as it first appeared. "Okay, I'll try to talk to him."

"Great! Look I'll take everyone on a tour of Cailkirn tomorrow, let them get to know the area. You go hang out with Rock."

Right. She'd just go *hang out* with the man that made her panties wet just being in the same room.

No room for disaster there. None at all.

Deborah pressed the buzzer on the gate for Jepsom Acres, startled when the voice that answered was female. Then she realized it must be Mrs. Painter.

"Hello, this is Deborah Banes, Carey's um..." Friend wasn't the right word but calling herself his costar right now would be pretentious. "Coworker."

"Is Mr. Rock expecting you?"

"No, I'd hoped he could give me a few minutes."

A moment of silence ensued and then, the woman said, "Come up to the house. You can have a cup of coffee at least."

"That would be lovely, thank you." Deborah didn't drink coffee, but she wasn't about to offer that little tidbit as a reason to go away.

The gate slid back, allowing her to drive the rental car up the long, but well-maintained drive. Following her instincts, Deborah pulled around behind the house and parked next to a late model bright yellow compact four-wheel-drive. Deborah didn't see a large man like Rock driving such a small car, much less one in such a cheerful color. It must belong to the housekeeper.

And he must pay his housekeeper better than most of Deborah's jobs paid her because that particular car didn't come cheap, despite its size.

Mrs. Painter opened the back door on Deborah's knock, the older native Alaskan woman's smile welcoming even as she peered past Deborah. "Good morning. Mr. Carey isn't with you?"

"He wanted to take some of the others on a tour of the town." Chilled in the morning Alaskan sunshine, Deborah was glad for the teal, double-breasted short trench coat she'd donned before leaving the hotel. The low seventies were winter temperatures for Southern California.

"I see." Mrs. Painter waived Deborah inside. "I hope he had the sense to book it with the MacKinnon boys."

"I'm not sure." But Carey hadn't said anything about having a guide.

The kitchen was as impressive as the rest of the house. Immaculate stainless-steel appliances complimented beautiful beams and exposed wood.

Mrs. Painter nodded toward a tall stool at the far side of the large island that held the range top. "Give me your coat and have a seat."

Deborah laid her quilted Chanel knockoff on the counter, then slipped out of her coat before handing it to the housekeeper. "Thank you."

"I'll just hang this in the mudroom." Mrs. Painter went back into the small annex to the kitchen they had just come through.

Deborah was sitting on the stool the other woman had pointed out when Mrs. Painter returned to the immaculate kitchen seconds later. She smiled at the older woman. "Carey is very lucky to be able to call this place home."

"That boy. He doesn't have the sense God gave a cat." Fondness along with a good dose of exasperation laced Mrs. Painter's tone.

Deborah did her best to stifle the laugh that wanted to bubble up. "He's young."

Not sure if it was Carey's apparent intention to guide the film crew around town on his own, or more likely his signing a contract turning his childhood home into a film location that had upset Mrs. Painter, Deborah forbore commenting any further.

Mrs. Painter filled a silver coffee percolator with water. "Mr. Rock was taking care of him and their little sister when he was that age. It wasn't easy either. You think those flighty Jepsoms left their kids more than a barely improved lot of land and a tiny life insurance policy? If it hadn't been for the payout from the airline after the crash, they wouldn't have had more than a pot to piss in."

"I didn't realize that." She'd thought Carey was wealthy and said so.

"Oh, he had a decent inheritance by the time he reached the age of eighteen. But that was Mr. Rock's doing. He's a financial genius."

And stubborn. And as sexy as any man Deborah had ever met.

Deborah cleared her throat. "Um, I don't actually drink coffee."

Mrs. Painter didn't stop what she was doing. "Oh, I remember, but Mr. Rock does. So, do I."

"Oh, okay. I just didn't want you going to trouble for me that would be wasted."

Mrs. Painter smiled. "Would you like water again today, or can I tempt you with ice tea?"

"I don't actually do any kind of caffeine." All part of keeping youthful skin.

"Not even chocolate?" Mrs. Painter demanded, sounding shocked at the idea.

"Especially not chocolate." Which was usually laden with fat and sugar, two things on her carefully moderated list.

"Mr. Rock would die. Chocolate is his weakness."

The idea of the overwhelming man being a chocoholic made

Deborah smile. "Maybe I should have brought a box of fudge as a peace offering on behalf of the film company."

"Maybe Carey should have thought of it," Mrs. Painter said with a frown and a shake of her head. "He doesn't mean to be thoughtless. I know he doesn't."

"He has a good heart." Deborah wasn't sure it was true, but it seemed like the thing to say.

"He does," Mrs. Painter agreed with an expression that said she knew Deborah wasn't convinced of the fact. "Rock raised him right, even if he doesn't always show it."

Deborah was impressed with the other woman's loyalty and the kind of sacrifice she alluded to on Rock's part. "He must care about his younger siblings a great deal."

"Are you surprised?" the other woman asked with a smile. "He practically raised them single-handedly a long time before they lost their parents."

"I couldn't have done it without you." Rock's deep tones rolled along Deborah's spine and settled right between her thighs. She squeezed them together in an involuntary movement.

"Well, you wouldn't have eaten nearly as often or as well, that's for sure." Mrs. Painter grinned. "And I wasn't there in the early years. You didn't move to Cailkirn until you'd about raised yourself. Not that you ever taught yourself to cook."

Rock's laugh was warm, and Deborah felt like she was lucky to be witnessing it. "They say charcoal is good for you."

Mrs. Painter shook her head. "For soaking up poison maybe."

"So, cooking is not your forte?" Deborah found herself smiling along with them, enjoying the proof that Mr. Amazing wasn't perfect after all.

"Not even a little." He inhaled appreciatively. "Is that fresh coffee I smell?"

Mrs. Painter patted his arm. "You know it is."

"Just what I've been needing."

"Well, it's about time for your midmorning coffee break."

"You take good care of me, Mrs. Painter." What would it be like to be the recipient of that affectionate and clearly appreciative look?

"Someone has to." Mrs. Painter gave Deborah a conspiratorial smile. "You don't want to know what he can do to a simple box of macaroni and cheese."

Deborah laughed, charmed by the color that slashed along Rock's chiseled cheekbones. "I wouldn't have survived the early lean years if I couldn't cook *that*."

"So, you can boil water and read instructions?" Mrs. Painter teased, clearly implying Rock couldn't.

"Yes, but I'm no gourmet." Considering the limitations of her diet to maintain her figure, learning to cook anything fancy would be a complete waste of her time. "I do make a mean smoothie though."

When she had the money to support it, she practically lived on organic smoothies.

"Too busy acting for normal meals." Rock made it sound like hers was the only job that interfered with regularly scheduled life and she knew it wasn't.

She was a waitress at a health food café on the side. Talk about demanding hours and odd schedules. Working in the food industry was no picnic.

She lifted one shoulder in a partial shrug. "Or working so I can keep trying to act."

She might not eat eighty percent of what they offered on the catering tables during a job, but when she was acting, Deborah's meals were actually more regular and elaborate than when she was on her own.

Rock nodded, his expression somber. "It's a hard life."

"But worth it." The words came out more by habit than intent. She just wasn't sure anymore if it really was.

There had been many more lean years than easy ones, starting with college, and Deborah missed having a family. She missed having friends who wouldn't stab her in the back for a chance at a role. Not that everyone in the industry was like that, but it was a cutthroat business with thousands of hopefuls for every success.

Deborah had been burned enough she stayed away from the tempting flame of friendship with her coworkers now.

Rock settled onto the stool next to her. "Did Carey send you here to talk to me?"

CHAPTER FOUR

"Yes." Deborah wasn't about to start this conversation with a lie. "I'm not sure if he convinced Art and Ms. Morganstein that it was a good idea, or the other way around, but they're all convinced you'll listen to me." Deborah had her doubts and she figured Rock could tell.

"I told Carey I didn't want to talk about it until after I'd read the contract and had done some research on the film company as well as Gamble and Morganstein."

Deborah would like to go back to the night before and smack Carey on the back of his head. Why hadn't he told their bosses that? Or had he taken Rock's words to mean more than they did?

Communication was rarely about what was said, but what was heard. Even so, Carey should have realized his brother's words were a heck of a lot better than Rock's outright refusal the day before.

"Maybe I could help," she offered.

Rock measured her with his sherry brown gaze. "With what?"

"The research. I did a fair amount before accepting the role they offered me and signing my own contract." She'd heard of Gamble and the film company, of course, but she'd required deeper and more specific information on both before signing a contract.

"You didn't just jump at the chance? According to Carey, this movie is going to be the making of both your careers."

So, Carey had gotten to say *something* and Rock had listened, despite all evidence to the contrary.

"It certainly has the potential to be. But if I've learned anything over the years, it's that there are as many con artists out there as legitimate opportunities, maybe more. Some of them even work for the companies with the best reputations."

"Have you been in the business since you were a child?" he

asked.

"No." Hadn't he looked her up on IMBD? She wasn't sure if she was relieved or offended at his apparent lack of interest in her particulars.

His brows rose in question. "You said *years*."

"How old do you think I am?" she asked with real curiosity.

She didn't think this man would flatter her for the sake of trying to get her into bed.

If she was honest with herself, she'd admit they both knew he didn't need to.

"Same age as Carey. Your eyes say you're probably older though."

"I'm twenty-nine."

The surprised widening of his own eyes was flattering and better affirmation than her mirror that her skin regime was working.

"Old enough to know that taking a part without knowing what I need to about the people making the offer would be a mistake," she added.

"If that's true, you showed more caution than your bosses."

She didn't take issue at his use of the word *if.* No matter how attracted to him she was, Deborah wouldn't just take Rock's word for anything either.

"You mean how they believed your brother, that he owned this land?"

Mrs. Painter made a scoffing sound, reminding Deborah she was there. "They believed a boy that age owned this spread?" *Tsking*, she shook her head, indicating how little she thought of Deborah's bosses' foresight.

Rock gave the older woman a nod of agreement. "A rudimentary title search would have revealed he didn't have the authority to sign that contract."

"But they didn't see the reason to run one," Deborah had to point out.

Rock looked less than impressed by that argument. "They should have and their lack of foresight casts some real doubt on the potential success of this film altogether."

Deborah squirmed on her stool, uncomfortable in the role of defending actions she would not have taken.

But she had to convince Rock that those actions did not indicate a serious lack of business acumen. One thing she was sure of after their short acquaintance, was that this man did not involve himself, even peripherally, with ventures doomed to failure.

She appealed to him with her eyes. "Both Mr. Gamble and Ms. Morganstein are savvy business people, but they're even better at making movies."

Rock made a sound of obvious disagreement.

"Give them the benefit of the doubt." Deborah sighed, hurt by his skepticism when she knew she shouldn't be. "They never would have anticipated a no-name actor like your brother risking his future in Hollywood to promise a location he couldn't deliver on."

"And yet they gave that same no-name actor a lead role in their movie."

"I said no-name, not *no talent*. Your brother is an extremely talented actor." Deborah had no problem admitting that. "His screen test was one of the reasons I accepted my role."

Rock turned so his body faced her, his jean-clad legs stretched out on either side of her stool. "I got the impression yesterday that my brother annoyed you."

"If I refused to work with every actor that annoyed me, I'd have no career." And didn't that make her sound like a crank who'd been in the business maybe a year too long?

But while there was no lack of professionalism in Hollywood, there was also a big dose of the artistic temperament.

"Point taken."

Mrs. Painter put a tray in front of Rock with a fragrant pot of coffee and a carafe of chilled water already forming condensation on the sides of the glass. "You two have things to talk about. Take this with you."

Despite the fact she called him Mr. Rock, there was no question who ruled the man's house.

Rock stood and grabbed the tray. "Good idea, Mrs. Painter. We'll get out of your hair."

"If Miss Banes wants to stop by to visit on her way out, she's welcome."

Deborah didn't make the mistake of assuming that, since the other woman was speaking to Rock and not her, she shouldn't reply. "I'll look forward to it and, please, call me Deborah."

Mrs. Painter smiled. "Very well, but you will have to call me Lydia."

Rock made a choking sound. "I've been asking you to call me Rock for years and you've always refused."

"Deborah and I are going to be friends," Mrs. Painter, no *Lydia*, asserted.

"What are we?" Rock demanded, his voice filled with sarcastic humor.

"Family."

Rock laughed. "Who call each other by a title?" he teased.

"Just so. Don't be asking me to change my ways this late in the game."

Rock shook his head, but he didn't argue. Just took the tray and headed out of the kitchen.

When Deborah didn't follow him immediately, Lydia said, "You'd better go, dear. He doesn't like to be kept waiting."

"Right." Deborah jumped off the stool. "I'll stop by and visit if he doesn't kick me off the property when I've had my say."

"That's not going to happen," Lydia scoffed. "He's angry with his brother, but at his heart, Rock would do anything for Carey or Marilyn. He seems pretty taken with you, too."

Deborah didn't reply to the latter, but she filed the first assertion away as an important element in the discussion to come and went after Rock.

After a couple of unintentional detours, she caught up to him in his office. He'd put the tray down on the desk and pulled a second chair around to face his computer, which was open to the film company's IMBD page. So, despite his clear knowledge of the industry public database, Rock hadn't bothered to look her up.

What did that say about his interest in her? Was it so purely physical, he had no interest in even knowing her filmography?

Regardless of what form his interest took, his impatient glare said Lydia had not been overstating how little he liked to be kept waiting.

"What?" Deborah asked. "You can't have been waiting more than a minute." Or two, at the most. Okay, maybe three. She'd run, darn it. And he'd clearly been busy the entire time anyway.

His brow rose, his expression mocking. "What did you do, go to the living room first?"

What if she had? And maybe she'd gotten the doorway to his office wrong, too, after realizing it made more sense for him to have come here. So, sue her.

She'd been paying more attention to him than the layout of his home the day before. "Don't be arrogant. If you didn't want me going to the wrong room, you should have told me where you were headed."

"I assumed you would follow directly behind me." The smile in his voice belied the irritation his words implied. The man liked to push, and he really did have a bold streak of arrogance.

She sat down and crossed her legs, gratified when his gaze strayed to the skin revealed and flared with heat. "You assumed wrong."

"Aren't you supposed to be charming me?" His look was assessing, his focus on her legs making her question her own motives in the decision to wear the borderline flirty black, not-quite-knee-length skirt. She was enjoying his attention way too much, despite her intention not to use the obvious physical attraction between them to convince him to honor the location contract.

He was right though, darn it. She was supposed to be charming him, or at least making her best effort to convince him. She focused on smoothing the folds of her black A-Line skirt, so she didn't have to look at him. "Yes."

"So? Charm me." He smirked when she raised her gaze to meet his.

"Now, you're being an ass." And he wouldn't respect her if she didn't call him on it.

The increased heat in his sherry brown eyes said he approved her spunk, even as he teased her. "And you are not doing your job."

"I can play any role you want, but this is me." She indicated herself with a wave of her hand. "More inclined to sarcasm than simpering."

Her white, crew-necked, short sleeved sweater followed her curves, but didn't cling to them. Her outfit was stylish on a budget and it flattered her figure, but it wasn't anything like LA sexy. She could play "L.A. Vamp" but that wasn't *her*. For reasons she did not quite understand, herself, she wanted him to like her, Deborah Banes, not a role.

Rock's mouth opened and closed without a word coming out, his gaze going narrow and then heating. His light brown eyes spoke volumes...about bedroom games and bodies coming together.

She'd never felt such direct sexual intent from another man and if she had, she was sure she wouldn't have liked it. But her body thrilled to that look, even as she fought to keep any corresponding feeling from showing in her own expression.

He turned to pour her a glass of water with smooth movements, no tremor brought on by sexual awareness in *his* hands. No matter what message she'd read in his gaze. If it had been her, she would have been using the action as a diversion so she could gather her thoughts and her composure. She didn't think this man ever needed those kinds of tactics.

He was way too self-assured.

He handed her the glass, his gaze boring into hers. "I'm not sure I ever saw my parents out of character."

Deborah frowned, but had no trouble believing him. "How exhausting." For both his parents and for Rock.

"Yes."

"I've met people like that in Hollywood." And it left her feeling disjointed every time.

His expression turned grim. "More than a few, I bet."

"Less than *you'd* expect." Rock Jepsom thought everyone in Hollywood was as fake as the special effects played against a green screen. "And actors aren't the only ones who get lost playing a role. They're just the ones that get paid for it."

She took a sip of the chilled well water, just as sweet and refreshing as the night before, and wondered if Rock would acknowledge her point. How deeply did his biases go?

He leaned back and crossed his arms, muscles bulging distractingly even as skepticism lined his features. "You think so?"

"Oh, come on." She set her glass of water on the desk and leaned forward. "You can't tell me you've never met another businessman who pretends to be something he's not."

Rock jerked his head in a nod of acknowledgment, but his expression didn't change. "It's not the same."

"As your parents? Probably not. It wouldn't be as personal for you." Or as painful, but she was sure he would not appreciate her voicing that belief.

He frowned as he poured his coffee, adding nothing to the dark brew. "You're trying to say my parents were the exception."

"No, I'm simply saying that they aren't the rule either." Surely a man as intelligent as he was would have realized that by now.

Only, that didn't seem to be the case.

"You would say that," he said, proving how deeply his prejudices were entrenched.

"Because it's true."

He took a long draw of his coffee, his expression revealing nothing, the silence stretching until he deigned to break it. "One thing I learned before I was old enough to go to school was that actors have a very passing relationship with the truth."

Ouch. She wasn't going to convince him of her trustworthiness in a single conversation over coffee. She knew that. But it still bothered her to know he had such a low starting point for his assessment of her character. "Some. Just like *some* businessmen."

"You're right."

"I'm surprised you admit it."

"I'm not an unreasonable man."

"I don't think Art and Ms. Morganstein would agree with you."

"I don't like your industry." He spoke without a single shred of apology. "I hate that both my brother and sister seem as enamored of it as our parents were. But even if that were not the case, I would not want a bunch of strangers running around my land for three months. I don't consider that unreasonable."

"Ten weeks." But she understood his point.

He was clearly a private man. The gate at the entrance to Jepsom Acres said as much.

His laugh was singularly lacking in humor. "And when have you ever known filming to run to schedule?"

"It happens." Particularly when money was tight. "Art is known for a smooth-running production."

"Is he?"

"Yes." She would have been happier if Rock looked like he believed her. Even a little. "Listen."

"Yeah?"

"I'll make a deal with you."

"What deal?" he asked, his sherry brown gaze flaring with something she didn't understand in the context. Lust.

The zing of answering desire in herself was inappropriate under the circumstances, but also beyond her control. The man wanted her and everything between them did nothing to lessen that fact. She couldn't help responding to that. Because she wanted him too.

But she wouldn't allow herself to get sidetracked by that desire.

"I won't assume you're a dishonest businessman who made his fortune on the backs of child labor and destroying other men's companies while stealing their most profitable ideas..." She paused, letting her words sink in.

By the way his square jaw went as solid as his name and his eyes narrowed, she figured they had.

She finished, "If you won't assume I'm a liar who spends my entire life living a part."

"I'm not going to automatically believe everything you say."

"And I'm not going to assume you're a good man."

The way he caught his breath and then scowled said he didn't like that at all. "I am no saint, but I am not a bad man."

She shrugged. "I'll give you the benefit of the doubt if you return the favor."

He cocked his head to the side, his blond hair cut in a short businessman's cut barely shifting with the movement. "You'd do well in the boardroom."

"Good to know." Considering the direction she wanted to take her career. She stuck her hand out. "Do we have a deal?"

He looked at her hand for a full five seconds before taking it and shaking it firmly. "Yes. Deal."

"Thank you."

He inclined his head but didn't let go of her hand. "I guess this is where you start into your pitch."

No way could she concentrate with him holding her hand. It felt too good. And he didn't look like a man about to hear a business proposal either. More like one prepared to make a proposition of the salacious variety.

More reluctant than she wanted to admit, but determined not to lose sight of her goal, Deborah tugged away from the physical connection. "I know you don't need the money."

His sexy mouth twisted wryly. "No."

"And considering your attitude about the film industry, you probably haven't given any real credence to what the movie could bring to Cailkirn as a good thing."

"So far, you're not making much of a case."

"But even if you don't like what we do, do you really want to deny all the benefits our being here and this movie could bring to the town?"

"Like what?" he asked.

"Like jobs now, increased tourism in the future, and even town pride."

He managed to surprise her again when he didn't dismiss her claims or express derision for them with his ruggedly handsome features. The man really would have taken Hollywood by storm if he'd followed in his parents' footsteps.

He had the kind of presence you just couldn't teach in an acting class.

"Cailkirn isn't short on jobs during the summer," he said mildly.

She'd read up on the town and discovered it was a cruise ship port. "If not for locals, for others on the peninsula."

Rock nodded. "You're assuming this film is going to reflect Cailkirn in a positive light."

"I know it will. The script is fantastic, Rock. It really is."

"Tell me about it."

She stared at him, too shocked by the request to answer right away. If she'd been asked, she would have said he was the type of person that eschewed movies and television entirely.

"I'm not a hermit. I have a television and I take in the occasional movie," he said, reflecting he'd correctly gauged what she'd been thinking.

Even though he despised the industry that produced them. Maybe Carey was right. Maybe deep down, Rock didn't hate what his parents had been as much as what it had done to their family.

Relieved in a way she couldn't define, she said, "Okay."

"So, are you going to tell me?"

"Didn't Carey?"

"No."

"Why not?" Carey's role was risky for him, but he was really excited about it.

"I refused to hear anything about the movie on his first visit home in three years."

Right. Carey had said that, or as much as. And Deborah could understand Rock's viewpoint, even if it made things harder for her. Carey clearly hadn't bothered to tell his older brother about the movie, much less his promise to use Jepsom Acres for the location shoots.

Shoots that would comprise of more than ninety percent of the filming, both for artistic and budgetary reasons.

She imagined Rock had been hurt by his brother's long absence from home, as well, though you couldn't tell it by his stoic appearance.

"Why hasn't he been home? Carey talks about Cailkirn like it is Paradise."

And there was no way this man had told his brother not to come home like her parents often told Deborah. Rock had made it clear from the moment he answered Carey's page at the gate that he considered his brother welcome in his home.

If grumpily.

Rock's face lost all expression, a trick she wouldn't mind learning. "You would have to ask him. He told me he was too busy with his career. Funny thing is, his IMBD credits are almost non-existent."

"Family can be complicated."

"Yes, it can."

"So, the film..." She paused, making sure he really wanted to hear this.

He made a rolling motion with his hand. "Go on."

"It's a coming of age and coming out story about two young people who have to break away from their Old Money families' expectations to be who they were meant to be. Both lead roles are rich with subtext and emotional appeal. They start out dating and end up friends closer than siblings. It's an amazing story that will touch audiences in ways they haven't been in a long time." If they did their job right, but she didn't mention that.

For her, that was a given. It should be for Rock too, considering his brother's aptitude to the craft. If it wasn't, he wasn't going to take it on her say-so.

"Coming out." Rock frowned. "One of you plays a gay character?"

"Yes." This could get dicey. Particularly coming from her instead of Carey.

Rock crossed his arms over his broad chest. "Which one?"

"Carey," she paused. "But you know that doesn't mean he's gay."

Rock's look was wry. "Of course not. Plenty of gay people play straight characters and vice versa." The reply had come too quickly, and his tone was too matter-of-fact for it not to be sincere, but when Rock finished speaking, his expression turned thoughtful.

"Would it matter if he was?" she couldn't help asking.

"I love my brother, Deborah." Not even a frisson of doubt made it into Rock's tone. "He could become a vegan and start protesting Alaska's fishing industry and I'd still welcome him home with both arms open."

It probably shouldn't have, especially after seeing them hug the day before, but his claim made her laugh softly. She couldn't help herself.

At his questioning look, she shrugged helplessly. "I don't see you as the effusive type."

"You barely know me." But he didn't deny it.

She could imagine him hugging his siblings after a long absence, but waiting on the front porch with open arms? Not so much. The sentiment was nice though.

The sudden thought that she could seriously fall for this man wasn't any more welcome than it was avoidable.

"Anyway, I have no idea if your brother is gay or straight." She wanted to make that perfectly clear. "It's none of my business."

"Mine either."

"You keep surprising me," she admitted.

"I don't know why. Since you don't know me, how can anything I say or do surprise you?" He was so pragmatic.

But he *wasn't* shy.   "Because you have given some very definitive impressions."

"Have I?"

Seriously? It was all she could do not to roll her eyes. "Yes."

"Like?" He leaned back in his chair and fixed those gorgeous sherry eyes on her.

"Like you had no intention yesterday morning of even considering allowing us to use your home for the location." He'd made that abundantly clear.

"I still don't."

If he was totally opposed to it, she wouldn't be sitting where she was right now. "I'm not so sure about that."

He set his coffee cup down and leaned forward, his eyes narrowed, every bit of his overwhelming presence focused on her. "What else did you decide about me?"

"I thought you were intransigent; now, I think maybe you just don't like being backed into a corner."

He nodded. "Smart woman. Go on."

The chairs hadn't seemed so close when she sat down, had they?

Had he moved closer? The heat from his body filled the space between them. Even though she was still in her own seat, she suddenly felt like their proximity was almost intimate. And the inexplicable desire to act totally out of character and join him in his chair simmered just below the surface of her every thought and breath she took into her body.

"You want me," she shocked herself by putting it out there, glad she controlled her tongue enough not to blurt out that it was mutual. "But that's not why you're going to let the film company use your home for location."

"You're so sure I'm going to?" He didn't sound angry. Not even a little worried. He sounded curious. He sounded dangerous.

The situation felt dangerous.

No, that wasn't right. Not exactly. Her heart was in danger and that shouldn't be possible. Not so soon, but she wasn't physically frightened. The air between them felt charged, though. Her breath was coming fast and shallow, but definitely not because of fear. More like anticipation.

CHAPTER FIVE

She forced herself to focus on the conversation, not the sexual tension ratcheting up between them by the second. "You said it yourself, you love your brother. You aren't going to allow his career to tank because he made a mistake."

Even one that was going to cost this man his privacy for more than two months.

"And what was his mistake?"

"Signing that contract before talking to you," she replied promptly, no doubt in her voice or thoughts.

"You're right."

"He should have called you from LA." She was certain about that one too, and not just because it would have prevented this situation from coming up. Carey had family he could rely on. Rock was as solid as his name implied. Carey should have trusted that.

Deborah would have given pretty much anything to have a family she could rely on with the same assurance of ultimate acceptance.

"Yes, but he thought I'd refuse." Rock shook his head. "Carey has always believed it was easier to ask for forgiveness than to ask for permission."

"It works for some people." That particular approach always felt sneaky and underhand to her, not to mention seriously risky.

Rock leaned back, his expression turning harsh. "And sometimes it blows up in their faces."

She'd suspected as much. "I wouldn't know. I've never done things that way." Her life might have been a whole lot simpler if she had.

Rock ran his hands through his short dark blond hair. "Yeah, me neither."

They shared a commiserating look that felt more intimate than it should have.

"So, I've done some preliminary research on Gamble and Morganstein. Their financials didn't hold anything I wouldn't expect." Rock leaned back, creating more than just physical distance between them.

She stifled the desire to lean forward and remove that distance herself. "Their financials? You ran credit reports on them? Don't you have to have their permission to do that?"

"Yes. They gave it."

She would have liked to overhear that phone conversation. As long as she wasn't expected to participate, minor production credit notwithstanding.

"I bet they weren't happy about it."

Rock's look said her bosses' happiness was not even on his radar of concerns.

"So, what else do you want to know?"

"Their reputation in the industry."

She indicated the computer with a jerk of her head. "Do you mind if we switch seats?"

"Why?"

"I could give you the highlights, but you're going to insist on reading the original sources anyway."

He shook his head. "Give me the highlights and then you can show support documentation if I require it."

"Do you try to be arrogant, or is that just natural?"

His eyes widened. "You offered."

"Right. It's that whole *if I require it* thing. Like you're deciding if you're going to believe me."

"I'm giving you the benefit of the doubt, like you asked."

"Oh." He was. Now that she thought about it that way, she smiled. "Sorry. I guess I'm feeling a little more defensive about your whole *actors have a passing relationship with the truth* attitude than I realized."

Which was kind of ridiculous. She shouldn't care what this man thought of her.

He sipped from his coffee, his gaze steady on hers. "People with integrity are usually offended when their honesty is questioned."

"So, getting annoyed with you is a point in my favor?" She gave him what she realized was a *very* flirtatious look over the rim of her own water glass. And didn't rein it in when she became aware of it.

Oh, wow.

This man.

He affected her like no other and turned her usually pragmatic brain to mush.

She'd better get it together. This movie was too important to let her attraction get in the way of convincing Rock Jepsom to make good on his brother's promises.

"Yes." Though desire flared in his eyes, he waited in clear expectation for her to talk.

So that was what she did. "Both Ms. Morganstein and Art are well-known in independent film circles. Most of their projects have done well at the festivals and gotten into theaters, if not the chains, as well as being picked up for DVD distribution by decent labels."

"Go on." His tone implied he'd already discovered most of that, but he didn't look impatient with her for telling him something he already knew.

"This film has a chance at getting into at least one of the national chains as well as digital distribution by a top label."

His eyes narrowed. "Who told you that?"

"Ms. Morganstein."

"Did she show you anything to support the claim?"

"Not on purpose."

"But..." His eyes invited her to continue.

"I was in her office and saw an email." She told him who it was from, one of the biggest distributers in the industry, not to mention a heavy hitter in original productions.

"You snooped."

"The monitor was on and she was on the phone. I was just looking around." Deborah drank more water, not sure why her throat felt so dry. "I'm not sure if you're interested in Art's reputation with actors."

"I am."

"He's good to work with, really cares about the script and the movie. It's not all about making the next blockbuster for him." He was no saint. No one she'd met in Tinseltown was, but Art Gamble was kind of her hero.

"Good thing since he hasn't made one yet."

"I'm not sure he's interested in moving into mainstream."

"I'm sure he's not."

She agreed, but didn't understand why Rock sounded so sure. "How do you know?"

"He's had offers from the big companies and turned them down."

"Really?" She didn't know that. Though it wasn't something Art would have advertised either.

There was a fine line between artistic integrity and career suicide. Still, she was surprised she hadn't heard the rumors.

"Where did you hear that?"

"From the studio exec who made the offer."

Shock coursed through her. "You have contacts in the industry?"

"I'm a venture capitalist." He set his coffee cup down on the tray, managing to invade her personal space again as he did so. "I have contacts in most industries, directly or by a degree or two of separation."

"Who was it?" she asked, unable and really not interested in stifling her curiosity.

He named a man so high on the food chain in Hollywood, Deborah would have said she didn't even know him by six degrees of separation. But now she knew she did. Through Art Gamble.

For the first time, she realized just how powerful this man who chose to make his home in small town Alaska was in the business world.

He didn't just have contacts, he had access to the power people.

"Art and Ms. Morganstein have no idea about who you really are, do they?"

Rock shrugged, like it didn't matter. And it probably didn't. To him.

She, on the other hand, faced the unenviable task of explaining to her bosses that Rock Jepsom wasn't a man they would intimidate or be able to push into anything he didn't want to do.

"If you have contacts in the industry, I'm not sure what I can tell you that they can't." Or why he'd even agreed to speak to her.

"Maybe nothing."

She looked at him, trying to read what he was thinking on his craggy features. "Then why listen?"

"Because I want to."

Again. Wow. This man didn't do anything he didn't want to. Full stop. Period.

"You're a very self-assured man."

He shrugged. "You want to convince me. I'm giving you the opportunity."

"You are." If there was a tinge of awe in her voice, who could blame her?

Rock Jepsom wasn't humoring her, he was giving her a chance

and that said a lot about his character. All of it good. At least in her eyes.

So, she did her best, sharing her own research into the film company, the production and its principles.

"You admire Ms. Morganstein." Rock steepled his hands and probed her gaze with his own.

Deborah wasn't sure if she wanted to go into production or get herself firmly behind the camera, but she admired Elaine Morganstein. "She's made a name for herself in a business that can still be very much an old boy's club."

"Is she someone you want to emulate?"

"In some respects, yes." Deborah pulled up a link she'd found early on. It was an article about Ms. Morganstein in an academic journal. "You see this?"

Rock gave her a measured look. "Yes."

"She's taken seriously."

"You want to be taken seriously?" he asked.

"I want to matter." That hadn't come out the way she'd intended it to, though the words were honest. "I mean, I want what I do to matter."

"And you can only achieve that on the other side of a camera lens?"

"We're not talking about me." And she'd revealed enough of herself to this man already.

"You have as much to gain, or lose, with this movie as my brother does."

"More." Carey was just starting his career. She was on the long side of hers. Fair, or not, male and female leads had a different longevity arc in their industry and she was on the tail end of hers.

No diet and exercise regime with the best skin care products was going to keep her looking young forever.

"You think so?"

"He's twenty-two. I'm twenty-nine."

"Not exactly in your twilight years."

"Hollywood years are like dog years. Exponentiated. Especially for a woman."

"Katharine Hepburn was eighty-seven when she made her last movie," Rock said, surprising Deborah with both his knowledge and attempt at encouragement.

"But she was twenty-six when she made *Morning Glory* and became a star, besides, that kind of talent doesn't live inside of every actor."

Deborah held no fantasies in that regard. She had never dreamt of achieving that level of stardom. She'd just wanted a big enough career that could justify her choice of film school over law school, something that proved losing her family to pursue her own dreams had been worth it.

"You understand the business better than I thought you would," Rock mused.

Was he kidding? The business was her life. "Condescending much?" she asked wryly.

His lips quirked. "Sometimes."

Okay, she was charmed. "Let me guess. You don't mean to be."

"Sometimes, but not that one."

"Thank you. I think. But let's just be clear on one thing. I am not an empty-headed actress, expecting my beauty to buy my big break." She'd never had the luxury of that level of naiveté.

"You are beautiful though."

"Thank you. I would say it was an accident of birth, but I work hard for this flawless skin and LaLa Land acceptable dress size."

"I have no doubt you do."

"Just so we're clear."

He nodded, his expression turning calculating. "So, your bosses and my brother believe you have a better chance of getting me to agree to this movie scheme?"

"It's not a scheme, but yes."

"I'm not sure what I've ever done to convince my brother I can be led around by my dick."

She choked on her sip of water. He'd gone there. He'd really gone there.

Taking the glass from her with one hand, Rock patted her back with the other. The touch turned into a caress as she got control of her breathing, his big hand rubbing a sensual pattern below her shoulder blades. "I'm not sure how I feel about the mention of my dick sending you into a choking fit."

She laughed, coughing and wheezing because her lungs weren't ready for that yet.

It took several breaths before she could assure him, "My body isn't up for grabs as an incentive."

His hand slid up to cup her nape under her hair. "Are you sure?"

"Yes." She should have been offended, but she was breathless with desire she refused to acknowledge instead.

"Can't we pretend it is?"

"What?" He...no...he didn't think...she wasn't... Her disjointed thoughts careened to a halt before she could think the word. He'd said *pretend.*

What did that mean?

And why did the idea of it turn her on so much? She wasn't kinky. At least, she never had been.

But aagh...this man, he made her think of things she didn't spend time thinking about. Like pretending to be a femme fatale in a role that would never see the silver screen.

Rock leaned forward again, his hand on her nape creating the sense of being in his arms, his gorgeous sherry gaze trapping hers. "Could we pretend for a minute that I *can* be led by my dick and that you *are* willing to sacrifice your body for the good of the film?"

"A minute?" she asked faintly, her mind plucking that word out of the provocative string.

"An hour, a day, a week, whatever it takes."

"What?" she asked again, her heart beating way too fast, her breath coming out in embarrassing pants. "I..."

"You. Me. Preferably my bed but any flat surface will do. Move in here for the duration, sleep between my sheets."

"Are you serious?" He couldn't be serious.

Men like Rock didn't make propositions like that, not in small towns like Cailkirn.

"One thing you'll learn about me, I don't have much of a sense of humor."

Just a really healthy imagination. "You're saying if I agree to stay here and have sex with you, you'll let us film the movie on Jepsom Acres?" No way.

People didn't really make deals like that. Not in this day and age. Okay, maybe they did, but not people like her. She'd never auditioned on the casting couch and she wasn't about to start now.

And this man? He didn't need to make sexual deals like this. Especially not with her. He had to know that.

Heck, she was practically hyperventilating with lust right now and he was smart enough to read the signs.

So, what was going on?

"Yes."

Disbelieving, she stared at him. "You have to know I'm as attracted to you as you are to me."

"It wouldn't be a lot of fun otherwise."

"You're not doing this to get me into your bed."

"Aren't I?"

"You're doing it for Carey, no matter how much you don't want to admit it."

Maybe Rock needed the fantasy to cover his emotional vulnerability to his brother. Or maybe the idea just turned him on and he *was* kinky. Shamelessly so.

"If you say so."

"So, you'll refuse if I do?"

He leaned in and kissed her, his lips taking possession of hers, no hesitation, no slow build, nothing but undeniable passion immediately taking over every one of her senses.

The kiss went on and on and she didn't want it to end. It had been too long since she'd been kissed like this. She wasn't sure she ever had. She couldn't remember feeling so much emotion, so much blatant sexual need sparking through her from a simple meeting of mouths. He hadn't even breached her lips with his tongue, but she wanted that. Wanted to taste him.

Deborah's hands found his shoulders of their own volition, but they felt right when they landed. Hard muscles bunched under her fingers. She squeezed, needing to hold him close. Craving more.

She'd never reacted to a kiss like this, but then she'd never been kissed with such intensity and focus either.

She'd never been kissed by Rock Jepsom.

He pulled her forward with arousing strength, and even more exciting eagerness, as he settled her on his lap. No question the man was every bit as turned on as she was. The hardness pressing against her bottom left no doubt either.

He broke the kiss. "Are you?"

"Am I what?" she asked in a breathy voice, her mind completely blank of anything but a crushing need to get back to that kiss.

"Turning me down."

Turn him down? Was he insane? Why would she turn him down? "No."

She wanted him.

"Good."

Suddenly, he stood and she automatically wrapped her legs around his torso, uncaring that her skirt hiked up to her hips, loving the way her naked thighs rubbed against him. She locked her ankles behind his back and her lips to his in uninhibited passion. She'd go wherever he wanted to take her.

He carried her out of the room. She took in the exposed beams of the hallway and then she was in a brightly lit room. It looked like an entire wall was glass, but she saw that it was a set of huge windows that peaked toward the ceiling.

The view was magnificent, mountains off in the distance, nothing but nature to impede their majesty.

The view inside the bedroom became too compelling to pay attention to anything else when she landed on the big four-poster, Rock looming over her, his handsome features cast in stark desire. Pure alpha male, he called sexual need from her very core.

His gaze raked her, no humor, no charm evident. Nothing but the kind of sensual approval she hadn't thought really existed.

"You are so beautiful, Deborah." His voice rumbled through her with the immediacy of a touch.

"I work hard at it," she admitted with a transparency she rarely offered.

His smile was predatory. "I bet."

"Take off your clothes." She wanted to see him naked. Needed to see skin and muscle and his sex.

She didn't care that women weren't supposed to be the visually stimulated ones. Who could deny the inspiration of a piece of art like the man standing before her?

That predatory smile shifted to a feral grin. "You're not shy about what you want."

"I am a woman, not a child." And her entire body was on fire. She'd never felt this way. She wasn't about to waste a second of it on polite pretense. "I want you."

He began stripping, his movements efficient but incredibly sexy to her. "You get me."

She nodded. No doubts were able to penetrate the haze of overwhelming lust she felt.

He revealed his body, one article of clothing at a time. His shirt came off, exposing golden skin and a V of blond chest hair. He might be a money man, but Rock did something to stay in shape. Blockbuster, male leads would kill for Rock Jepsom's abs. Heck, their body doubles would too. His shoulders were boulders, his thighs rippled with muscle, his calves belonged on a Michelangelo statue.

And his engorged penis was a work of art all on its own. Long and thick, it jutted from a nest of dark blond curls in an invitation she couldn't deny. Deborah rolled up on her knees and crawled to the edge of the bed.

"You got something in mind, hot stuff?" he asked, his voice gruff.

Hot stuff. She liked that.

"Yes." Kneeling up, she crooked her finger. "Come here."

Sherry brown eyes flared with lustful heat. "You have this ethereal beauty, but it's all a mask, isn't it?"

"What do you mean?"

"Other worldly you are not." His gaze roamed her body like possessive touch. "There's an earthiness about you that matches me fine."

She'd never seen herself that way, but she wouldn't deny it now.

Actors wore masks all the time. She'd never considered her looks a mask all on their own, but he might be right. She certainly didn't *feel* innocent. All she knew for sure was that she wanted this man in a primitive way that belied the satisfaction of every sexual encounter that had come before.

"I want to taste you," she told him, no attempt to hide anything. From him, or from herself.

He cursed and took a giant step forward. "You're so damned sexy like this."

"You bring it out in me," she felt compelled to admit.

"Good." His expression turned stern with a tinge of confusion in the depths of his eyes. "The idea of you like this with someone else pisses me off."

She shouldn't like hearing that, but she did. A lot.

"You like that," he said, calling her on it.

Unable to deny words she'd just admitted to herself, she nodded.

His expression turning feral, he dropped another guttural expletive. "You are annihilating my control."

She shook her head. He was the one who turned her on so much all her usual reservation had taken a rocket ship for the next galaxy, but she didn't have the words to argue the point. Only feeling and atavistic need.

She crooked her finger again. "Come on."

And then he was there, that magnificent piece of male flesh right in front of her face. His male musk calling to something primitive in her, she drew in a deep breath. Taking in his scent, she allowed her own need to spike and felt the corresponding increased heated moisture between her legs. Then she did what she'd been wanting to do since he pushed his jeans down his hairy, muscular legs. She closed her mouth right over the head of his sex and tasted.

Moaning, she savored his unique flavor as it burst over her tongue. A little salty, but mostly sweet. All Rock. Unlike any other guy she'd done this for. She didn't give head a lot, but she had discovered that pre-come was usually less bitter. His tasted perfect to her.

Rock's was sweeter than most, and his masculine sexual scent excited her in ways that modern women weren't supposed to admit to. The desire to have him inside her, *claiming* her body with his was growing by the second.

The logical part of her still knew this was casual. That despite his unexpected possessiveness, Rock didn't want to *keep* her any more than she should want to be kept.

But that voice was muffled to near silence by the rage of carnal feeling pouring like hot lava through her blood.

She tasted more of his essence, reaching with one hand to hold his steel-hard sex at the base. She brushed her hand up and down the column of flesh while using her tongue to play with his slit.

He groaned, long and low.

"So damn good, Deborah," he husked, one of his big hands landing on the back of her head, the other cupping her nape.

He didn't try to push her mouth further down on him, but she could feel the rigid control it took and that excited her even more. She jacked him while sucking and laving his head and the whole time he moaned and cursed.

His big body gave a huge shudder and he yanked away. "Not yet, damn it."

"You don't think you can get it up again?" she taunted, really enjoying her newly discovered inner vixen.

At twenty-nine, she'd figured she knew all there was to know about her sexuality, but she wasn't this way with other men and that knowledge was something she would have to take out and examine later.

His gorgeous gaze narrowed. "Oh, sweetheart, I think when it comes to you, I'll have no problem with that, but the first time I come is going to be inside your body."

"My mouth is my body," she snarked, not sure where this woman who challenged the alpha male in front of her came from, but liking her.

"You know what I mean," he growled.

And she did. Oh, man, did she! "I can't wait."

"Good." He smiled at her, the look making her insides clench. "Now, let's get your clothes off."

CHAPTER SIX

"Okay." But even as the word left her mouth, she hesitated.

What if he didn't like the very slim figure necessary for Hollywood screen time?

Her breasts were fuller than other actresses, but Deborah did not have a Kardashian butt or curvaceous thighs.

He wouldn't be the first man to be disappointed when the clothes came off. Her lack of stardom didn't stop men from wanting the woman they'd seen on screen. Unfortunately, reality didn't always match the image they had in their head.

Deborah wasn't a slut, but she'd had her share of star chasers masquerading as potential boyfriends.

Rock didn't seem disappointed though, as he got her sweater off and then her skirt. She lay on the bed, her bra and panties still on and for some reason he seemed intent on getting his fill of that visual.

"I'm not a Victoria's Secret model." Far from it.

Rock's brows rose. "I've screwed one and she had nothing on you."

"Oh." Damn. This man just kept surprising her.

He put his hands on Deborah's waistband. "Okay?"

The question shocked her, but she liked it. Liked that no matter how alpha this man was, he was still concerned with her wishes and not taking this moment just before complete nudity for granted.

She nodded. "Oh, yes."

He tugged the fuchsia lace down her legs and off before lifting the panties to his face and taking a whiff. It was such an earthy thing to do.

She knew he could smell her excitement there. She'd been wet since he first got into her space in the office. She got that he was that guy, the one totally unashamed of his sexual nature, but why did she find his action such a turn on? She wasn't *that* woman.

At least not usually.

Rock's eyes went heavy-lidded and he dropped the panties on the floor. "I want."

She didn't ask what he wanted. The way he was looking at her mound said it all. He was going to taste her like she'd done to him. And not in order to get a free pass to being inside her, but because he wanted to.

Her own desire ratcheted up several more notches as he knelt down between her legs, pushing back on her thighs to open her to him completely.

Her breath caught as sexual need surged through her at the way he took control.

He was man enough to let her do what she wanted and then unapologetically go after what he wanted too. That was rare in her experience. He was strong and dominant by nature, but not selfish.

Nuzzling into the apex of her thighs, he inhaled deeply and groaned. "You smell so good."

No one had ever said that, and she knew he wasn't just doing it to be sexy. This man was the real deal. Sensual and earthy and everything she wanted in a sexual partner and never knew.

He licked her, his tongue teasing the opening to her vagina, then running up her labia to settle flat against her clitoris. Oh... that was...it was so good. Almost magic, how he elicited a response from her body. Just that simple pressure had her ready to explode. Not quite there, but embarrassingly close for so little contact.

Deborah wanted to rock her hips, but she didn't because she craved more of *this* feeling. More of whatever he wanted to give her.

He tickled her with his tongue but rocked back onto his heels too quickly for her to go over the edge. "Sweet."

She grabbed for him. "Take another taste." Please.

"Don't worry, I will, hot stuff. But first..."

He started touching her, kissing spots on her body she knew turned her on and nibbling at ones she'd never had any idea. By the time he took off her bra and caressed her breasts and their turgid peaks, she was writhing on the bed with an abandon she didn't allow herself.

When he finally pulled one nipple into his mouth to suckle and pinched the other one in his fingers, Deborah had a mini-orgasm and couldn't help crying out, her body seizing in miasma of pleasure.

Her nipples had always been sensitive, but she'd never come from a touch like this before.

He didn't stop what he was doing and her body thrummed with delight, her womb contracting, her vaginal walls squeezing on the finger he'd inserted as she climaxed.

It was all too much and not enough at the same time.

When he knelt back minutes later, she expected him to get a condom so they could make love, but he didn't. He moved so his mouth was able to give her another of the most intimate kisses of all.

This time, he licked and sucked until she was rigid with the near painful need to climax again, whimpers falling from her lips, her mind awash with sensation.

With a gentle pinch to both nipples and a swirl of his tongue against her engorged clitoris, he took her over the edge into an abyss of pleasure so profound, nothing else registered but her body's enhanced response. She screamed again, this time, long and loud and ending on a wail as the pleasure didn't dissipate but grew and morphed until she simply couldn't take another second.

She grabbed his hair. "Too much!"

He gave a final swipe of his tongue before lifting his head. His smile was filled with primitive satisfaction, his big body dark with a sexual flush.

Blown away, she melted into the bed, satisfied lassitude pouring through her body.

He grabbed the sheet and used the corner to swipe the glistening wetness from around his mouth. "Yum."

Her own husky laughter surprised her. Oh, lord. This man was something else. Something amazing.

"I thought you wanted to come the first time inside me," she said when she could rub two words together again.

His look bordered on diabolical. "I plan to."

"But..." Thinking better of any protest she was about to make, she waved her hand languidly. "Do what you like."

"You think I'm just going to use your body to get off?"

"It won't be using me." But she wasn't good for much else right now. Her brain was barely functioning.

That diabolical cast edged over his features again. "I like having an active partner."

"You should have thought of that before mind numbing orgasm number two."

"You'll come again, sweetheart. Don't you worry," he promised for the second time.

She almost believed him.

"Um..." She loved the sound of that and she knew some women could, but not her. The fact she'd already had a mini climax and then a fully realized one was kind of a miracle in itself. "I never have."

"Never have what?" he asked, giving his dick a casual caress. He was just so comfortable with his body.

Most men in the industry? At least the ones she'd been to bed with, weren't.

She wasn't. "I don't do multiple orgasms."

"Are you sure about that? Because I could swear you just did." He winked, all sexy confidence.

"That was..." Amazing. Mind blowing. "Unexpected."

"Uh, sweetheart, you do know that as a woman you are wired that way?"

"Maybe some women, but not me." She was very sure of that.

Not even when she touched herself. She'd tried, but she could never get out of her head enough after the first orgasm to achieve a second one.

Instead of accepting his words as fact, he was looking way too challenged for her peace of mind. Alpha men took challenges as something that needed to be conquered.

And she just knew that was how this man saw any perceived obstacle in his path.

"I'm not saying I don't want to do it," she assured him.

He ran his hands up and down her thighs, the physical connection more intense than it should have been as blissed out as she was. "But you don't think you're going to get anything out of it."

"Oh, I'll get something out of it." Just not an orgasm.

He offered her a sinfully sexy smile. "I'll make you a deal."

"Another one?" she teased, convinced his original *deal* had been a joke.

He nuzzled her shoulder, licking at the moist layer over her skin and making her shiver. "Part of the same."

"What?" she asked, her thoughts splintered by his actions.

He leaned up until their gazes met, his filled with erotic determination and confidence, but not a trace of humor. "If you come while I'm inside you, you move your stuff in and we tell your bosses they can use my land."

"You don't mean that."

"I don't lie."

"You don't need to offer the bribe. You've already got me in bed." Her integrity and feminine pride insisted she point that out to him.

He kissed her, his mouth coaxing sensation forth she had been sure five seconds before she was too replete to feel.

"Maybe that's why I'm offering," he said against her lips. "You're not asking."

And suddenly with chilling clarity, she knew if she'd tried to flirt or cajole her way into his agreement, he would not have given it. Ever.

But now he was offering and somehow that made it different. Or at least different enough she didn't feel like she had to say, *no*.

"And the house?" The story needed it. And she knew now was the time to ask.

As screwed up as that might seem to someone else. He was all male naked above her, but his heart still beat in the chest of a mega successful businessman.

He smiled down at her now, a shark's look, not amusement. "Within reason."

"You'll make them sign another contract." She thought maybe she was starting to understand this man.

He shrugged, like that was a given, the movement rubbing the hard muscles of his chest against her massively sensitive nipples.

A sound escaped her lips, something between a moan and an aborted complaint.

Yes, it was almost too much, but she didn't want to stop feeling what his body moving against hers made her feel.

His borderline smug look said he knew it too.

"I can't believe we're talking about this right now." She was naked.

He was naked.

And he'd just given her the best and most intense orgasm of her life. If he was serious about it, she'd pack her bags and relocate to his home no extra climaxes necessary.

His dark chuckle went straight to her core. "Just giving you a second to catch your breath, sweetheart."

She didn't get a chance to answer because suddenly his body was rubbing against hers with intent and his mouth was claiming hers in a breath-stealing, mind-shattering kiss.

His big, talented hands were everywhere, touching her with the kind of confidence that she'd always found to be a huge turn-on. He rubbed his oversized, adamantine erection against the apex of her thighs, teasing her with what was coming.

And incredibly, unbelievably, she felt her body respond with want, with desire, with aching, voracious need that should not be possible after her last climax. Not for Deborah.

She spread her legs in blatant invitation, thrusting up toward him, returning his kiss with everything in her. When he broke their mouths apart to reach for a condom, she mewled in protest.

She, Deborah Banes, *mewled*. She didn't make that sound. She just didn't.

He rolled the condom over his shaft, his gaze fixed on her. "You ready for me, hot stuff?"

"Yes!" She didn't know how, didn't care. She definitely was.

He smiled and squeezed his hard-on. "You sure about that?"

"You know I am." Her body thrummed with pleasure while her vaginal walls tightened on a new sensation of emptiness.

He continued to kneel between her legs, in the same position he'd taken to don the condom and put his hand out. "Then come on."

At first, she didn't know what he meant and then she realized Rock expected her to get up and straddle him.

"I...can't we just do it like this?" She wasn't sure she could hold herself up. And while she wasn't passive during sex, she'd wasn't totally comfortable with that kind of active role either.

She'd didn't usually trust her partners enough to act on certain urges, but Rock was inviting her, giving a tacit promise her feminine aggression would be welcome.

"Come on, sweetheart, live a little. Isn't that what the kids say?"

"I'm not a kid."

"No, you're a beautiful, sensual woman." He reached and took one of her hands into his. Then he tugged. "You're going to like it."

No doubt. So would he. And it was that knowledge that allowed her to let go of the last vestige of her nerves.

Letting lust overcome common sense seemed to be a norm when she was around him anyway. Even though she knew her muscles were noodle soft, she let him pull her up and onto his thighs.

The head of his penis pressed against her entrance even as his arms came around her, supporting her. "Ride me. I know you want to."

And she did. No matter how weak her muscles were, how sated she *thought* she was, surprisingly there was nothing she wanted more. Driven by need too great to ignore, Deborah pressed down against that blunt hardness and felt his aroused flesh pushing into her filling her just like she needed him to do.

"You're so tight," he groaned out, his face a rictus of desire. "So good."

But he didn't move, didn't thrust up, didn't do anything but remain a solid - very solid - presence beneath her, a support around her and a very real presence within her. He was big and she was tight. It had been a while, but she thought maybe his size would have made her feel like a virgin regardless.

She rocked her hips in small backward and forward movements that helped her to take him inside until he was pressing against her cervix, her vaginal walls stretched around him. It felt amazing.

They both stilled, their bodies joined as close as possible, the scent of their combined musk teasing her nostrils, sexual need sweet on her tongue, the sound of their breathing not enough to drown out the beat of their hearts. The silence around them was redolent with anticipation.

Desire and pheromones thick in the air, sweat slicking the small of her back, his thighs rigid beneath hers, their breathing grew shallow and faster.

"Ride me, sweetheart," he said in a voice that made her inner walls clench around the thick flesh inside her.

She couldn't imagine doing anything else. She needed to be the one to move, the one to control the upward slide and downward glide. At first anyway. Deep inside, she knew that wouldn't last forever.

Where she'd been barely able to sit up moments before, now her muscles tensed with acute necessity for movement.

Tilting her pelvis forward, Deborah drew her body back and lifted up with her legs, every centimeter of slide along his fat column of flesh sending shockwaves of pleasure through her. She pressed back down, the angle of her body pressing his sex against her g-spot.

Sparks lit along her nerve endings and another climax didn't seem like such an impossibility. A few more slow glides up and down and it became more a glorious probability.

His jaw hard as granite, his eyes burning with sensual need, he still let her set the pace. Rock's big hands squeezed her backside rhythmically, but he didn't try to guide her movements. There was something incredibly arousing about such a powerful man giving her this moment of control over his body.

The pleasure was so intense, so consuming, everything around her faded into the background, going fuzzy and indistinct. Everything but him.

Every pore of his gorgeous skin stood in stark relief, his eyes locking her gaze to his, his body smelling and feeling like the best sex she'd ever had.

She could feel her climax building, but she couldn't go over. She didn't want to be right about that. Not even a little. Frustration made her whimper. Every up and down over his rigid penis felt so good. Amazing, but she was primed to explode again and she could tell that she wasn't going to.

"You ready to keep our deal, sweetheart?" he asked in that voice of sin she knew she'd never be able to turn down.

She glared at him, unrealized passion making her cranky, "I can't. I told you."

"And I told you that with me, you *would*." He grabbed her hips and started thrusting upward, taking over the pace and the angle, pushing more pleasure into her body than she knew she was capable of feeling.

The sound of skin slapping skin mixed with his earthy words of encouragement. "Come on, sweetheart, ride me like you mean it."

Their bodies moved together in a harsh, wild rhythm that sent shockwaves through her. And unbelievably she felt that imminent cataclysm of pleasure, not beyond her reach. *Right there.*

And then she went over, the feelings so intense she couldn't hold back the scream that tore out of her throat. His shout of completion mingled with hers and suddenly he was holding her body so close their chests expanded and retracted together with each breath.

She let her head fall forward onto his shoulder, her mouth pressed against his skin, her hands gripping his shoulders hard.

"Now that's sex worth compromising for."

She huffed out a laugh against him. "Jerk."

This wasn't about some deal. No way was what they'd just done about the movie or anything else. It might be casual. It might have no possible future, but it wasn't a deal.

"Be quiet about your deals while you're still inside me," she said, no edge to her tone but no give either.

She felt too good to even pretend annoyance.

His arms locked around her, steel bands holding her tight. "Watch out, or I'm going to think you want something real."

"Our bodies are connected in the most intimate way possible." And shouldn't he be shrinking and sliding out? "That *is* reality."

He laughed softly and rocked his hips. "Connected like this."

Aftershocks rocked her and she gasped. "Don't tell me you're ready for another round already." That wasn't possible for a man, was it?

But then Rock had proven that he was capable of decimating her concept of the impossible.

"Not without changing the condom." He sighed, but his arms spasmed around her, like he didn't want to let go.

Was he saying, he could go again, though?

She found out seconds later, when he laid her back on the bed, and took time to change to a fresh prophylactic. He *could* and he could do it for hours. Hours in which he shattered her belief that she couldn't have multiple orgasms. Hours during which he showed her the kind of sex she thought only existed in the imagination of people with more creative thoughts than her own.

They skipped lunch and napped after, but her phone ringing roused Deborah enough to realize Rock was working on his laptop as he lay beside her in the bed sometime later. She thought it was still afternoon.

"You didn't sleep?" she asked on a yawn as she reached for her phone.

"I'm an Alaskan man. I've got more stamina than those boys you play with back in LA."

"I don't play a lot." She wasn't a virgin, but she wasn't a player either.

It was safer for her that way, both for her heart and her equilibrium. She tended to get too emotionally involved when sex entered the equation. Which should have stood as warning to her in this situation.

But none of her usual cautions even registered right now. And she had no trouble dismissing the ones that did.

For that kind of sex?

She could dismiss a lot.

"That's not the first time your phone has rung. You were sleeping hard." He sounded proud of himself, like he took credit for that fact.

And well he could.

"Darn it. It's probably Ms. Morganstein, or Art." Deborah changed her mind and didn't answer her phone, but let it go to voicemail as she checked the call history.

One from Art. Two from a number she was pretty sure was Carey's and the last one had been Ms. Morganstein.

"Do you want me to call Ms. Morganstein and tell her you're willing to honor Carey's contract?" Maybe Rock would rather make that call himself, or tell Carey first.

"No way in hell am I honoring that contract."

She stared at him, still muzzy from sleep. "But you said..."

"I'll renegotiate a contract with terms I find acceptable."

"Of course." She knew that. "I didn't mean the actual contract."

He cocked his head in acknowledgement, but his expression remained serious. "Be careful of exactly what you say when it comes to business."

"I know that." Only maybe in her cutthroat business she had never been quite as cutthroat as the businessman in bed with her.

"Maybe I'll just go take a shower while you make that call then."

He nodded, his expression saying he saw it has his job, not hers. "Good idea."

She liked that unlike everyone else, Rock clearly didn't think she belonged in the middle of this fiasco, regardless of his teasing her about their deal.

Rock didn't bother to dress before picking up his phone to make the call. He had every intention of keeping the conversation short and joining Deborah in the shower.

He called Carey.

"Hey, Rock," Carey answered in a cautious tone.

Rock appreciated that his brother seemed to finally realize he'd screwed up. "Hey, kid. How did the tour go?"

"It was kind of flat, to tell the truth. I guess I wasn't cut out to be a tour guide."

"Why didn't you book with Tack or Egan?"

"It was a last-minute thing." Carey paused like he knew that admission made it clear he'd expected to start filming today. "Anyway, Cailkirn is the size of a postage stamp. It shouldn't have been that hard."

"This movie is important to you, isn't it?" Rock knew the answer, but he wanted to hear about it from his brother.

He should have heard about it before Carey had ever left LA.

"I need it," Carey said baldly and without any of his usual artifice.

That, more than anything, told Rock that he was talking to the boy he'd raised, not the Carey James, star in the making. "You're going to explain to me how you ran through the damn inheritance I worked so hard to build for you and a lot of the money from me purchasing your interest in Jepsom Acres, all without any significant credits to *your* name."

Carey made a wounded sound. "How did you know?"

"I'm still on most of your accounts, Carey."

"I...just...it's complicated." The pain in his brother's voice said it was worse than *complicated*.

"I love you, kid. You know that."

"People say that."

"I'm not people. I'm your brother and I've been taking care of you since Mom brought you home from the hospital."

"People don't get that, you know."

"I know."

"They think no way could a ten-year-old boy take care of twin babies, but they don't know you."

"They don't know our past."

"Even when you tell them, they think you're dramatizing." Carey kept saying they, but Rock got the feeling his brother was talking about someone specific.

Rock didn't know who had made Carey feel like talking about the pain of their childhood was being dramatic instead of real, but whoever it was had a new enemy. Carey was his baby brother, Rock's to protect and he wasn't letting anyone get away with messing with Carey.

"I'm never going to abandon you, Carey." Rock had proven himself time and again to his siblings. He wasn't going to take off for a business deal, or die on them, or anything else. Damn it. Not like their parents.

"I forget." Carey's voice caught on tears he was clearly trying not to let out.

"Well, don't."

"So, the contract?"

"I've drawn up a new one."

Carey gave a choked laugh. "Ms. Morganstein isn't going to like that."

"Not my problem."

"No, it's not. I messed up, Rock. I'm sorry."

That's all he'd needed to hear. From his *brother*. Not the actor. "I forgive you."

"Thanks." Carey took an audible breath. "I guess I better go break the news to Art and Ms. Morganstein."

"Bring them to dinner. I'll have the new paperwork for them to sign."

"I will. Thank you, Rock." Carey was sounding more like his clueless, enthusiastic self when he hung up a few seconds later.

And damned if that didn't make Rock happy. Now, to join his temporary lover in the shower.

CHAPTER SEVEN

Rock stopped in the doorway of the bathroom, arrested by the visual feast in front of him.

Deborah stood under the shower, her eyes closed, her head thrown back as water cascaded over her head and ran in rivulets down her beautiful body.

Her dark brown hair looked like a mass of black silk slicked to her head and rippling over her shoulders. Rosy nipples, still blood swollen from his earlier attentions tipped her breasts, tempting him to taste again. Her feminine hands ran over her stomach, dipping down to the neat patch of dark hair covering her mound.

A primal growl rose in his throat.

That was his to touch, but damn. Watching her bathe herself was erotic torture.

He pulled the glass door on the shower open and stepped inside the oversized enclosure, blocking some of the multiple jets from Deborah's body.

Her eyes fluttered open, sultry sensuality glowing in the dark chocolate depths. She didn't tense with embarrassment at being caught washing herself intimately, like some women would, and he found that an amazing turn on.

Her eyelids dropped to half-mast and she smiled. "Done with your phone calls?"

"I only made one. Carey is bringing Gamble and Morganstein for dinner later."

"Am I staying for it?" she asked, not sounding particularly interested in the conversation as she reached for him.

He wrapped her in his arms, surprised by the desire to hold her. Because it wasn't entirely motivated by sexual need. "We'll get your things and bring them back beforehand."

"So, I'm really moving in."

"You agreed." Was she trying to back out now that he'd agreed to location shoot?

"I did. I guess I still find it a little incredible you're inviting a total stranger to live in your home for the next two months." She rubbed her hands down his back and over his buttocks.

"After this afternoon, I wouldn't call you a total stranger."

She laughed, the soft feminine sound going straight to his dick. "No, I suppose not."

He pulled her closer, so their wet, naked bodies touched from chest to thighs. "I ran a background check on you."

Would that piss her off?

She nuzzled into his chest, licking a trail of water up his pectoral. "You said you didn't know how old I was."

"The file came in while you were sleeping." Fire erupted along the trail of her tongue against his skin.

He did nothing to stifle his groan of appreciation at the sensation.

"Are you going to let me read it?" she asked between gentle bites of the flesh she'd just licked.

Was he supposed to keep thinking while she did that?

"If you want." His voice broke on the last word as her teeth closed over his nipple, pressing down just until it began to sting.

She laved his nipple before pulling away to move across his chest with more biting kisses. "It only seems fair."

He didn't reply as her mouth found his other nipple, sending unexpected pleasure stabbing through him.

Her uninhibited enjoyment of his body excited the hell out him.

She would be the perfect lover if she wasn't in the acting business.

Shoving that disturbing thought away, Rock cupped her delectable ass and lifted.

She didn't hesitate to lift her face for a wild kiss. Her lips were soft and swollen from earlier, her mouth just as sweet and hot.

Her legs came up around his hips as he adjusted their position so the apex of her thighs pressed against his swiftly growing erection. She undulated against him, rubbing her clit against his cock, their kiss going incendiary.

As often as they'd already had sex today, this time should be slow and leisurely.

He wasn't feeling it though.

He wanted to be inside her body. Right now.

Rock helped Deborah get better friction between them with his hold on her fleshy curves as they moved together.

It felt so damn good, but he wanted more.

She broke her mouth from his. "Want you inside me."

"No condom." He'd had every intention of getting sexy in the shower, but hadn't thought they'd end up doing the Full Monty.

Not just because he'd already been inside her more times than even he had expected to happen, but they were under time constraints.

If they were going to get her things before dinner, they didn't have a lot of time for their shower antics.

That didn't stop his body from demanding full penetration though.

"Get one," she demanded even as her legs tightened around him and she increased the tempo.

"You'll be too tender." It was the one consideration he could not ignore.

Something shifted in her expression, approval mixed with awe sliding over her beautiful features. "I'm not."

"Are you sure?" Did he still have that extra box of condoms under the sink?

"Yes." Her undulations grew more frantic. "I want."

He felt that particular tight sensation in his balls and at the base of his cock that told him even if he didn't get inside her, he *was* going to come.

"You have to let go, if you want me to get the condoms."

"No." She wasn't letting go.

"Fine."

He shoved the shower door open and stepped dripping onto the tile, her body latched around his like an octopus. He bent down and flipped open the door on the under-sink cabinet.

She giggled, the sound going high and breaking as his movements shifted the position of their bodies.

Score. The condoms were there. Unopened. Damn.

It took precious seconds to rip through the packaging and get to a condom. Then he had to open that without destroying the damn thing in the process.

Not an easy task with her mouth burning another pleasure trail along his neck and collarbone.

He sat her on the edge of the vanity, stepping back far enough to get the condom into place. His damn hands shook as he rolled the latex over his aching dick.

Without preamble, he hooked his arms under her knees, spreading her wide for his penetration. She leaned back, her hands supporting her on the countertop, breasts offered up in tempting relief.

He groaned. "That picture right there is enough to make me come."

"You better not!" But her expression said she was pleased to have this effect on him.

He pressed the head of his cock against her entrance.

It was her turn to moan, her head falling back, her body flushed with desire. "Yesss..."

The word drew out into a long, pleasure filled moan as he pushed inside her.

It should be easy. She shouldn't be so tight. Not after their hours in bed.

But wet, silken flesh pressed around him in a snug grasp that stole his breath. "You're so tight."

"You're big."

Maybe he was, but he didn't remember another woman holding him so closely.

"Perfect fit," he groaned out as he pulled back until only his head remained inside her.

She gasped. "Don't tease."

He didn't answer. Couldn't answer. He wasn't drawing it out on purpose. Rock was running purely on instinct right now.

Doing what his body required.

Nothing more. Nothing less.

She made a needy sound and he plunged forward, barely bottoming out before he was pulling back in one long glide. Deborah cried out and tilted her pelvis up to meet him, to draw him in? He didn't know, couldn't stop to figure it out.

Swiveling his hips on each downward thrust, he pistoned in and out of her, driving them both deeper into the maelstrom of pleasure.

It consumed him.

Her cries and demands for more said she was drowning just like him.

And then he couldn't even think that much anymore as he pounded into her with uncontrolled, primitive rhythm. Pleasure roared through him, exploding out of his cock into the condom. His muscles locked as he shouted his approval.

Deborah tightened around him, her own scream rending the air as her vaginal walls convulsed and squeezed him to maximized pleasure.

She was so beautiful in her satisfaction, it hurt him somewhere deep inside to see Deborah abandoned so completely.

One thing he was sure of. In this moment, she wasn't playing a part.

No matter how good an actor she was, the flush of her body, the involuntary tightening of her muscles, the glazed looked in her eyes, they all told a story he wanted to read again and again and again.

Deborah waited nervously for Art, Carey and Ms. Morganstein to arrive for dinner.

She was less concerned about how they were going to react to Rock's new contract as the news she'd moved in with him for the duration of their filming in Alaska.

She could barely believe she'd agreed to it herself.

But there was something about Rock. He wasn't like any other man she'd known and the sex was mind blowing, just like he'd promised. She'd pinch herself to make sure she wasn't dreaming, but she'd never imagined sex could be this good.

Even in her dreams.

"Deep thoughts?" Rock asked, coming into the living room.

Deborah shrugged. "I'm just not sure what everyone is going to think of me moving in here for the shoot."

"Carey is staying too."

"He is?" Did that make it worse or better?

Rock poured himself a whiskey from the drinks cabinet. "I want to spend more time with my brother."

That wasn't surprising, considering how Rock felt about his family. She'd been surprised Carey's initial plans hadn't included staying at Jepsom Acres.

Well, until she'd realized he'd signed the land use contract without his brother's knowledge or approval.

She had a thought. "Does Carey know he's staying?"

"He will tonight."

Nope. No alpha dictator in this man at all. She wasn't about to examine too closely why that trait seemed sexy instead of annoying either.

She simply said mildly, "He is an adult, you know."

"Even adults need the support of their family once in a while."

"Do your sister and brother know that about you?"

Sadness? Weariness? Something flickered in Rock's gaze. "I'm the exception to that rule."

Or he'd been forced to be for so long, he didn't know he needed other people.

Without thinking about why she felt the need to do it, she walked over to him and reached up to kiss the underside of his jaw. "You're exceptional, that's for sure."

His smile took her breath away. "Thank you."

His kiss was on her lips and held a lot more passion than hers had. She was lost in the feel of his lips when the sound of a door opening and voices barely registered.

With a final press of his lips to hers, Rock stepped back. "They're here."

She was still translating those words in her desire fogged mind when Carey came into the living room, followed closely by Art and Ms. Morganstein.

"I'm glad Carey was able to talk sense into you about the contract." Art put his hand out Rock.

Rock shook the other man's hand, but his expression wasn't warm. "Funny, I was under the impression you sent Deborah to do that."

Art shrugged. "It never hurts to have more than one perspective."

That sounded so much better than the reality, which Deborah was now pretty sure had been an expectation she would exploit the sexual chemistry between her and Rock to convince him.

Which she had done.

An unpleasant weight settled in her stomach.

"Knock it off, Rock." Carey shook his head. "You have your own reasons for letting us use Jepsom Acres for the film, but the day you let a woman lead you by the nose - or anything else - I'll give up acting."

Since she was certain that was the very last thing Carey would *ever* do, Deborah appreciated the sentiment.

She wasn't so sure, but she would cling to the belief Rock's *own reasons* had more to do with his love for his brother than the amazing sex she and Rock had had that afternoon.

"We're all hoping that doesn't happen any time soon, Carey." Ms. Morganstein's tone wasn't effusive, but was all the more believable for its dry sincerity.

And that was one of the reasons Deborah had wanted to work on this project. Art might have his cynical side and Ms. Morganstein might be hard as nails, but they appreciated artistic talent.

Carey's smile was nearly as gorgeous as his brothers, but it didn't affect her the same way. Not even a little. "Thank you, Ms. Morganstein."

Rock wasn't smiling, but he wasn't glaring either as he surveyed her bosses. "Carey, get our guests a drink."

The younger man immediately offered the contents of the drinks cabinet with the confidence of familiarity.

Art didn't surprise her when he asked for soda water and a lime. The director didn't drink when he was talking business. Ms. Morganstein, however, wanted a Manhattan and Carey showed his mixology skills making it with practiced ease.

Rock's brow rose, but he didn't comment on his brother's adeptness as a bartender. "I assume you brought the revised contract with your witnessed signatures."

Art settled into the same chair he'd used before. "I wasn't happy with some of the restrictions you placed on hours for filming and locations."

Carey poured himself two fingers of whiskey and swallowed half in one large gulp.

Rock frowned at his brother basically doing a shot for courage and then at Art. "I told you the terms weren't negotiable."

"Everything is negotiable."

"You don't know my brother," Carey muttered before tipping back the rest of the amber liquid in his glass.

Ms. Morganstein's lips pursed, her eyes casting censure at the director. "We talked about this, Art."

"And I told you I thought Mr. Jepsom was a reasonable man, Elaine."

Taking Deborah's arm and tugging her toward the sofa, Rock ignored the by-play. "Did you know Cailkirn was settled primarily by members of three Scottish clans?"

"I read something like that. There was an Englishman and Russian fur traders too, weren't there?"

Rock's mouth twisted sardonically. "That's right. The town has a website. Sloan said we needed to move into the twenty-first century."

"Sloan?" she asked.

"Mayor Sloan Jackson. Wasn't his picture all over the website?" Rock asked with mockery.

She remembered the letter from the mayor now. "Not really. Just with his letter."

"He does like his publicity photo."

"It's a good one." She might have infused her voice with just a tad extra clear feminine approval.

But if the man was as good looking as his photo made him out to be, he could give Rock a run for his money in the gorgeous alpha male race.

"You think so?" Rock asked with narrowed eyes.

"Oh, yes. He's pretty young for a mayor, isn't he?" She gave Rock her best guileless look.

"Especially in this town," Carey inserted.

Rock shook his head at his brother. "Sit down, kid, before you topple."

"I'm fine," Carey insisted, though his cheeks were flushed from his double shot.

He sat down however, and Deborah gave a mental sigh of relief.

"He was only thirty when he got elected. Sloan's the one that got us on the cruise route." Carey nodded sagely.

Deborah refrained from rolling her eyes. All they needed right now was a tipsy dinner companion when things were already tense between Rock and the others.

"He had the right business and political connections to make it happen." Rock didn't seem bothered by his brother's tipsy demeanor.

But then he wasn't giving off much of any emotion at all.

"Yeah. Lucky him. You're one of his friends. Right, big brother?"

"Yes." Rock gave Deborah a sideways look. "I could introduce you if you want."

"No, thank you." She would have laughed if she was sure he was teasing like she'd been.

After their hours together in bed, she had no interest in meeting another man. No matter how good looking and politically savvy.

"Getting back to the contract..." Art inserted.

Rock turned his sherry gaze onto her director, no give in his granite set features. "You can leave the signed contract on the coffee table before you leave tonight or start looking for a different location tomorrow."

Art opened his mouth to speak, but Ms. Morganstein forestalled him. "Would you please try to remember, Art, that Mr. Jepsom has not signed the contract himself?"

In other words, Rock could still withdraw his contractual offer if Art's insistence on trying to negotiate what had been presented as nonnegotiable annoyed him enough.

"Come now, Mr. Jepsom. You have to realize the difficulties you are putting in our way with some of your stipulations. You are not a neophyte about this business."

Ms. Morganstein let out a hiss of annoyance.

Carey just shook his head and muttered something too low to hear.

"Call me Rock. Using Mr. isn't going to convince me of a respectful attitude when you use it just before trying once again to adjust terms I have been clear are already set."

"I'm not trying to offend you, Rock, but I've got a movie to make."

"And you can make it somewhere else if you don't like my provisions for making it here on Jepsom Acres."

Art seemed to finally get a clue that Rock meant what he said because the director opened and closed his mouth without speaking again. His expression turned thoughtful, but not calculating.

Finally.

Art looked at Deborah. "What do you think about the contract?"

"I haven't seen it."

Art's brows beetled, his eyes narrowing on her. "What were you doing here all afternoon then?"

"Getting to know me better," Rock said without missing a beat.

While she sat and called on every drop of her talent as an actor to hide her gasping shock at the colossal disingenuousness or lack of perception in Art's question.

"I'm sure she took the time to tell you about the movie then," Ms. Morganstein said drily.

"She did."

"What did you think?" Carey asked, trepidation seeping through his tipsy demeanor.

"That the subject matter and intent behind the film were worth investing in."

"Oh." Carey's head dropped. "I thought..."

"We can talk about what you thought later. We'll have plenty of time. You and Deborah will be staying here for the duration of the filming."

Carey's head shot up at that. "We will? I mean, that's great. I thought I'd want to stay with the rest of the cast and crew at the lodge, but I miss home."

"I'm glad to hear that."

Carey gave his brother a smile that nearly broke Deborah's heart. He so obviously wanted his brother's approval.

While Rock, in no way, could be said to approve of their chosen profession, the man's love for his brother was undeniable. A pang of longing for family, for that kind of unconditional love, hit Deborah so hard it became a breath-stealing pain.

She wanted to call her younger sister, but Deborah knew that, ultimately, she would feel just as empty afterward, if not more so. Alicia had chosen her primary allegiance a long time ago and it wasn't to the sister who had chosen to buck family tradition and expectations.

Rock's hand landed on her shoulder.

Maybe that should embarrass her in front of her bosses because it implied at least some level of intimacy had been achieved between them. But she didn't care.

Deborah needed the human connection right then.

Their gazes clashed, his seeing too much.

"It turns out it's a good thing they are both staying here," Art said, interrupting the silent communication between Rock and Deborah. "There was some kind of mix-up with the rooms booked for our cast and crew. Right now, some of the rooms have four people staying in them."

"Sounds crowded," Rock offered laconically.

The look he gave Deborah said that once again, he wasn't impressed with the director's forethought and planning.

"I don't know what happened." Ms. Morganstein frowned. "The directorial first assistant assured me that the proper number of rooms was reserved, but the Lodge did not agree."

Rock looked ready to say something Deborah was pretty sure would be derogatory or incendiary.

"Do you think Lydia's ready to serve dinner?" she asked with classic, and not very subtle, misdirection.

"Who's Lydia?" Carey demanded.

"Mrs. Painter." Rock grimaced. "She has decided she and Deborah are friends."

"What does that make us?" Carey asked in unconscious duplication of his brother's same question that morning.

"Family," Rock said, giving Lydia's answer.

Carey's brow furrowed, but he didn't say anything else.

"As to your question," Rock said to Deborah. "She left it warming before going home."

"She doesn't live here?" Deborah asked in surprise.

"She used to. When the twins were younger, but she finally married her longtime beau when they started high school."

Carey made a disgusted sound.

Rock rolled his eyes. "My brother never forgave Levi Painter for taking her away."

Carey shrugged, embarrassed, but he didn't deny Rock's words.

"Art, put the signed contract on the coffee table and then might I suggest we all celebrate with dinner?" Ms. Morganstein worded it as a question, but she was already standing in anticipation of everyone's cooperation.

"I'd prefer to see Rock sign the contract before we go into dinner."

"My assistant acts as my notary, but he went home hours ago."

Deborah hadn't realized anyone else was in the house. Who else did he have working for him?

Art handed a set of documents toward Rock. "Deborah and Carey can witness it."

Rock didn't reply, but he took the contracts and checked both copies had the required signatures before adding his own.

Deborah and Carey both signed as witnesses and then Rock passed one copy back to Art and laid the other on the coffee table.

Carey jumped up like that had been a signal. "Now, we can eat."

CHAPTER EIGHT

Dinner was surprisingly pleasant. Deborah expected tension, but it turned into the celebration Ms. Morganstein had suggested they make it.

They talked about the movie and the amazing roles both she and Carey had in it, with no overt hostility on Rock's part.

"This movie is going to make your brother's career," Art said as he sipped complacently at his second glass of dinner wine.

"Are you worried about being typecast?" Rock asked Carey.

"No. I'm making a statement. It's who I am."

Rock's smile was the first genuine since the others had arrived. "Then it's a good statement to make."

"I don't want to live a lie, trying to build a career pretending to be something I'm not."

"I'm proud of you."

When Rock didn't add a caveat, making sure his brother knew that he wasn't proud of the decision Rock hadn't agreed with - going into acting - Deborah wanted to hug him.

Carey's eyes grew suspiciously moist, but he blinked several times and smiled. "Well, yeah, what's not to be proud of?"

Rock didn't smile. Serious as a banker under audit, he said, "Nothing."

"Let's not go overboard." Something in Carey's tone said he wasn't joking either, though he was trying to.

"Not to break up this little love-fest, but we need to agree on tomorrow's schedule." Ms. Morganstein pulled out her smart phone and started swiping and tapping. "We can do the initial scene blocking at six."

"In the morning?" Carey squeaked.

Ms. Morganstein gave a barely-there nod, but focused her attention on Rock. "Will that suit?"

"Yes. Carey can show you the areas mentioned in the contract."

"Since you are limiting the days we film in the house, we won't do any work inside until we've done all the scenes we can with the outbuildings and outside."

Rock relaxed back in his chair. "Good idea."

In other words, he wasn't budging on those limits.

Art frowned, but he just said. "We'd better get back to the lodge then. If we're going to be back here at the ass-crack of dawn."

"I'll bring my stuff with me tomorrow morning," Carey said to his brother.

Rock nodded. "Good."

Ms. Morganstein gave Deborah a questioning look.

"I brought my things over this afternoon." She didn't offer any explanation beyond that.

As awkward as the situation felt, it was none of their business. Deborah's decisions were her own.

"Are you sure you prefer to stay here?" Ms. Morganstein asked, a wealth of meaning in her words.

"Who wouldn't?" Seriously. Even without the phenomenal sex, Rock's home was beautiful and quiet.

The Northern Lights Lodge was nicer than she'd expected of the small town, but it couldn't compete with the millionaire's home. And the chance for quiet to study her lines and regroup after a day of filming was something she would never turn down.

Ms. Morganstein studied Deborah for several seconds before giving a sharp nod. "All right then. We will see you tomorrow."

The others left, and Deborah found herself helping Rock clean off the dining table.

"I'm surprised you don't leave this for Mrs. Painter."

"I would never."

"I like that."

He stopped in front of her, putting the dishes she was holding back on the table before pulling her into his arms for one of those shattering kisses he was so darn good at.

When he stepped back, she had to force herself to focus. "What was that for?"

"Do I have to have a reason?"

"Other than finding me irresistibly attractive? Nope," she teased.

"Good thing I do then."

She'd been admired for her beauty, her body coveted by men

who liked the idea of taking someone *famous* to bed, but no one had ever found her sexually irresistible.

Not like this man.

"You're really good for my ego."

"You're not good for my self-control. Let's get this stuff to the kitchen so I can take you to my bed."

"I don't get my own room?" she teased.

"Sure, but you're sleeping in my bed."

"You're not even a little shy about what you want, are you?"

"Should I be?"

"No." She liked him fine just the way he was.

His smoldering look told her they had better get the table cleared or she was going to end up being made love to on it.

She didn't want that memory the next time she ate in here with her colleagues.

Deborah grabbed the stack of dishes and hotfooted it to the kitchen.

She was putting the serving dish to soak when she felt heat against her back. Rock's hands came around to cup her breasts, his hard body pressing into her from behind. "You look damn sexy at my sink."

"Some women might find that comment sexist."

"Good thing you're the one standing here." He bent down and pressed heated lips against her neck. "I like the way you look in my home. The only improvement would be you standing here naked."

She would have laughed but didn't have enough air. She'd known that was what he meant.

"I don't usually do the dishes naked."

"No?" he asked, teasing along her neck with his teeth.

She shivered, electric shocks of pleasure jumping like lightning from one nerve ending to the next.

He tugged at her earlobe with his teeth. "Feel good?"

"You know it does." Her voice rose an octave as his tongue came into play.

Rock Jepsom knew way too much about how to give pleasure to a woman. To her.

Dizzy with that pleasure, Deborah dropped her head back. She let herself rest against his muscular chest, taking advantage of the stability and giving him better access.

The ultra-masculine sound of approval he made went right through her. Heat and pleasure coalesced in her core. A molten swirl of sensations she should be too tired, not to mention sated from earlier, to be experiencing.

What was it about this guy?

Everything about him turned her on. Every touch was perfectly targeted, causing a conflagration of desire in her.

She made a stab at reason. "I have an early call time tomorrow."

"Not as early as Carey's." There was definite satisfaction in Rock's voice.

"You sound a little too gleeful about that." Her words came out more breathy than the teasing tone she'd intended.

But his hands worked sexual black magic on her body, even through the layers of her clothes.

"I may still be a little bit pissed at him," Rock admitted against her ear, blowing soft puffs of heated air in more shiver inducing sensation. "Even if his actions brought you here."

Warmth unfurled inside her at the knowledge he saw her as a benefit to his brother's undoubtedly annoying finagling.

"You were really nice to him at dinner." Kinder than she'd expected.

"He's my brother."

Who Rock didn't mind waking up a couple of extra hours early to guide the director and his crew, but who he would ultimately protect, even from himself.

Rock slid his hand under her sweater and up the naked skin of her belly to cup her breasts, the silk of her bra no barrier to the calloused pads of his fingers. "Why are we talking about my brother?"

"I don't know." She inhaled sharply as he pinched her taut peaks.

"Flip that switch." He directed her head with his own so she saw a single switch to the right of the sink.

She reached out and pressed it, dropping the kitchen into immediate darkness. The shades had not yet been drawn over the five-foot-wide, countertop to ceiling window over the sink.

Moonlight bathed the meadow beyond in a silver glow, the sky such a dark blue it was almost black, the stars blinking through the break in the clouds, ethereal in their beauty.

She gasped again, this time from the sheer gorgeousness of the night sky.

How had Carey managed to leave this behind?

"You would understand better than I," Rock said, indicating she'd asked the question out loud. "You have the same passion for the business."

"It's our dream." Though what part of it was her dream and how much of her efforts were meant to prove something to people who stopped acknowledging her existence eleven years ago, she couldn't really say.

"Dreams." The wealth of disparagement in that single word was mind-boggling.

She turned in his arms, so she could look up into his face. Though cast in shadow, it wasn't hard to see the granite set to his jaw.

She reached up and laid her hand against his stubble roughed cheek. "Dreams feed our heart."

"It's a good thing I don't have one then."

"I don't believe that."

He looked down at her, his sherry eyes glittering blackly in the darkness of the kitchen. "Don't make the mistake of thinking because I love my siblings, I have anything resembling a real heart."

"That doesn't make any sense."

"This between us is sex. You know that. It's all you could possibly want."

"Why? Because I'm an actor?"

"Because your life is in LA and mine is very clearly here."

"You have to travel, Mr. Big Time Venture Capitalist."

"You're not looking for a long-distance relationship."

"I'm not looking for anything right now." This whole thing had come out of left field for her.

She'd come to Alaska to make a movie, not find a boyfriend, or something more. Honestly, she was still reeling from how quickly she'd responded to him.

It didn't help that with all the thoughts swirling through her head, her desire had not abated even a little bit. She was supremely aware of how close he stood, of every point which their bodies connected.

"Good." The finality in his tone said the conversation was over for him.

His lips covering hers insured it was over for her, too.

Not ready to talk about things still confused in her own head, she gave in easily, responding to his kiss and reveling in the knowledge that he was going to make love to her again.

After minutes of the mind-shattering lip-lock, he broke his mouth from hers to tug her sweater over her head. He didn't stop there but stripped the clothes from her body interspersed with kisses and caresses that kept her heartrate in the stratosphere and the pleasure inexorably building inside her body.

He looked down at her, her body pale in the moonlight from the window. "That's better."

"You said you wanted me naked." And this man was used to getting what he wanted.

It might even be a religion for him.

"I did."

"I think I'd like you naked too."

His brow rose, his craggy features cast in taunting lines. "Would you?"

"Oh yes." And she wasn't going to wait for him to acquiesce.

She immediately started on the buttons of his shirt, loving the glimpse of whorls of hair over a chest way too muscular for a man who made his living behind a desk.

He dropped his slacks even as she finished the buttons on his shirt. She let him shrug it off while she reached for the waistband of his briefs obscenely tented in front, his broad head already peeking out of the top.

She dropped to her knees in front of him, pulling the briefs down his legs as she did so. His big hard-on jutted toward her face. She accepted the invitation it presented without a second thought, leaning forward to kiss and then lick the weeping slit.

His flavor burst on her tongue and she went back for another taste, keeping him inside her mouth this time, licking and sucking with more enthusiasm than experience.

He didn't seem to mind, the demands and sexual praise falling from his lips a solid indication she was getting something right.

She wrapped both hands around his dick, rhythmically squeezing and rubbing while she played over his big, round head with her mouth.

He groaned and grabbed her under her armpits. "You've got to stop."

Her mouth came off him with a pop. "Why?"

"I've got a plan."

"Maybe mine is better."

He lifted her like she weighed nothing, bringing her body flush to his, her mouth close as she came up onto her tiptoes. "Trust me."

She gave her agreement in her kiss. He accepted it as his due and she didn't even mind. His hands were everywhere on her body, molding her curves, exploring her skin.

When he broke the kiss and turned her body around to face the window again, she made a sound of protest.

He leaned down and bit gently against her neck. "I'll make it good for you."

Of that she had no doubt. The man was a master at the art of pleasure.

He maneuvered her so she was leaning forward, her hands curled around the front edges of the sink for support, her legs spread, her bottom tilted up, completely open to anything he wanted to do to her.

What he wanted was to touch her, with his fingers, with his lips, with his teeth and tongue.

When she felt the broad head of his penis pressing into her entrance, she was so hungry for the contact she canted her hips back, tilting as invitingly as any temptress in history.

He speared her, his shaft stretching her and caressing her to new heights of ecstasy. The beauty of the night outside mixed with the silence of the kitchen broken only by their breathing and his promises of unending pleasure.

His angle rubbed her g-spot even as his hand came around so he could caress her clitoris with knowing fingers.

"You're going to scream as you come and I'll be the only one here to hear it." The dark promise skated over her skin leaving goosebumps in its wake.

A few more surges of his hips and she was doing just that, screaming and climaxing, her body not hers in that moment, but completely given over to the delight of his possession.

She was barely aware when he carried her up the stairs and laid her in his bed, dozing almost immediately, but waking enough to curl into his body when he returned some time later.

He'd probably picked up their clothes, discreetly discarded the condom and removed any evidence of their lovemaking from the kitchen so Lydia wouldn't be shocked in the morning.

Rock was that kind of man.

Rock tuned out the voices coming from downstairs. They were filming inside today. It was only the third day doing so in the two weeks they had been making the movie on Jepsom Acres. Art Gamble had shown his savvy in scheduling as much of the filming outside as possible.

Even so, discomfort climbed along Rock's spine at the knowledge his home was filled with strangers.

Maybe now would be a good time to go for a ride on Orion.

He was quiet walking down the hall into the kitchen.

Mrs. Painter smiled in greeting. "You're a little early for your midmorning coffee."

"I'm going riding."

"In the middle of a work day?"

"How am I supposed to get any work done with all the commotion?"

"Don't be silly. They're staying on the main floor just like you instructed."

"They're in my home."

"It's Carey's home too."

"I have never denied it."

"It's good of you to give him this. I'm proud of you."

Rock scowled, though he was secretly warmed by the older woman's praise. "I wasn't going to let him go to jail for fraud."

Mrs. Painter's eyes widened. "That wouldn't have happened, surely."

Rock shrugged. Probably not. Not with his lawyers, but things could have gotten ugly before he contained it. He was a venture capitalist, not a fixer.

"Maybe you should ask Deborah to ride with you."

"She's working."

"Actually, she's not in this morning's scenes."

Then why in the hell had she had an early morning casting call?

"I supposed Mr. Gamble likes to have everyone on set regardless," Mrs. Painter answered as if he'd asked the question aloud. "I think he'll survive you stealing his leading lady for a little while."

Rock thought so too.

Spinning on his heel, he headed to the sound of Art's booming voice yelling, "Cut!" followed by a barrage of commentary.

Apparently one of the actors hadn't done their homework and didn't have his lines down. It wasn't Carey, so Rock tuned out the older man's lecture as he looked around the living room for Deborah's beautiful form.

Wincing in sympathy to the actor getting his ass handed to him, she stood against the far wall. She noticed Rock immediately, like she was tuned into his arrival.

Her smile was warm and inviting.

Too damn sexy for his peace of mind.

He made a *come here* gesture with his hand. She cast a sidelong glance at the director and bit her lip, clearly undecided.

Rock wasn't so reticent. He crossed the room in long strides, enjoying the way her beautiful face reflected both concern and welcome.

He stopped in front of her. "Mrs. Painter said you aren't in this morning's scenes."

He made no effort to lower his voice. Gamble was still yelling, so quiet-on-the-set wasn't a consideration.

He ignored the way everyone's attention shifted from the incensed director to Rock and Deborah.

"I'm not, but Art likes me to watch the other scenes filming, for a sense of continuity."

"You've read the script." About a hundred times, if the number of times she went over it every night was any indication.

"Yes."

"Then you know what happens."

"Was there something you needed, Rock?" Gamble asked from where he'd finally stopped berating the unprepared actor.

Rock shifted his body so he stood between Deborah and her director, but faced the other man. "Does Deborah's contract require she be here for scenes she is not in?"

"No, but I prefer all my actors watch the filming, and her particularly." Gamble cast Deborah a censorious glance. "Which she is aware of."

"And I prefer not to have strangers in my home. There are times when everyone must make compromises." Rock let a hint of warning infuse his voice.

It was clear the director's anger was spawned by the realization he was going to need more inside filming time than he'd planned for today, which could put future filming days in jeopardy according to *their* contract.

Gamble's expression turned crafty. "I could probably see my way to releasing Deborah for some R&R time if we could have an extra couple of hours filming today."

Carey, who was in the scene with the hapless actor, gasped. He knew his brother well enough to know that wasn't something he'd be likely to agree to.

What he didn't know was how much Rock wanted to take Deborah into his world, even if it was just for a few hours.

He turned to her. "Are you on the afternoon filming schedule?"

"Actually, no."

So, Art had planned to have his leading lady spend the entire day watching other scenes film instead of preparing for her own part or taking a much-deserved day off?

Rock turned glacial eyes to Gamble. "Deborah and I will be

busy until eight. I expect my home to be quiet and empty of your crew and equipment when I return."

Gamble took a step back, his eyes widening in clear surprise at Rock's anger, but he nodded. "I can do that."

Rock turned his attention to Carey. "Make sure it happens."

"I've got your back, big brother."

Rock tamped down the desire to make a derisive sound. In his own way, Rock knew his little brother did have his back.

Rock put his hand out for Deborah. "You ready?"

She took his hand in silence and allowed him to lead her out of the room.

He stopped at the bottom of the stairs. "You'll want to put on jeans and boots. We're going riding."

"What if I don't know how to ride?"

"Amanda is a patient horse. You'll be fine."

"What if I wanted to watch today's filming?" she asked, a bite to her tone.

"Did you?"

"No, but that is beside the point. You and Art negotiated my time like I'm a commodity."

"On the contrary, *I* negotiated *for* your time. No one is forcing you to spend the free time I negotiated with me."

"Are you sure about that?" Her director would be pretty angry if she messed up the valuable hours Rock had extended him.

"I am. Are you?"

"You're saying, if I choose to return to the filming or do my own thing, you aren't going to renege on the extra hours you gave Art?"

"You are always free to *do your own thing*."

Deborah's sigh ended on a pout he didn't think she was aware of. "That's at least marginally better. Though I'm not sure what I think of my director considering my company a commodity up for barter."

"Are you saying that when you film in Hollywood, you're never expected to attend a certain party, or go to an investor's home for dinner?" He knew he was right. Rock had made his own command performances as the charming young son of Georgia Howell and Errol Jepsom.

"I'm not sleeping with those investors or party hosts."

"I'm glad to hear it."

"You're impossible, you know that, right?"

"I've been accused." By his siblings. By business rivals.

It was a thing.

She shook her head and spun on her heel, heading up the stairs.

"I'll meet you in the stables."

"Can you ride?" he asked, planning their afternoon in his head.

"I had to learn for a commercial."

Well, that was good to know anyway.

CHAPTER NINE

Deborah found Rock saddling one of the most beautiful mares she'd ever seen with a gorgeous white mane and dappled grey coat. It was also one of the biggest horses she'd ever seen. Full stop. "I know the state of Alaska is all about everything being oversized, but do you really need giant horses?"

"Humans have increased in size over the centuries, few equines have been bred to accommodate that change in size safely. These two have been."

She noticed the black stallion already saddled then. He was patiently waiting on Rock, no throwing his head or snorts of temper, but still intimidating by his sheer size and leashed power.

"What's her name?" Deborah asked.

"Amanda. She's gentle enough for Marilyn."

"Your sister?"

"Yes."

"I would think she was an accomplished horsewoman, being your sister and all."

"She's not fond of horses. Carey isn't either. Both only ride under duress."

"Do you have another horse?"

"No. They fight over which one has to go riding with me. We've never needed a horse for all three of us."

She laughed at that, such a homey, *family* kind of argument. "Carey's probably thrilled I'm here to go riding with you then."

"You have no idea. Last time we went riding, he was so nervous, even Amanda got skittish after a while."

"Maybe if you had smaller horses."

Rock shrugged. "They have to be able to carry me for their

exercise when the twins aren't around."

Which Deborah realized was most of the time. Rock, at six-foot-four inches of pure muscle, probably did need a giant horse.

He finished saddling Amanda and led the mare out of the stable, the stallion following behind without a lead.

"Doesn't Lydia ride?" Deborah asked as she swung up onto the mare's back with a leg up from Rock.

"Her off hours are her own."

Unlike Deborah's. She'd heard the reprimand in Rock's voice. "Making a movie isn't like a regular job. It takes over your life."

Rock swung into the saddle and kneed his horse into movement. "I'd say that's pretty much true of any role."

"Which is why so many actors take breaks between movies."

"It still makes for a pretty narrowly defined life."

"You can find balance, if you look for it hard enough."

"Do you look for it?"

"I'm here with you, aren't I?" As he'd confirmed it had been *her* choice to take the day off with him.

He didn't answer but urged his horse into a faster walk. "Can you canter?"

"Yes, but I prefer galloping." It was a smoother gait and she was no professional.

"If you trust the horse, she knows the trails around here well enough."

"I trust you not to put me in jeopardy."

His smile made her stomach flip. Their pace increased until the horses loped at a relaxed gallop across the meadow and into the trees.

The mare did seem to know the trails because she followed the stallion and his rider without a single misstep.

Thank goodness. Deborah wasn't keen on the idea of falling off such a tall horse.

The forest was beautiful, but Rock was headed somewhere special and the horses seemed to know it. They'd ridden about an hour, slowing to a walk when the trees and brush thickened, the ground grew rocky and the sound of rushing water could be heard. A few minutes later, they broke into a clearing of sorts, a waterfall-fed pool in the center surrounded by rocky outcroppings, the Alaskan sun dappling between the leaves of the surrounding trees and covering the open spaces in beautiful, bright light.

"It's gorgeous," she said with awe. A reaction that was becoming almost familiar in her weeks here in Cailkirn. "If Carey had shown them this place, we'd have filming scheduled here."

"It's a hike in. The ride takes about an hour, walking longer."

"I'm pretty sure Art would think it was worth it."

"It's not my land."

"Who owns it?"

"The State of Alaska."

Even better. She had a feeling the state would be easier to deal with than Rock. "I can totally picture the big failed love scene set here."

Rock swung down off the big stallion, patting its midnight black flank before the horse ambled over to the pool and bent down to drink.

Her stallion came over to help her down off of Amanda's back. Rock put his arms up and she let herself slide into them.

He held her to him as the big, grey Percheron mare moved away to join Orion at the water. "Do you ever take it off?"

"What?"

"Your acting cap?"

"Do you?"

"What?"

"Ever stop being Mr. Responsible, Scary Venture Capitalist."

"I'm not scary."

"Tell that to Art's assistants. They offer bribes to each other to get out of taking messages to you."

Rock rolled his eyes. "I haven't bitten anyone yet."

"Good thing, seeing as how you're not a vampire."

"Does he have to hire them so young?"

"At the salary he's paying? I'm pretty sure the answer is yes. Besides, only Dino could be considered young. The second assistant is at least ten years older than me."

"Some boy carrying cable asked me if I was excited about being an extra."

She couldn't stifle her laughter. She pitied the hapless crew member who asked something so dumb, but man, Rock's look of disgusted chagrin was funny.

"Most people would love to be an extra in a movie."

"I noticed. The number of casual visitors I've had in the last two weeks is more than the past five years combined."

She had no trouble believing that. The man liked his privacy.

"Even Sloan wants a bit part," Rock said with disgust.

"The mayor?"

"Yes. He said it will be good for his image."

"Does he need help with his image?"

"The man likes attention. He is a politician."

"And your friend."

Rock's lips twisted. "Yes."

"Don't sound so happy about it."

"He made me introduce him to Art."

"I bet Art was thrilled." Getting the mayor's support would mean a lot to the director.

"You know your boss."

"I do."

"Not as well as you know me." Rock's tone dropped an octave to that husky timbre that sent shivers through her.

"I should hope not."

He leaned down and kissed her, the pleasure of their lips coming together blowing through her like a storm wind and leaving just as much devastation in its wake.

She stepped back from him. "Don't tell me you brought me here to go skinny dipping. That's so cliché."

They hadn't brought swim suits though.

His laughter filled the air around them. "The tributary that ends in that waterfall is off a glacier-fed river. It would take a braver man than I to go swimming in that water."

"But it's so beautiful here."

"Be my guest." He waved toward the water.

"You don't think I will?"

"It wasn't a dare, Deborah."

"Wasn't it?" Surely it wasn't that cold. The summer sun was high in the sky, the temperatures not exactly those of Sothern California, but definitely warm enough for swimming weather.

Before she could think better of it, Deborah stripped her clothes. "Is it deep enough to jump into?"

"Yes." He measured her with his sherry gaze. "You sure you want to go swimming. There's other things we can do now that you're naked."

She wasn't having him call her a flat-footer or city slicker. His home was filled with luxury, but he looked at the film cast and crew like they were a different species. Even her sometimes.

He wasn't going to look at her like a coward.

She turned and took a running leap into the beautiful pool.

The cold hit her with the power of a fist, surrounding and covering every inch of her body with ice prickling intensity. She was so shocked, she just sank at first.

Unexpected terror burst inside her, her body's reaction to cold so intense it hurt.

She kicked for the surface, her movements feeling sluggish and awkward, the freezing water sucking the coordination from her muscles.

She broke the surface and sucked in air before giving vent to her shock with a long, dedicated scream.

The sound of his laughter was nearly as loud, the big man clearly breathless with mirth.

She glared over at him. "It's not funny."

Her body gave a jolting shiver, her teeth clacking together in the cold.

"I warned you."

He had, which made it worse. "So, you never swim here?" she demanded, her stuttering from the cold detracting from the effect of the annoyance in her voice.

"Not in years and usually not until later in the summer."

"You're a peach."

"Come on out of there and I'll warm you up."

"I would if I could. My legs and arms don't want to move."

His expression turned serious in the blink of an eye. "Stop playing and get out of the water. You could end up with hypothermia if you're not careful."

"Maybe you should have thought of that before letting me jump into glacier runoff." A terrible idea formed in her mind.

He was standing on the edge of the water now. "I'm serious, beauty. Get your pretty ass out of that water."

She moved like she was trying but couldn't quite coordinate her movements. Which actually wasn't a huge stretch. "I'm trying."

He stripped so fast, his movements were almost a blur. Her conscience told her to warn him off, but the devil inside her wanted him to jump into the icy water like she had.

Even if she would have given into her better instincts, he didn't give her the chance, diving straight into the water.

Big hands curled around her waist even as he rose out of the water, bringing her up with him, so her breasts broke the surface. The grunt he gave in acknowledgement of the cold of the water was nothing like her scream.

She'd been prepared to laugh, but she couldn't. Not when he was looking at her like *saving her* from her own folly was all that mattered.

Her legs wrapped around his torso of their own volition, but she very consciously leaned forward and pressed her chilled body against his heat.

His eyes narrowed. "You said you couldn't move."

"I was teasing."

"You've got a mean streak."

"Maybe."

"This water is damn cold."

"You're not."

He didn't say anything as he maneuvered them to a big flat rock slab beside the water. Rock set her on the smooth surface warmed by the sun. The difference in temperature from the water made her gasp and she made to scramble to her feet, but he pressed her onto her back so her body was warmed from heel to shoulder by the warm stone.

"Stay there. I wasn't joking about the hypothermia."

"I'm sorry. I shouldn't have teased you into coming after me." Though honestly, she never expected him to act so fast.

"On purpose or because you couldn't help it, every second in that water was lowering your body temperature."

"You're a very protective guy." It ran through his veins as sure as red blood cells.

He shrugged, his big body moving over hers in intriguing ways. "Someone had to be in my family."

"Tell me about it."

"Now?" he asked, giving a significant look to their naked bodies pressed together.

"Did you have something else in mind?"

He did. And it started with him licking every droplet of icy water from her rapidly heating body.

They were laying together afterward, her head on his chest, his heartbeat a steady rhythm in her ear, when he said, "I'm not sure why my parents decided to have the twins."

Deborah made an encouraging sound, but didn't speak, not wanting to break to spell of Rock opening up to her.

"Carey and Marilyn weren't accidents. Not like me."

She patted his hard stomach and couldn't help the small, quiet denial. "You weren't a mistake." He was planned by somebody. Anyone this amazing wasn't anyone's definition of a *mistake*.

"I think they had fantasies of being that Hollywood legacy family. Everything in their life was fantasy."

"But children need reality."

"They need real food, real clothes, real care."

He painted a bleak picture. "Your parents didn't offer those things?"

"When they remembered." His body went tense beneath hers. "They forgot a lot."

She couldn't hold back the wounded sound straight from her heart.

He tugged her closer, running his hand over her back. "It wasn't so bad when it was just me. I learned to fend for myself early. But when the twins came..."

She waited for him to continue, but he didn't. "You really did take care of them from birth."

"I was ten years old. Learning to change a diaper was hell. There was a part-time nanny at first. She fit Georgia's view of the fantasy, but when it came a choice between buying a designer dress for a red carpet event and keeping the nanny, they let her go."

"How old were the twins?"

"Six months maybe? Georgia was very proud of her newly slim figure."

"When did you all move to Alaska?"

"They bought Jepsom Acres as a *retreat* when the twins were five."

"Another fantasy they wanted to live out," she guessed.

"Exactly. They hired Mrs. Painter, Miss Bearcliff back then, the first time they flew down to LA without us."

"She stayed with you."

"Even when they forgot to pay her. Yes. She helped me with the twins, getting them into school, making sure they had food to eat, clothes to wear."

"Lydia is an amazing woman." And no wonder Carey was possessive of her like a mother.

"She is."

Deborah shifted so she could look into Rock's eyes. She wanted him to listen to her words and believe what she was about to say. "But you were an amazing kid and even more incredible man."

"I made mistakes."

"You were a child with the responsibilities of an adult."

"Georgia and Errol meant to sell Jepsom Acres when they got back from that last trip." Rock grimaced. "It didn't matter to them that Carey and Marilyn had made friends, that they had a life here. I'd already offered to keep them here with me."

"They refused?"

"They had a new fantasy."

"But then their plane crashed." She could imagine the conflicting emotions Rock must have gone through when that happened.

"My first reaction when the news came was relief. The kids weren't going to get uprooted again." The guilt in his tone tore at her heart.

"You grieved them though. I know you did." She leaned down and placed a kiss right over that strong heart he did such a good job of hiding from everyone but his family.

"Yes. I even missed them, but in that first moment of knowledge I felt relief."

"And you've never forgiven yourself."

"What is there to forgive? They never cared how their choices impacted their children. They never made a single decision with the twins' welfare in mind."

"Or yours."

He made a dismissive sound. "I was used to that."

"But you didn't get over it."

"I'm not a broken child."

"No, you are a very strong, highly intelligent man with a work ethic that rivals my own."

His chuckle was warm. She was glad he hadn't taken her words wrong.

Hopefully he wouldn't take these the wrong way either. She reached up and traced the line of his brow and down his cheek. "Your parents weren't neglectful because of their chosen profession."

"It didn't help."

"No." Most careers in the arts were consuming.

He trapped her hand against his face with his own. "But the choices were still theirs." It was a concession.

But she really needed him to understand. "And not the ones we all make."

She hadn't thrown her family away; they'd exiled her. And she'd tried so many times to make peace with her parents. They weren't interested in a daughter who wouldn't follow their plan for her life. They considered her a defect and had thrown her away like anything else that didn't work properly.

"How often do you see your family?" Rock asked, in tune with her thoughts in a way she did not question.

He might see their connection as purely sexual, but she hadn't since their first night together and she was fully aware that was her problem. Not his.

Her choices being evasions, lies or honesty, Deborah put the truth out there, raw and painful. "I haven't seen my parents since I was eighteen."

"Why?" he asked, judgment surprisingly lacking from his tone, his sherry gaze compelling more honesty from her, no matter how painful.

"They cut me out of their lives when I accepted a scholarship to a school for the performing arts instead of going to university and then law school like they expected."

"That seems pretty harsh."

"I thought so." What kind parents rejected their child because she didn't follow their plans for her life? Her parents. "My mother is a judge and my father is a surgeon on the board of his hospital."

"Med school wasn't an option?" Rock asked, his tone curious.

"They decided my aptitude for science wasn't strong enough in primary school."

Rock's body went rigid with tension, his expression tinged with disbelief. "And started grooming you for law school then?"

"Yes."

"But you rebelled."

"If you call excelling at something they didn't approve of well enough to land a decent scholarship rebellion, then yes."

"I bet they did."

He was right. Her mother had been livid, her father *disappointed.* "Yes, along with a lot of other less than complimentary things."

"They've never softened?" Rock rubbed her back, like he was comforting her for the decade old pain, for once nothing sexual in his touch.

"I invited them to my graduation."

"They didn't come?" He sounded like he couldn't imagine it.

He probably couldn't. As much as her industry had cost his family, he would never have made the same choice with his brother or sister, Deborah was positive of it.

"Not to that and not to a single thing I invited them to after." Not to a single movie premier. Not to a single industry award night.

Of course, she'd never been the star, or won something big and her mother had pointed that out when she'd told Deborah to stop pretending her *little accomplishments* meant something.

"Do you have siblings?" Rock asked.

"A younger sister." Deborah laid her head against his chest again, cuddling in for comfort she never allowed herself in a life where she was well and truly on her own. "We have a secret relationship my parents don't know about."

"That's bullshit."

"She doesn't want to lose them too. She has two children. They don't even know who I am. They think I'm an old friend she sees once or twice a year when Grandmother and Grandfather are conveniently out of town."

"Your parents have serious control issues."

"Oh, yes." But they hadn't been able to control her.

He tipped her head up with hand under her chin, his own expression suffused with approval. "You fought to make your own way."

"Sometimes, I wonder if I didn't take the path I did in order to break away from them."

"Their rejection hurt you." He tugged until Deborah was fully on top of him, his big arms locked around her.

She nodded, acknowledging a pain she never shared with anyone else. But with his past, Rock would understand. "I knew they'd be mad, I didn't think they'd dump me like a car that turned out to be a lemon."

"And your sister toes the line, even now she's an adult." Disgust laced Rock's tone. "Did she become the lawyer?"

He wouldn't understand her sister's behavior. He'd spent his life taking care of his siblings and sacrificing for them. Rock couldn't conceive of not having Carey or Marilyn's back, even when it came to something he didn't agree with or understand.

"She's a doctor."

"Who lacks both a backbone and compassion. I pity her patients."

"Maybe she agrees with my parents."

Rock shook his head, like that was just crazy, but when he spoke it wasn't about Deborah's family. "Speaking of sisters, Marilyn is coming in next week."

Relieved they were off the topic of her painful past, Deborah smiled. "I thought she was going to stay on campus and work on her master's thesis during the summer break." Carey had mentioned it the week before.

"Marilyn wants to see a film in production. She's really excited about the whole making a movie in our home thing."

Unlike her big brother, who barely tolerated it.

"I look forward to meeting her," Deborah said with genuine anticipation.

"She'll love you."

For some reason, Deborah really hoped that was true. Fitting in with Rock's family was more important than it should be for what could only be a short-term relationship. But it was a relationship, no matter how short-term. Regardless that Rock classified it as just sex, there was nothing *just* about how he and Deborah interacted.

It had only been two weeks, but every day she spent in this man's world and in his bed, the less she wanted to leave it. She might have no more choice over that than she'd had over leaving her family, but she was determined to squeeze every drop of experience out of their time together she would get.

She wiggled suggestively against Rock. "So, you told Art he had until eight."

"Yes."

"I'm guessing we're not going to spend the rest of the day and evening lying naked on a rock in the middle of the forest." Not that she'd mind.

He shifted so she was suddenly on her back and he was looming over her. "You have a problem with that?"

"My body might. I'm going to end up with bruises if I'm not careful."

CHAPTER TEN

Just like that, he was up and pulling her to her feet. "We can't have that."

"I didn't mean we had to go right now."

"But I've got plans for the afternoon."

"Oh? Are we going to sneak back into the house?"

"I'm taking you into town. You haven't seen much of Cailkirn yet."

To be accurate, she hadn't seen *anything* of the quirky little town. In two weeks, she'd never left his property. "True."

The drive into Cailkirn was shorter than she remembered, the views along the highway enough to keep Deborah's gaze fixed firmly out the window. "Is there anything not gorgeous about this state?"

"It's home."

"By choice. You could have taken the twins back to the Lower 48 after your parents' deaths." But even as she said the words, something told her Rock wouldn't have done that.

"They don't remember the fear and stress of moving to the next *perfect* address constantly. I wouldn't revisit that for them."

"Did *you* ever want to move?"

"No. Cailkirn was the first place that felt like home." The first place he'd felt safe. It was in his voice. Not to be missed.

"What was so special about it?"

"It's a small, close-knit community. No child is going to get lost here. If the twins didn't show up to school, their teachers stopped by to make sure everything was okay."

She wondered how much of that was the usual way of doing things and how much came from Lydia letting others in the community know how absent their parents had been.

"So, that whole no child left behind thing really works here."

"Yeah, but maybe not the way it does other places." Rock shrugged, cast her sideways glance before focusing back on the road. "Kids get help if they aren't getting it in school. The level of volunteerism here and in other small Alaskan towns is higher per capita than most other towns in America."

"That's impressive."

"It is. It means the whole community takes responsibility for the well-being of the town." The words might be just information, but the way Rock said them, that tone in his voice? The set to his shoulders?

It all made her feel like he was telling her something really personally important to *him*.

"It sounds idyllic."

"It can be."

"There have to be drawbacks."

"We don't have a mall. The nearest movie theater is in Kenai. According to Lydia, groceries are worth their weight in gold."

"I noticed you have a garden."

"Lydia has a garden."

"She has time?"

"I hire her nephew to help her out."

"Because she wants fresh produce."

"I would do anything for that woman."

"You've offered her enough money to retire, haven't you?" Deborah wasn't sure how she knew, but she was positive Rock had done that.

"She says she'll retire when she wants and not one day before."

Deborah laughed. "That sounds like her." She'd gotten to know the woman and they had indeed become friends.

Rock pulled his SUV into a parking spot on Main Street. The kitschy shops were crowded with tourists, the real wood boardwalk filled with more people moving from shop to shop.

After so much time spent at Rock's place, Deborah felt herself drawing inward at the sight, despite the usual crowds of her LA home. "Wow. It's a lot busier than I expected."

"There are two ships in port." Rock sounded dismissive. "We don't usually have more than one at a time."

"It's like this all summer?" she asked in surprise.

"Yep. Then the last cruise ship sails and suddenly it's as quiet as the middle of National Park lands right here in downtown."

"I bet you prefer that."

He shrugged, his expression wry. "I do, but I appreciate the new life the cruise ships have brought to our home."

He got out of the SUV and came around to open her door. Deborah wasn't such a feminist she minded small courtesies like this one. She smiled and stepped out. "Are we going shopping?"

"If you haven't been in them, the tourist shops can be fun." Rock placed a warm, proprietary hand to the small of her back.

"But you've been in them." And she couldn't imagine Rock enjoying the tourist crowds.

"Don't worry, hot stuff." He winked down at her, flirtation glowing in his sherry brown gaze. "I'll have fun showing you around."

"There you go, reading my mind again." He was way, way, way too adept at that.

"You haven't got much of a poker face for an actor, beauty."

"I don't play roles around you."

"I'm beginning to believe that."

Her heart skipped a beat, but before she got a chance to say anything else he guided her inside a rustic store filled with dozens of display cases of jewelry. It wasn't high end, but it was enchanting and Deborah was soon lost among the colors and unique designs.

She didn't know how long they spent there, but Rock never grew impatient, or rushed her. From there, they moved next door to an old-fashioned emporium.

She couldn't believe how crowded the stores were. Not only with people, but with merchandise. The oddest assortment of goods sat side-by-side on shop shelves.

Right beside authentic *ulu* knives with their half-circle and wicked sharp blades would be a display of rubber moose that when squeezed, offered a colorful gas bubble. Beautiful, handmade jewelry shared shelf space with cheap t-shirts adorned with cheesy slogans.

One of which she thought would make a great gift for her sister. Bright pink, there was a female moose on the front in a tiara. Below were the words *Coffee Queen*.

"You don't drink coffee," Rock observed.

"Alicia, my baby sister, mainlines it." Deborah grabbed the t-shirt, surprised at the affordable price. The necklace that had caught her eyes was twice what she'd expected though.

Weird. And cool.

Rock maintained his patient, protective presence (keeping

enthusiastic tourists from knocking into her several times) as Deborah perused the shelves and collected a decent pile of things she'd determined she couldn't live without, or without sending to the small amount of family she still had left.

Rock presented her with a small bag on the way out of the store.

She stopped in the middle of the busy boardwalk and looked up at him, trying to find a clue, as to what might be in the sack, on his handsome face. There was none.

She bit her lower lip, stopping almost immediately, shocked at herself for reverting to an old habit she'd broken herself of long ago. "What's this?"

"Look inside and find out."

"You thought there was one more thing I needed to take home with me?" she asked with a laugh, strangely reluctant to open the bag.

"Yep."

She shook her head. "I'm pretty sure there wasn't."

He just waited, not moving, but forcing the flow of people to split around them.

She pulled out a small black velvet bag. Not the tacky stiff kind, barely a step above paper, but soft and luxurious, a little nice for the tourist shop, she would have thought.

Inside was the hand crafted natural stone necklace she'd decided was too much of an extravagance. The beads interspersed with graduating sizes of leaves, culminating in one that would dip toward her cleavage in the right dress shining in swirling blues and greens.

"I didn't mean for you to buy this for me."

"I know."

"Are you sure?" She wasn't looking for a sugar daddy. Not that the necklace had been diamonds-and-gold expensive but it had been out of *her* price range.

His laughter was as shocking as it was welcome.

"What?" she demanded, borderline cranky.

He shook his head, like he she was just oh so ridiculous. "The look on your face. It's a necklace, not a contract to become my mistress."

"Can a woman be a mistress if the man isn't married?"

He shrugged. "Doesn't matter. It doesn't apply."

Okay. Maybe she was being a teensy bit ludicrous. She took a deep breath and let it out along with the sting to her pride that wasn't meant to be there.

She smiled. "Thank you."

He leaned down and kissed her, making her feel like maybe she should have been the one to offer the sweet token of affection. "You're welcome."

"Rock, who is this lovely young lady?"

Rather than looking embarrassed to be caught kissing Deborah in the middle of the boardwalk, or even a little annoyed as she might have expected by the nosy interruption, Rock turned a clearly welcoming smile on the elderly woman who had stopped beside them.

"Miss Elspeth, may I present Deborah Banes, soon to be film star and already hard working actor." It was a much more positive introduction to her career than she would have expected.

"Deborah, this beauty is Miss Elspeth Grant." He indicated an elderly woman with chin length red hair (though surely it wasn't a natural shade any longer) and sparkling blue eyes, the patina of loveliness still evident on her features. This woman had been a knockout back in the day and would still turn heads with her porcelain skin and air of youthfulness.

Miss Elspeth blushed and fluttered her hands. "Oh, you. The men in this town are too charming by half," she said archly to Deborah. "You'll have to watch yourself."

"I'll keep that in mind," Deborah replied dryly.

Rock gave the older woman a teasing smile. "Don't scare her off, Miss Elspeth."

"Oh, I wouldn't do that. Not at all. Rock's quite the catch, my dear. A real man's man."

"*Miss Elspeth.*" Rock sounded pained.

And was that an embarrassed tinge on his cheeks?

Deborah made no effort to hold back to her smile. "Is he?"

"Oh my, yes!"

Rock glared at Deborah and then turned a pained smile on Miss Elspeth. "Deborah is here making a movie."

He *must* have been desperate to change the subject if he was bringing the movie up voluntarily.

"You're all staying at Northern Lights Lodge." Miss Elspeth's words had a bite of accusation in them. "I suppose Carey *James* thought our Knit and Pearl wasn't sophisticated enough for a film crew from Hollywood."

"I'm not sure Carey had anything to do with the arrangements for accommodation. It probably had more to do with the number of rooms available than anything else."

"But you're a small film company. I'm sure Alma said so."

"Even a small film crew is still a crew. There are technicians, actors, and production people." Deborah shrugged, hoping the older woman's feelings were assuaged.

She felt a peculiar reluctance to offend Elspeth Grant.

"You know it's owned by the Sutherlands, don't you? The Grants own the Knit and Pearl."

"Um, that's nice." What else was she supposed to say?

"The Sutherlands aren't all bad, of course. Even if Josiah has far too high an opinion of his lodge." Miss Elspeth muttered something else that sounded like *and his matchmaking skills*.

"It's rustic but very nice," Deborah felt compelled to say. "Though I'm sure the Knit and Pearl is lovely."

"You'll have to come for dinner."

"I'm not sure I'll have time."

"The mayor is a Sutherland too, you know?" Miss Elspeth said as if she hadn't heard Deborah demur. "On his mother's side. I hate to imagine how insufferable Josiah Sutherland would be if Sloan Jackson carried his name as well as some of his blood."

"You don't like Mr. Sutherland." The innkeeper had seemed nice enough to Deborah during her brief stay at the lodge.

"I like him fine, not that way, of course." Miss Elspeth blushed. "I lost my one true love overseas. He was a Marine."

"I'm sorry."

Miss Elspeth nodded. "I'm sure Josiah's glad Sloan Jackson doesn't carry his name when it gets bandied about with his proclivities."

The small-town mayor had acknowledged *proclivities*? Deborah wasn't sure how well that would go over, even in Hollywood.

"The man only takes his *lovers* from the cruise passengers." She whispered the word *lovers*. "They're here one night, two at the most. I'm sure that suits his purposes."

"His purposes?" Was the man a pervert? She was sure Carey had said Mayor Jackson was Rock's friend.

"He likes to tie his women up."

"Maybe you shouldn't be telling me this." In the middle of Main Street, in front of Rock. Deborah felt her own blush heating her face. And wasn't even sure why. They weren't *her* proclivities.

"Oh, we all know. We pretend we don't, naturally, but it's a small town." Miss Elspeth winked conspiratorially at Deborah. "He doesn't think any of the local women would like his bedroom adventures, but I'm not so sure he's right about that."

"Um, Miss Elspeth--"

"Don't you worry, dear. It's all safe, sane and consensual, I'm sure."

Deborah stared at the elderly woman, not a single word to say coming to mind.

"Don't look so shocked. I like to read." Miss Elspeth grinned, her blue eyes glittering with mischief.

Deborah looked up at Rock for rescue, but for once, he looked as lost she felt.

"Well, you two will want to get back to your date. Don't let Rock get away with too much, dear, but don't be too hard on him either. What's the fun in that?" Miss Elspeth dismissed them as if she hadn't left them both speechless with a little finger wave and a wink for Deborah.

Deciding the whole frozen fish look wasn't a good one for her, Deborah forced herself to start walking again, her new necklace tucked securely in with her other packages. "She's quite a character."

"Most of the long-term residents are, one way or another." Rock's hand slid into hers, his big fingers lacing between hers.

"Even you?"

"I'm a millionaire who feeds his own horses and participates in the Highland Games."

"You're of Scottish descent?"

"You heard Miss Elspeth. I'm an honorary Grant. The Knit and Pearl sponsor me in the Braemar Stone toss."

"Like you need them paying your entrance fees."

"No, but I wear their colors."

"Like a kilt?"

"Exactly like." And he didn't sound at all like a man who would be bothered in the least showing off his gorgeous legs in the Grant colors.

"And you throw a heavy rock?" she asked, picturing the rather primitive event and deciding that while she should probably think it was barbaric, she thought it sounded exciting instead.

"About twenty-five pounds of heavy."

For a man who tossed around fifty-pound bales of hay taking care of his horses, that was probably not a big deal, but still. Yum. "I can't wait to see."

"The games are in September," he dismissed easily. "You'll be gone by then unless Gamble runs way over schedule."

"Maybe I'll have to come back for them." It was the first time she suggested anything like maintaining their friendship beyond the making of the movie, but not the first time she'd thought of it. She wanted to hear his reply. Needed to hear it.

Best case scenario. He'd come to realize how well they clicked and wanted to explore that further too. He'd say something like his door would always be open to a friend's visit, or something.

Only he didn't answer, just gave her an unreadable look.

So, not worst-case scenario, but definitely not best case either. It hurt, but she hadn't really expected Rock to have figured out his heart this fast. Or admit he had one just yet.

Had she?

"So, more shopping?" she asked, beyond ready to change the subject.

Could anybody say *awkward*?

"Aren't you shopped out?"

She forced a grin. "I'm guessing you are."

"I had hoped to go for a walk along the water."

"That sounds almost romantic."

"Aren't we allowed romance?"

After buying her that necklace, making love to her in the sun? She thought they were already heavily planted in romance territory but didn't think he'd appreciate her saying so.

"A romantic walk along the water sounds wonderful."

"No jumping in."

"I don't skinny dip in front of witnesses."

"Oh really? What was I?"

"My lover."

"For the summer."

Her heart did a little flip at the reminder, but she forced a smile. "For the summer."

So, he *wasn't* keen on the idea of her coming back to visit. She didn't think her hint had been too subtle. Rock Jepsom was a smart guy. And maybe his silence had been more of an answer than she'd wanted it to be.

Miss Elspeth wasn't the only interesting character they met in town and by the time they sat down for dinner, after their walk along the water, Deborah was thoroughly charmed with Cailkirn and its inhabitants. If she was maybe on the verge of being just a little in love with one of them, well that was her business, wasn't it?

She looked around the restaurant, filled with tourists and locals alike, finding it easy to tell which was which by the way the wait staff interacted with them. "I can understand why you decided this was a good place to put down roots for you, Carey and Marilyn."

Rock's eyes widened with surprise. "It's not exactly big city."

"But it is a wonderful little town where the people clearly care about one another." His shock that she could appreciate things besides bright lights and big cities was starting to irritate her.

Hadn't he gotten to know her at all? Or romantic walks, thoughtful gifts and kind gestures aside, maybe his only interest really was her body. He knew it better than she did at this point, she was pretty sure. A little frisson of excitement at memories of how well he knew went zinging through Deborah.

Rock made a sound halfway between disparagement and awe. "You got that from a few nosy neighbors trying to figure out who my date is?"

"Everyone who has stopped us to talk has been a neighbor?" She found that hard to believe. Especially considering how far out he lived.

"Everyone in Cailkirn is a neighbor."

"Well, that makes sense."

"I notice you didn't ask if this was a date," he drawled with a tinge of sarcasm.

She gave him her best prim look. "Some might call it a kidnapping, but I prefer the term date."

"I gave you a choice about coming."

"So, a date."

"Does that mean you don't want anyone joining you?" a deep masculine voice asked from behind Deborah.

She turned her head, surprised to see the mayor. She'd seen his bio and picture on the town's website, but it didn't do him justice. Former Army Ranger, Sloan Jackson, was a definite hottie. With his brown hair cut and styled in the latest trend, molten grey eyes, a body on par with Rock's and features an action star or a rival politician would envy, he was the whole package. And a bag of chips.

"Sloan." Rock nodded in acknowledgement of his friend.

Unable to forget Miss Elspeth's words about at the mayor and his preferences in sexual partners, Deborah felt her cheeks heat in an uncharacteristic blush as she met the mayor's undeniably flirtatious grey gaze.

"This is Deborah Banes, one of the film people."

"Nice to meet you, Deborah. Elaine Morganstein mentioned you when we met."

Deborah smiled. "It's good to have the town's support of the film."

"We came to an amicable agreement after some discussion," Mayor Sloan said. Which wasn't exactly agreement but wasn't denial of her words either.

"Surely filming is good for the town." She understood Rock's attitude but was surprised the mayor would have taken any kind of convincing.

The information she'd found on him and the town seemed to indicate he courted publicity.

Sloan smiled, the expression every bit as shark-like as anything she'd seen back in LA. "This time of year is busy around Cailkirn. Businesses are already stretched to their limits managing the tourist trade off the cruise ships."

"But surely our small crew doesn't stretch the town's resources too much."

"As I've said, Elaine, Art and I worked out an agreement that's good for your movie and our town."

She wondered if that had anything to do with the change in filming schedule for town shots. Then realized, of course it did. It probably explained why the catering service was out of Kenai as well, when originally, she knew the intention had been to use someone local.

Everyone local was probably already fully booked. Just like this diner, with not a single open seat, unless friends shared a table.

She wasn't surprised, or even really disappointed when Rock invited Sloan to join them. He stood up to sit beside her though, putting Sloan opposite them and got a little a growly when Sloan flirted with her over the menu.

"What's the matter, Rock, worried she's going to realize she might be interested in seeing what else is out there while she's visiting our little town?"

Deborah laid her hand on Rock's thigh before he could answer and whatever words he was about to say turned into a glare and a growl but remained unspoken.

Sloan smirked. "Don't tell me she's tamed you already."

"Damn it, Sloan."

The unleashed power she felt vibrating off Rock felt anything but tamed to Deborah. "Are you being an ass on purposed, Mayor Jackson?"

The mayor threw his head back and laughed.

Rock turned and kissed Deborah right there in the middle of the busy restaurant. And not like he'd done on the boardwalk either. This kiss was anything but sweet. It was fast; it was hot, and it taste of both passion and possession. And no, she didn't mind that even a little. This wasn't about being a possession, it was about being possessed.

And it turned her on. A lot.

When he pulled back, she took a second to catch her breath and then asked, "Not that I'm complaining, but what was that for?"

Would he admit it out loud? His need to possess her? She was still smarting from his clear intention for their relationship still to end when filming did. Things had changed for her, but they hadn't for him. Or he simply wasn't willing to admit it if they had.

A man as stubborn as him probably never would be.

Rock looked at her, catching her gaze and keeping it, making her feel for that moment like she was the only other person in the crowded restaurant. "I like you."

"I do too, Deborah Banes." The mayor's voice was an unwelcome intrusion, but not one she could ignore. "And it's just Sloan to my friends."

She flicked her gaze to his and saw that the other man's eyes glittered with speculation. It was a familiar look, one she'd seen in other men's eyes many times in her life. And if she hadn't met Rock, she might have explored that look. Or not. This man was far too confident in his own attraction.

"I can't say the feeling is mutual." Deborah took a sip of her water and gave the mayor a reproving frown over the rim of her glass. "So far, all I've seen is your annoying side. How about you show me something else for the rest of dinner. Rock's your friend. There must be a reason why."

Both men laughed; Rock put his arm around Deborah and pulled her close to his side. "He's annoying all right, but he's got his good points. He was there for me when my parents died. He helped me with Carey and Marilyn."

"And that was a good thing?" she asked dubiously.

Mayor Sloan chuckled. "I tried not to be too bad of an influence."

"So, it wasn't your idea for Carey to affect an English accent."

"Is he still doing that?"

"Enough that you notice when he doesn't."

Sloan shook his head. "He's still hiding from who he is."

"Maybe not so much." Rock sherry gaze darkened with satisfaction. "He said the role is a statement, so he doesn't have to hide who he is as an actor."

"That takes guts," Sloan said. "I'd like to see that boy stop running."

Deborah pointed out, "He's not going to stop chasing his dreams."

"That's not the same thing as running from himself." The mayor sounded like he knew what he was talking about.

Dinner was nice, and Deborah did end up liking the mayor, but she was glad when she and Rock left the restaurant and were alone again. They were so rarely alone. Even when the film crew left, Carey was there. Their time alone was usually in bed and that always led to sex, then exhaustion...then sleep. Especially as early as most of her casting calls were.

CHAPTER ELEVEN

Tension he hadn't realized had been gripping him dropped away as Deborah followed Rock into his bedroom. She'd been distant in some indefinable way since dinner.

He'd thought at first it might be Sloan, but as annoying as the mayor had been with his damn flirtation, Deborah had handled him just fine. No, it was something else. If he were a betting man, he'd put five thousand on the probability she was upset he hadn't wanted to talk about her coming back to visit after the movie was over.

But what was the point in letting her make promises she wasn't going to keep?

He was doing her a favor, even if she didn't realize it.

Deborah started peeling her clothes off with deliberate movements, her expression pure feminine provocation, no distance in her expression now. "I've got plans, Rock, and they require your cooperation."

"I like plans, hot stuff."

"I know you do." She stepped out of her underwear, no signs of self-consciousness, every glorious inch of her pale skin uncovered.

He could look at the feast in front of him for hours. Her breasts were a perfect handful, even for his big hands, tipped by dark pink nipples, already drawn tight with desire. The curve of her waist flared to perfect hips going down legs he wanted wrapped around him while he pounded inside her, or rubbed against her.

Damn it. He didn't care how they pleasured each other. He just wanted their bodies to be together, moving in unison.

His dick took immediate, near painful notice. "Damn, beauty, I've suddenly got some plans of my own."

Her laugh was as sultry as a Caribbean summer night. "Maybe

you should lose the clothes, Alaska Man." She started moving backward toward the bed, her body all sinuous grace.

He yanked his shirt over his head, not bothering with buttons, jerking his jeans and shorts off over his already hard cock with impatient movements.

She laughed at him. "In a hurry, Rock?"

"Yes."

She ran her hands down her torso, over those perfect pink tipped breasts, touching herself in ways meant to provoke. And damned if it didn't work spectacularly. He dove for the bed without a thought of playing it cool.

It didn't matter they'd already made love earlier today, or that they had a steady diet of daily sex, his need for her was as strong as if he'd had a long dry spell and met this sensual beauty for the first time. She was pure primal sexy.

Her laughter turned into a long, sensual moan as his mouth landed on the bare, soft skin of her throat. She undulated against him.

More provocation.

"You trying to make me lose my mind here, hot stuff?" he asked against her ear, his voice gruff with want.

Her foot slid up his thigh, caressing, taunting. "What if I am?"

"You're doing a damn fine job."

"Good." There was something there. Something in her voice. Something in the way she was teasing him.

But damned if he could focus enough to figure it out. Rock was used to being to aggressor. Even with this woman.

His beauty didn't lack confidence, but she wasn't like this. Pure heated desire rubbing against him with unadulterated intent.

She was all sinuous grace, soft skin so hot against his, he'd caught fire with a need that would consume him if he didn't meet it.

He pressed down, his hard cock aching, pure pleasure shooting from his groin to the rest of his body as his rigid sex rubbed against her moist flesh. She gyrated her hips, giving him delicious friction and making him groan.

"You like that, Rock?"

"You know it."

"Do you want more?"

Was she kidding? "You know I do."

She hitched her leg higher on his hip, opening herself to him, allowing his hard-on to rub against her swollen clitoris. They moaned together. And damned if her obvious pleasure didn't turn him on more.

The knowledge that his body was exciting hers, that not only was she allowing it, but inviting it, making it happen? That was intense in ways he did not want to think about.

This woman did it for him on every single damn level.

He surged forward with his pelvis, pressing against her, pleasuring them both, wanting to be inside her, but loving the feel of rubbing against her too much to stop what they were doing.

"Feels so good," she moaned in a voice laced with decadent pleasure.

Had any woman ever been as honest in her body's desire with him? If she had, Rock couldn't remember it. Deborah was special. And she drew forth a level of desire in him he'd never felt with another woman either.

"You are something special, hot stuff," he admitted just before taking her mouth again.

He poured feelings he would never give words to into that kiss. This relationship couldn't last beyond filming of the movie she'd come to Alaska for.

Deborah wouldn't be back to Cailkirn, but that didn't mean he wasn't going to take advantage of every day and night he had with her. Including wringing every last ounce of pleasure out of their current situation as he could right now. For both of them.

Rock continued to rub off against Deborah until he brought her to a shattering climax that had her screaming in his ear and arching up against him. He was coming moments later, his ejaculate splattering between them, marking her in a way that satisfied him on an atavistic level.

For several long minutes, they lay there, bodies pressed together, both their breathing harsh in the aftermath, the scent of spent pleasure mixing with sweat and pheromones in a fragrance Rock didn't find offensive at all.

"That was amazing," she said breathlessly as he cleaned them both up after he'd convinced himself to move.

Fighting the primitive urge to rub his come into her skin, he remained silent. He wasn't some kind of caveman that had to mark his woman with his scent. Deborah wasn't even really *his*. She was his temporary lover. That didn't justify the feelings of possessiveness twisting his insides.

Other lovers had never engendered these feelings and he'd be damned if he gave into them now.

"Didn't you think so?" she asked, sounding a little peeved.

He smiled, letting her see just how sated he was, his cock

hanging against his thigh at half-mast. "It was good, beauty. Damn good."

"I mean I know we didn't, *you know*."

"For a Hollywood star you sure can be an innocent," he teased as he tossed the wet washcloth at the laundry hamper and pulled her close.

She snuggled in, no attempt to maintain any kind of distance between them. "I'm no star."

That was one of the things he loved about having her in his bed. She matched him perfectly as a lover, but she was a great *sleeping* partner too.

"We don't have to screw to get off." And he was starting to resent the condoms for some crazy damn reason.

It wasn't like he couldn't get off wearing one. He wasn't some selfish kid that claimed he couldn't feel anything wearing a glove.

He just didn't like the sense of separation. So, he'd gone for making love in a way they didn't need them. Yeah, it made so much sense. Not.

He wasn't ever going to admit that issue out loud. He'd deal with it.

"I have an IUD."

"What?"

"And clean test results from the month before we came up to Alaska. I guess you'd have to trust me when I tell you that I haven't been with anyone since six months before then."

"What are you talking about?" But he knew. She was talking about not using condoms. Like she'd been reading his mind. Or maybe, she wanted that intimacy too.

Which should scare the shit out of him. Neither of them should be looking for *intimacy* in their *relationship* such as it was.

She slapped his chest, and looked up at him, her glare pretty fierce for how relaxed into the afterglow she'd been. "Don't play stupid. *Do* you have recent test results?"

He didn't even consider prevaricating. "I do."

"I'll show you mine, if you show me yours." Her voice was teasing, but there was a thread of seriousness he could not ignore.

This was serious stuff. It was the kind of thing they shouldn't even be considering. Not for a few weeks-long affair.

"I'll pull them out tomorrow morning."

"Okay." She yawned, dropped her head down on his chest and went boneless against him.

He loved that moment, when her body told him she trusted him enough to let go of all her worries and trust him to watch over her sleep.

He lay there thinking about the other trust she'd just given him, trust neither of them should be giving each other, but a step he was infinitely glad they were taking.

When her phone range later, waking her out of sleep, Rock was not happy. The expression on Deborah's face as she listened to whoever was on the other end wasn't anywhere near pleased either.

"Okay." Pause as the other person spoke, the agitated masculine tones coming through the phone if not the actual words. "I said, all right. I'll talk to him."

She hung up and gave Rock a worried look, her bottom lip tucked between her teeth.

"What's going on?"

"They somehow managed to lose all of yesterday's footage. Art only just discovered it."

"How the hell did they do that? Who did it?"

"Art doesn't know. The files were on the computer and the backup server, but they're gone, now and no one knows how."

"That's ridiculous. Someone had to have deleted them."

"Whoever did it isn't fessing up and it's not like we have major security on set. There's no way of knowing who signed into the computer. The whole editorial crew has access, not to mention Art and Ms. Morganstein's people."

"Is he sure it was an accident?"

"What else would it have been? Everyone on the crew and cast has a vested interest in this movie succeeding."

Rock looked thoughtful. "I suppose Gamble wanted you to ask me to amend the contract, giving you another day for filming."

"He did, yes." Deborah sighed. "I know that even if you say yes, you aren't going to be happy about it."

"If he agrees that when you're not filming, your time is your own, I'll let him have the day. I won't even bitch about it."

"So, I can spend that time with you?"

"So, you can get more sleep, spend time preparing during the day and yes, if you want, spend more time with me."

Deborah felt a grin split her face. Oh, she was so falling for this man. "I'm sure he'll be just fine with that." She knew she was. An extra hour of sleep some mornings would be very welcome. "And sometimes, I *want* to be on set when I'm not in the scene."

Rock tugged her back down into the warmth of his arms. "Just as long as every night you want to be here."

Rock was *not* hiding in the barn with the horses while the film crew took over his damn house *again*. Carey had convinced him to add an extra day of indoor filming to the contract for *Marilyn's* sake.

She had arrived that morning, all smiles, and hugs for her brothers and pure fascination for the movie being filmed on Jepsom Acres.

Rock had hung around the kitchen for an hour or so, but Mrs. Painter had shooed him away. He'd tried working, but he'd cleared his calendar for Marilyn's arrival.

Finally realizing his sister was not here to visit her eldest brother in any shape or form, Rock had come out to the barn to take care of the horses. There was always something to be done in care of the big animals.

Maybe he'd go for a ride. It didn't matter that despite having a lover in residence and both his siblings being home, he had no one to accompany him. He was not feeling sorry for himself. Millionaire businessmen were too busy for that kind of wasted emotion.

He pulled out Orion's tack and began to saddle the horse, talking to the big, black Percheron. "You'll be happy for the exercise anyway. Too bad we don't have someone to exercise Amanda."

He'd have to have Mrs. Painter's nephew take the mare for some circuits of the paddock at least. The boy was a passable rider.

"Hey, big brother. I thought I might find you here."

Rock turned in surprise at the sound of Marilyn's voice. "You're busy with the movie people."

"I was." She grinned, and he saw the little girl she'd been and the woman she was. "It's amazing you're letting them film inside."

"It's in the contract."

"Carey said you allowed them an extra day so I was guaranteed to see some inside filming while I was here."

Rock shrugged. He'd been seeing to the twins' needs since their birth. He didn't see what was surprising about this.

"You're an amazing brother, you know that?"

"Don't go getting all sentimental."

"Right. You're not emotional at all." His baby sister's voice was just dripping with sarcasm.

He chose to ignore it.

"What are you doing out here? All the filming is happening inside the house."

"Yeah, well, as cool as it is, I missed my big brother."

"You didn't take a break from your thesis to visit me." If she was going to do that, she would have planned to come home before she found out they were filming a movie in Cailkirn.

She frowned and shook her head at him. "It wasn't an easy decision not to come home this summer."

"You and Carey decided on a different life than this one." Rock tightened the saddle on Orion.

"We didn't decide to leave you behind."

"He hasn't been home since he left for LA."

"He wanted to come home a star."

"Hollywood breaks a hell of a lot more actors than it turns into stars."

"He knows that, but he wanted to prove he'd be different."

"Until he had a use for me."

"*Rock*. It wasn't like that."

"Wasn't it? Neither one of you came home until there was something here for you besides your family." Besides the man who'd given up his own childhood to raise them.

No, he wasn't feeling sorry for himself at all.

Damn it.

Marilyn surged forward and threw her arms around him in one her patented hugs. He'd never been able to resist his baby sister when she needed comfort and as much as it might seem like she was offering that commodity to him, he knew she was really seeking it.

Rock put his strong arms around his sister and gave her a firm squeeze. "It's okay, Marilyn. I'm never letting go, you know that."

"We didn't leave you."

They had, but she was his baby sister. So, he just hugged her.

She sniffled. "We were always coming back. I wasn't even going be gone the whole summer."

He gave another tight hug and the pushed her just far enough away that he could look down into her pretty face so much like their mother's. "How's the thesis going?"

"Good." She winced. "Okay, honestly? It sucks. Maybe this whole me being a film director with vision and a message for the masses isn't all it's cracked up to be. I don't know if I can do it, Rock."

He frowned. His can-do sister was doubting herself? No way in hell was he going to allow that to happen. He might not like where her dreams were leading her, but he'd be damned if he'd allow her to doubt her ability to make them happen.

"You listen to me, Marilyn Jepsom. Mom and Dad may have

gotten a lot of things wrong, but one thing they had in spades?"

She gave a watery chuckle. "What's that?"

"They never gave up and neither will you. You are brilliant, kid. You can do this."

"You really believe that? I'm not like you. I can't take a few thousand dollars and turn them into several million and raise my sister and brother while doing it."

"Well, we can't all be financial geniuses," he said with obvious sarcasm.

She punched him. Hard. "Don't you make light of it, Rock Spencer Jepsom! You are the best, smartest man I know. No other man can live up to you. And that's another thing. I keep breaking up with guys because they're not good enough. None of them live up to my big brother. It's a problem."

Rock couldn't be happier. "Well, now, that puts my mind at rest."

"Oh, put a sock in it, big bro. A girl has her needs."

"Not something I *ever* wanted to hear about."

She burst out laughing. "So, you're going riding."

"What was your first clue?"

"Don't be a smartass."

"Don't swear."

"Rock, I'm twenty-two years old, not twelve."

"Still my baby sister."

"You are such a Neanderthal about some things."

"This is not something new."

"I suppose not. Did you want some company?"

"You're offering to go riding with me?" he asked suspiciously. "What do you want?"

"Nothing." She glared at him. "I really did miss you, you big jerk. Do you want my company, or not?"

"I do."

It only took a few minutes to saddle her horse and then they were on their way, but they were only a short distance into the ride before Rock realized what Marilyn was after. Information. On Deborah.

"We're not dating."

"Carey said she sleeps in your bed."

"I don't appreciate you two gossiping about my love life."

"So, it is a *love* life."

"No, damn it."

"Oh, you swore!"

"Don't be a pain in my as... backside! Deborah and I are

friends."

"With benefits."

"Don't be smart."

"But you said I am."

For that, he took their horses to a gallop and only slowed down when his sister started using some of his favorite cuss words.

When their horses were walking again, Marilyn turned to him in her saddle. "Carey says you really like her."

"I do like her." Too much.

"She's an actor."

"I am aware."

"Is that why you insist you're not dating?"

"We aren't dating."

"Carey said you took her into Cailkirn, showed her the sites."

"There are no sites in Cailkirn." It was a popular refrain with the twins.

"You know what I mean. You two went to dinner, but Sloan horned in on your romantic evening. Did he try to make a move on Deborah?" Marilyn's eyes gleamed with more interest than was healthy in either their town mayor or her brother's current non-relationship. "Did he flirt with her?"

"Sloan flirts with every beautiful woman who crosses his path. He's a politician."

"He's something all right." Marilyn frowned.

"Deborah didn't flirt back."

Marilyn's grin was blinding. "Carey said she didn't."

"How would he know? He wasn't there."

"Town gossip." Marilyn looked pityingly at Rock. "You do remember how that works? Miss Elspeth has repeated your conversation on the Boardwalk word for word."

"I'd think she'd be embarrassed to."

"Ooh, was she talking about Sloan's proclivities again?" Marilyn demanded.

Rock felt real dread settle in his stomach. "You keep your mind off of Sloan's bedroom preferences, young lady."

Marilyn kneed her horse into a canter as she headed back to the house. "Gotcha!" Her laughter trailed her as she rode away.

The arrival of Rock's sister ate into their already limited time alone together, but the upside was the instant almost sister-like rapport Deborah shared with the younger woman. She couldn't remember ever being as free and easy with Alicia.

Maybe because she'd had to walk away from the family a decade ago, but Deborah loved the way Marilyn teased Carey or Rock and invited Deborah to join in on the joke. They'd had late night snack sessions in the kitchen and because Marilyn got the business, she got that Deborah had to do that in a healthy way.

They chatted and laughed, and Marilyn never judged Deborah or treated her like she was less because she was an actor. She talked to her like Deborah had wisdom Marilyn was eager to hear.

It was a gift. Rock might not be willing to give their relationship a chance, but he'd given her a taste of family she hadn't had in ten years.

And the kind of family she'd never experienced before.

"So, you and Rock?" Marilyn asked Deborah with exaggerated widening of her eyes and raised brows.

"For the duration of the film."

"Oh, you don't like that do you?"

Deborah rubbed her arms, feeling cold for some reason. "How can you tell?"

"Well, it's not like it's written all over your face. Okay, it kind of is. You don't have a very good poker face for an actor who has been in the business for like a decade. You're practically a *veteran*."

"Rock says the same thing. I don't put on roles for him."

"Or his family, apparently," Marilyn said with a wry smile.

"Should I?"

"No." The younger woman shook her head vehemently. "I'd say that's the worst thing you could possibly do. Especially if you're hoping to make this thing last beyond the movie. What's it like?"

"Being with your brother?" Deborah asked with a squeak, genuinely shocked Marilyn would ask.

The blonde was confident, bold even, but this was brash, even for her.

"Ewww. No. Being in a movie, dork."

Deborah laughed, relaxing a little. "Exhausting. Exhilarating. Terrifying."

"Why terrifying."

"I lost my family over my desire to be an actor. This is my chance to prove that decision wasn't the wrong one."

"And if the movie fails, you didn't prove anything." Marilyn's expression was filled with understanding.

More understanding than Deborah would expect Rock's sister to have.

Deborah grimaced. "Other than I make sucktastic choices."

In careers and men and friends. Really. Her life wasn't peopled with them, was it?

"Don't get so down on yourself." Marilyn gave her a tight hug. "Everybody has flops, but this isn't going to be one. I can feel it."

"Has Carey let you read the script?"

"No."

"Did he tell you about it?"

"Well, no."

Deborah couldn't help laughing. "Then you're not exactly an informed observer, are you?"

"Don't be snotty."

"Don't be bossy."

"It's in my DNA. You have met Rock, haven't you?" Marilyn's laughter was infectious.

"Touché."

"Carey said he wants to talk over dinner tonight. Like a family meeting or something."

"Oh." He hadn't told Deborah he didn't want her there. Maybe she should make herself scarce, regardless.

One thing she was not, was family.

She didn't have family, not really, not anymore. "Good thing I've got dinner plans with Art then. Direction stuff to go over."

"You do? Carey didn't say anything about dinner."

"That's because it's not about his role. Just mine. Just some notes I want to go over with Art." She made a mental note to let the director know about the plans too.

"Oh, okay. Is that usual?" Marilyn asked suspiciously.

"It's not unusual."

"He's not like putting pressure on you to spend a lot of time with him outside of filming is he?" Marilyn pressed.

Deborah got where the line of question was going and let her disgust with the idea show on her face. "Like you said, *ewww*. Marilyn, Art is a good guy. He has real integrity. He doesn't just talk about it."

"That's good then."

"I think so. I wouldn't have signed onto the project if he was that type of director."

"So, there *are* those in Hollywood."

"Of course, there are, just like there are corporate sharks that seduce their admins and dump them with pink slips." Deborah reached out to the younger woman. "You take your time researching the people you'll be working with, if you're smart. And I know you are intelligent. No project is worth getting in a bad situation over."

"You're right. I'm lucky. I have a cushion. So does Carey."

Deborah wasn't so sure that was true any longer, but she wasn't going to be the one to spill the beans to Marilyn about her brother's reversal of fortunes.

CHAPTER TWELVE

Rock watched his brother and sister trade affection disguised as insults over the dinner table. Deborah was eating with Gamble, going over scene notes, or something.

She wouldn't tell him how long she thought it would take. Irritated, Rock stabbed his steak and sawed at it with his knife.

"What did that piece of meat ever do to you?" Marilyn asked with a teasing smile.

"Nothing." He chewed his food, barely tasting the organic beef Mrs. Painter had marinated and grilled to perfection.

Carey pushed his food around his plate, but so far as Rock could tell the boy hadn't eaten any of it.

Rock put his cutlery down and waited until his younger brother met his gaze. "All right, kid, out with it. Ever since you've been home, there's been something you've wanted to say. Marilyn's here now. Say it."

Carey gave their sister a pained look.

Rock wondered if she knew what this was all about, but she just looked back at her twin in confusion.

"I'm not like Marilyn," Carey practically yelled.

"I am aware."

"That right there!"

"What?" Rock asked mildly.

"I know I'm not perfect."

"You don't have to be."

"Really?" Carey asked defiantly, but with an underlying hope Rock couldn't ignore.

He'd raised this young man, no matter how improbable that might seem to some. He would never allow Carey to doubt that

Rock accepted him, failings and all.

"I love you, Carey."

"I lost my money, Rock. All of it."

"I'm on your accounts, kid. I knew that."

Carey deflated, his expression still tense, but his body as slumped as a balloon with a slow leak. "I wondered."

"There's more," Rock prompted, certain there was.

It was time for Carey to come clean with all of it, for his sake. Not talking round it, saying vague stuff like he wanted to be himself. He needed to say who that self was. Out loud.

And find out his family loved him for being him and nobody else.

Marilyn's mouth was open in a shocked 'O,' but she hadn't said anything, no recrimination, no demands of how Carey had squandered so much money. For that, Rock was grateful. He thought the explanation was going to be a painful one.

"I'm gay."

"You always have been," Marilyn said, like maybe Carey was slow or something.

He glared at her and opened his mouth.

Rock quelled them both with a look.

"Are you out in Hollywood?" Rock asked.

Carey shook his head, pain and something like shame shining in his eyes. "Not yet. I told you I wanted this movie to be a statement. About me, but he said it would be career suicide."

"Who?" Marilyn demanded, with that tone that said things weren't going to go well for someone.

Rock appreciated the sentiment.

The story came out then. Carey had fallen in love with an older actor. The man had convinced Carey to bankroll *his* role in an indie action adventure that had subsequently tanked. Just like their relationship.

"He used me." The pain and shame resonating unmistakably in his tone now.

Rock reached out and squeezed his brother's shoulder. "People do that."

Carey looked up at him. "You don't."

He wasn't sure Deborah would say the same, but they'd both gone into their relationship, such that it was, with their eyes wide open. Not like his baby brother and that damn lothario in LaLa Land. A currently out of work actor who would be damn lucky if he ever got another role outside of porn again in his natural life.

"So, you don't mind?" Carey asked them.

Marilyn and Rock stared at each other and then at Carey and then Marilyn socked Carey in the arm. "Don't be an idiot! You're you. How are we going to mind you being you? Should I mind you having brown hair instead of blonde like mine? Gosh boys are dumb sometimes. I wish I was gay so I could marry a girl sometimes!"

Rock burst out laughing at that one, but then he sobered and stood up, pulling his brother from his chair so they faced each other. This was too important not to face it like men.

"You listen to me, Carey Jepsom. You are my brother. I raised you like a son. I will love you to the end of time. Nothing will ever change that. You get me?"

Carey swiped at the moisture spilling over his eyes. "Yeah, I get you."

"Now, I'm going to tell you something else. I can't make choices for you and I'll never try to push you into doing something you don't believe in, but I don't think a man who stole from you and used you is the best source of advice on how to live any aspect of your life. The world has changed, maybe not as much as we'd have liked, but every person who lives in courage changes it a little more. Isn't that what your movie is about?"

"It is, yeah." Carey looked shocked, like he was surprised Rock had listened when he'd talked about the movie.

"I raised you to be yourself. To be honest. Do you really want to deny an aspect of who you are to pursue your dreams?"

"I'm making this movie and it's so good and it's so real...I don't think I can."

"Then don't, Carey. I'll stand with you, whatever you decide, but you remember that. No matter what, I'll always have your back."

"Thanks, Rock. You've always been our Rock."

Then Marilyn and Carey were hugging him and he put up with it. For a little while anyway.

Deborah let herself into the house with Carey's key before dropping it and his gate opener onto a table in the hall like she'd arranged with him earlier.

"Dinner went late."

The sound of Rock's deep voice stopped her forward momentum toward the stairs and Deborah turned, adjusting her course toward the living room. She found him sitting in an armchair with his e-reader, his long legs encased in jeans stretched out in front of him crossed at the ankles. One lone lamp cast a soft glow over his ruggedly handsome features.

Undoing the buttons on the coat made necessary by the drop in temperatures night brought, even in summer, she smiled. "Where are the twins?"

"Watching an old Carey Grant movie in the media room." Rock set the e-reader down and reached for her. "Why so late?"

She let herself be pulled into his lap. "It sounded like Carey had things he wanted to say. And it ended up Art did too. One of the cameras isn't working and we had to reblock tomorrow's scenes to stay on schedule."

"Sounds like a lot of work." Rock's tone said he wasn't sure he understood why she'd been the one doing it.

"Not so much, but it was tedious. I guess that's all part of being behind the camera."

"Is that something that interests you?" Rock asked.

"It is."

He nodded, like fitting another piece of the puzzle that was her into his brain.

"And Carey?" she prompted.

"He said what he needed to."

"And it went okay?" she probed, unable to tell how dinner had gone by Rock's demeanor.

Messy family confrontations she got. Cold family dinners, filled with disapproving silences, she understood. But the Jepsom family dynamic was outside her experience and she wasn't sure what to expect from the way Carey had been behaving when he'd leant his keys and gate opener to her earlier.

He'd been nervous. Stressed. Clearly worried about the coming conversation.

Though from Rock's reactions to his siblings so far, Deborah wasn't exactly sure why. No doubt the man could be a hard ass. The new contract for property use with the film company attested to that, as Art pointed out at least once a day during filming, but with his own family? Not so much.

"Sure." The shrug was in Rock's voice if not his shoulders.

Deborah doubted Carey felt half so sanguine about their conversation. "You're so informative," she teased.

Rock pulled her coat off and nuzzled into her neck, sending shivers along nerve endings she'd only discovered having since meeting him. "You smell good, beauty."

"I smell like I need a shower." She tipped her head back to give him better access though.

"Shower after."

"You are insatiable."

He pulled back and met her gaze, his so intense it went to her very core. "Are you complaining?"

She shook her head, her mouth suddenly too dry to speak.

"Did you get everything settled with Art that you deeded to?"

"You want to talk about that now?" she croaked.

"I want to make sure you are okay."

She wasn't the one who'd had a family *discussion*. "I'm fine."

"You haven't had to meet with Art before."

"We've met lots of times."

"Here, for an hour. Not in town, for hours." The whole time they were talking, Rock was kneading Deborah's backside, his hands staking a claim she was more than happy to succumb to.

Technically, she hadn't needed to be there for the new blocking and Rock must have realized that. "Carey isn't usually staging a big reveal scene over dinner."

"Oh."

"Yes, oh."

"Carey was done telling us his big news hours ago."

"How was I supposed to know that?" she asked reasonably.

His sherry gaze glowed with desire. "I didn't like you being gone."

"Has anyone ever told you that you're a spoiled man?" she demanded.

"No."

"No?" she asked incredulously. Because really, the guy had a serious hard on for her presence.

"I am not spoiled."

"But you expect me to be here all the time."

"That was part of the deal."

She rolled her eyes, even as pleasure surged through her body at his expert touch. "Whatever you say."

"I say I didn't like you being gone."

"You missed me," she teased, hope springing anew in her heart.

A man did not miss a woman after only a few hours' absence and then simply let her walk out of his life with no desire to ever see her again a few weeks later. That made no sense. No matter what Rock thought he wanted.

Rock growled and then kissed her and pretty soon, Deborah wasn't thinking anything at all.

The morning sun glowed brightly through the skylight, allowing Deborah to appreciate the sight of the naked man still in bed with her. He was sitting up, the blankets and sheets in a pool that barely covered his hips, every inch of his well-defined torso on display for her pleasure. Or at least that had been the plan.

She had a rare day off and Rock had cleared his calendar as well. The automatic shades had receded to let the light in from the big picture windows and skylights only moments earlier, but both she and Rock were already awake.

She'd woken with the intention of starting their day with some sexy play, but the sound of his phone's insistent ringtone had interrupted her before she'd barely gotten started. With a quick, "I have to take this," that sounded way too alert for the early hour, he'd leaned across her body and grabbed his smart phone from its charging cradle. Rock was now speaking in rapid Japanese, his face set in lines that meant all business.

This was not part of the plan.

Today was supposed to be a day for play. Today was supposed to be a day for *them*.

Feeling mischievous, Deborah moved sinuously against Rock. Letting her hand slide precariously close to his sex.

Not by a single hitch in his breath did her businessman give away what was happening to the other man on the phone, but Rock let his thighs part, giving Deborah tacit approval.

She nearly shook her head.

This man was willing to take whatever risk. He wasn't afraid of losing control on his phone call no matter if she touched him right on his semi-tumescent flesh.

What woman wouldn't take that as a challenge?

A woman a lot less competitive than Deborah. That was all she knew.

Filled with determination to get some kind of reaction, Deborah let her hand cup his warm sac, trailing her fingertips over the silky skin, gently rolling his balls, oh so careful not to jostle or hurt the most tender masculine orbs.

Rock's legs moved farther apart. The only indication her touch was affecting him.

She kissed his shoulder, moving her mouth over his hot smooth flesh until she reached the tiny brown disc she sought and then she gave it all the attention it deserved, pulling the nipple into a tiny rigid peak with her teeth and tongue, using what she knew of his body to entice and excite him away from his phone call.

Reminding him, today was supposed to be theirs.

She moved across his chest, depositing small nipping bites as she went until she reached his other nipple. There. That was a hitch in his deep, oh so masculine voice.

He went on speaking, but the hitch had been there.

She was inclined to agree with Carey. Rock would make an amazing leading man in Hollywood. His acting skills were top notch, but he wasn't exactly lacking success in the business world, was he?

She continued down his stomach, her hands busy on his sex, bringing the warm thick flesh fully erect. He smelled like clean male skin, his scent entirely familiar and all Rock. They'd showered after making love the night before and she thoroughly enjoyed the natural fragrance of skin after a night of sleep wrapped in one another's arms. The warmth of his body amazing against hers, part of her just wanted to cuddle against him and revel in the stolen moment, when they had no place to be and no agenda but each other.

Even the phone call felt like a peripheral. Maybe even something good. Up to this point, she'd never had the opportunity to touch him without him taking over, or even getting his sexy seductive side going on.

Rock Jepsom had the kind of body that excited and delighted Deborah. He turned her on like no one ever had. Touching the sexy businessman's muscled limbs felt like a special privilege, one that could be denied her at any time. So, she had to take advantage while she had the opportunity. He was everything she'd dreamed of in a boyfriend, in both a physical and emotional sense.

If only he wasn't so sure that sex without commitment was the only way to go.

Pushing the depressing thoughts away, she kissed down his stomach with sucking little busses, bringing up marks that would disappear in a few minutes, but for now, marking him as hers.

He kept talking in Japanese, the cadence of his voice barely changing, but she lived for every minute shift in decibel, every tiny exhalation change, each inhalation he might not have intended to make.

Then she allowed her mouth to find the tip of his erection. Score! He made a hoarse sound which he turned into a cough. Grinning deep inside, she sucked.

A quick spate of Japanese and the phone call was over. Both of Rock's hands landed on her head, his fingers tunneling through her hair to knead her scalp. "What the hell are you doing to me, hot stuff?"

She gave a gentle tug to his balls in answer and continued sucking on his hard flesh.

A harsh shout sounded from deep in his chest, his voice filled with pleasure and loss of control that made her vaginal walls contract with a need to be filled.

Oh, yeah! Indie actress *one*, business concerns *zero*.

She kept going until Rock's powerful hips were jerking, his hands squeezing in convulsive movements against her scalp she found a total turn on.

Deborah loved knowing she could do this to the big man, reveled in the certainty that she alone could turn him inside out like this.

"Deborah!" His hips arched upward. He pulled at her head. "I'm close," he gritted out, the words tense and guttural.

She refused to be denied.

She and only she would take him over the edge.

Her jaw was stiff, but she increased the suction and bobbed up and down on his oversized prick, intent on taking him to full on orgasm.

Pre-come coated her mouth, surprisingly lacking in bitterness. She'd read somewhere that when two people were chemically compatible they tasted good to each other. She wasn't sure about the science of that, but Rock sure as heck tasted better than any other guy she'd had in her mouth.

Not that there'd been many.

Especially without a condom.

Her thoughts scattered as he shouted and came, filling her mouth with thicker, stronger tasting ejaculate. She swallowed and pulled off, jacking another two shots from him before he grabbed her wrist. "Enough."

"Is it?" She looked up at him. He was still hard in her hand.

Rock's sherry gaze burned with intent. "Come up here, beauty."

"You got plans, Rock?"

His smile was answer enough. Their day didn't get started for another hour, or so. He proved that she wasn't the only one with an oral fixation and found the taste of their partner pleasing.

Despite their morning lovemaking, it was still early when they pulled up in front of a large sprawling Victorian house just on the other side of Cailkirn proper from Rock's spread. The sign in front proclaimed it the Knit & Pearl Inn.

"What are we doing here?" Deborah took in the well maintained, but small patch of grass and flowerbeds in front of the house.

"Picking up our picnic lunch. Don't you dare tell, Mrs. Painter." Rock grinned as he unbuckled his seatbelt. "But no one can beat Miss Elspeth's chocolate chip-pecan cookies."

"Lydia's cooking has been amazing."

"She didn't need the extra work either."

Deborah nodded. "You can be considerate when you want to be."

Rock shrugged. "Do you want to come in and meet the Grant sisters?"

"Of course." Deborah followed Rock into the inn, loving the way the sisters had the bed and breakfast decorated.

From the name, she'd expected something fussy and grandmotherly, but instead it was warm and welcoming. The furniture was a mixture of antique and clearly newer pieces designed to a more traditional aesthetic.

Everything was clean and freshly polished, the fabrics unfussy and unfaded.

"It's nice in here."

"I'm glad to hear you think so," a rather formidable looking older woman said as she walked up.

Rock smiled at her. "Miz Alma. I'd like you to meet Deborah Bains. She's working on the film."

Miz Alma smiled and extended her hand. "I'd heard about you from Elspeth. It's a pleasure to meet you Miss Bains."

"Deborah please, Miz Alma. A pleasure to meet you as well."

"You're here to pick up a picnic basket?" Miz Alma asked Rock.

He nodded. "That we are."

"Lydia won't be pleased to hear that."

Rock treated the older woman to one of his rare smiles. "I'm hoping she doesn't hear at all."

Miz Alma gave Rock a look but didn't reply. Simply moved behind the desk and started working on something.

Rock didn't seem bothered by the dismissal as he led Deborah to the back of the house. They found another woman in the kitchen. She was talking to herself. At least that's what Deborah thought at first.

"I know, Ardal. I'm sure it will work out between them, but things aren't looking as good as they could right now," the redheaded woman said with a sad shake of her head.

"Who is Ardal?" Deborah whispered to Rock.

Rock put his arm around Deborah's waist and gave her a light squeeze. "Her dead husband. Don't worry about it." He cleared his throat. "Miz Moya, we're here for the basket."

Miz Moya looked up and smiled, seeming unfazed by being caught talking to her dead husband. "Oh, Rock. I didn't hear you come in. Ardal and I were conversing." She winked at Deborah. "You mustn't think me a batty old woman. Ardal left Cailkirn in life, but his ghost hasn't been able to leave it in death."

"Perhaps he has unfinished business." Wasn't that what they always said about ghosts that couldn't move on?

If you believed in them anyway.

Miz Moya nodded her head, red curls too stiff with hairspray to sway with the movement. "Just so." She stood up and started bustling around the kitchen. "Now, Elspeth made those cookies you like so well, Rock. I made your favorite stacked sandwiches and cranberry Waldorf salad."

"That sounds delicious." Rock's voice rang with clear sincerity. He didn't seem bothered by Miz Moya's propensity for talking to ghosts either.

Deborah smiled at the older woman. "It really does."

"Where are you two headed?" Miz Moya asked.

"I'm taking Deborah to get a taste of the area."

"You're not taking her hiking dressed like that?" Miz Moya asked, looking aghast.

Deborah wasn't sure what was wrong with what she was wearing. She'd put on jeans, a teal t-shirt, a grey short sleeved knit cardy that fell into points mid-thigh and she was wearing a darker teal scarf for both style and well, warmth. Alaskan summer just wasn't as warm as LA summer.

She'd opted for sandals, but she'd walked miles in these shoes back home. They were stylish, but comfortable.

Rock laughed, himself clad in jeans, two-tone knit tee and Cole Haan shoes. "We're driving to see the sites, not going on a hiking tour. I'm not Tack."

Moya made a face at the mention of the other man. "Kitty started working at his tour guide agency. I thought it was the right thing, at first."

"Don't you still?" Rock prodded.

"I'm not sure. She's been sad lately."

"She's a grown woman, Miz Moya. You have to trust her to make the right choices for her life," Rock said.

"That didn't work so well before."

Deborah reached out to the older woman. She couldn't help herself. Miz Moya just seemed so grief stricken. "It'll work out."

She didn't know if that were true, or not, but she felt almost compelled to reassure to the older woman.

Miz Moya smiled at her and patted her arm. "You're a good girl, Deborah. Elspeth was right, I think. You'd fit in well around here."

Rock made a scoffing sound. "She's from the big city and going back to it. Don't go thinking Deborah is moving to Cailkirn, Miz Moya. That's not how things work."

"Why not?" Miz Moya looked unconvinced. "You came here from LA and stayed."

"As a ten-year-old."

Miz Moya gave him a chiding glance. "Others have come and stayed."

"Not actors."

That again? Deborah felt like screaming. Hadn't they made any progress on that front at all? Or was Rock determined to forever lump Deborah in with his parents and every other flaky actor he'd known or heard of?

"Your parents stayed." Miz Moya pointed out.

Rock just shook his head. And Deborah felt her heart constrict. He'd never told anyone his parents had planned to leave the tiny Alaskan town before their tragic deaths. That they'd planned to rip the only security their children had known away from them...again.

Yeah, Rock had his reasons for doubting that Deborah might want to make a life in Cailkirn, but couldn't he ask, couldn't he even consider the idea of compromise?

CHAPTER THIRTEEN

Deborah made a little surprised sound when Rock turned south on Sterling Highway.

"What?" he asked.

She turned to him. "I don't know. I guess, I just expected us to go toward Kenai."

"There's more to the peninsula than the town it's named for."

"Yes, of course." Deborah's soft tones washed over Rock's body like her fingers had earlier that morning. "Where exactly are we going?"

He was glad she was talking again. She'd gotten quiet after meeting Miz Moya. He didn't know if it was meeting an old lady who still talked to the ghost of her dead husband, or what, but Deborah had seemed to pull into herself. Rock didn't like it.

He answered her question now without hesitation. "Ninilchik."

"Where's that?"

"About an hour south. It's one of the oldest villages in Alaska, much less on the Kenai peninsula. Before the Russians came, it was a Deni'ana Athabaskan lodging area." She was going to love the mixture of Russian and Native American culture in the small town. It was a lot like Cailkirn without the cruise ship culture and influx of hundreds of thousands of tourists in the summer. It was missing the Scottish influence as well.

"You'll love the Russian Orthodox church. It's really old and beautiful." He told her its history, knowing from past discussions it would interest her.

"You know a lot about your adopted state."

"It's home." He might not have been born in Alaska, but he was proud of his home. It was unlike any other place on earth.

She gave him a speculative look. "Carey said you fly to New York at least once a month."

"And Tokyo, sometimes Europe, even South America when necessary." That didn't mean he ever wanted to move to the Lower 48 to live. "I like to travel. There's things I can do in the city I can't here, but I always come home."

And he always would.

Cailkirn was home for him in a way it never could be for a city girl with stars in her eyes like Deborah. The woman was an older version of Carey. She wanted to be a star, just like his brother and that didn't make for settling down material. Not that Rock was looking.

He'd raised one family that had walked away already. He wasn't sure he'd ever open himself to another one.

"You're lucky." Her voice was soft, wistful.

"Am I?"

"You know what you want out of life and you have it. Do you have any idea how rare that is?"

"Are you saying you don't?" He passed a slow moving RV running his gaze over Deborah's face as he looked over to move back into the lane.

Her beautiful face was set in serious lines. "I thought I knew exactly what I wanted when I walked away from my family. I'm not so sure anymore."

"That must feel like hell, considering what you gave up for your dreams."

"My family was never like yours. If my parents could reject me just because I didn't go into the vocation they wanted me to, they could never have loved me like a mom and dad are supposed to love their daughter."

The pain in her voice did something Rock's inside. "You sure about that? Maybe they didn't want to see you spend your life chasing a dream that might break you."

"So, they tried to break me with their rejection?" she asked in a voice laced with bitter memory.

"I'm sure they didn't see it that way."

"My parents aren't like you, Rock. They don't love me like you love your siblings. Their love has as many conditions as the US Pacific Trade Agreement and I broke one of them, so they withdrew their love and my place in the family along with it."

"And now you're doubting the dream you followed?" he asked with some disbelief.

"I don't know. Maybe. We're not all as self-assured as you are, Rock."

"You seem pretty sure of yourself to me, beauty. You're one hell of an actor."

"Thank you. That's high praise coming from you."

"I told you. I don't like your industry. Doesn't mean I'm ignorant of it."

She made a sound between a laugh and disbelief. "You're just a little arrogant, you know?"

"Just a little?"

"Maybe more than."

Rock was right, Deborah loved the small town of Ninilchik and its historical Russian Orthodox church. But most of all, she loved spending the day with Rock. They held hands as they walked through the graveyard, making up stories about the lives the people buried there.

"I think that man must have been one exhausted puppy by the time he died. Three wives and all those children?" Rock shook his head, like the idea of all that family was an anathema to him.

Deborah wasn't buying it. Not from the guy who did family so well. "He probably died fat and happy."

"He outlived all three of his wives and half of his children. That's a lot of loss." Rock frowned. "I don't think fat and happy comes into it."

"But think of all the grandchildren he had by then."

"Do you think they made him forget the ones who had gone before?" Rock asked in a tone that had lost all the humor.

"I think we have to allow the gains in our lives to balance out the losses or we'd never survive." She couldn't dwell on the loss of her family and how they'd rejected her.

Deborah had come to recognize that early on. Although, she realized there was still a part of her that was trying to prove that her decision hadn't been the wrong one, she didn't spend her days in an emotional abyss because her parents didn't love her and her sister's familial affection extended only so far.

"Does your career fill in for the loss of your family?" Rock asked her bluntly. Almost brutally.

So, she replied in kind. "I'm not sure I ever had a family. Not the way you, Carey and Marilyn are connected."

Maybe he would never understand that, because for all his

parents' faults, because of who *he* was, Rock *had* always had a family. He'd made one.

There *had* been a time she wasn't entirely alone though, when she'd had people she'd believed were *hers*. A time when she didn't wake in the middle of the night terrified by a sense of loneliness so heavy she thought she was going to suffocate from it.

"Anyway, school was very fulfilling." Her friendships there deep and intense as college relationships so often are, but only one had lasted beyond school.

"And your career since?" he pressed. Was he baiting her? Drilling home what she'd lost?

He really didn't understand she'd never had it in the first place. Her nightmares weren't new. She'd had them as a child too. Only now she knew she was alone. Back then, she'd had the illusion of a family.

She did something she'd told herself and him she'd never have to do with Rock. Deborah pulled her actor persona around her and gave him a flip answer. "It's had its moments."

"I'm going to assume this film has been one of the good ones." Rock turned her to face him, pulling her body into his, his heat engulfing her, making her feel warm, safe, cared for even as she marveled that he hadn't noticed what she'd done. His sherry brown eyes burned down into hers.

Letting go of any thoughts of loneliness, knowing her future would be what it would be, she grinned up at him. "That's a very safe assumption."

"When you smile like that, all I want to do is kiss you."

"What's stopping you?"

"Nothing." He leaned down, let his lips slide over hers. "Nothing at all." Then he was molding her body to his and kissing her with possessive intent.

She opened her mouth, letting him taste her, returning the favor, reveling in the amazing sensation. Kissing Rock sent bites of electric shock along her nerve endings and heat to her core. Every. Single. Time.

Her past. Her future. None of it mattered when Rock was kissing her.

Loneliness wasn't even a concept when his mouth claimed hers, when his body was pressed so tightly against her own.

She locked her hands behind his neck, diving headlong into the kiss, pushing tighter into his body.

He growled softly and broke his mouth from hers. "We'd better stop, hot stuff, or we'll be doing things in this cemetery that have a lot more to do with life than death."

She let her throaty laughter be her answer as he took her hand and led her toward the white church with green trim. The quaint building had definite Russian flair with its rounded brass spires topped by crosses with three horizontal bars, rather than the more familiar Western cross of a single horizontal bar. Deborah found the building both fascinating and beautiful.

Stepping inside was even more surreal. It was not entirely unexpected. The iconography, the stark white with gold accents, the beauty of the altar, all were within what she understood of the Eastern Orthodox tradition. But to find them amidst this small village on the outer reaches of the Kenai Peninsula in Alaska?

It was almost magical.

"This is amazing," she whispered to Rock, feeling that to speak any louder would be wrong somehow.

He nodded, his expression both understanding and approving at the same time. He slid his arm around her, his hand settling on her hip.

His voice near her ear was soft, his deep timber sending warmth through her. "Unexpected beauty is the best kind."

She looked up, their gazes locking, and she knew she hadn't imagined the double meaning behind his words.

"Was I a surprise, Rock?" she asked.

"I guarantee I never expected to find a woman like you on a movie set, beauty."

That had to mean something, didn't it?

She didn't ask him what. The moment was too perfect to ruin with reality.

Later, they drove back toward Cailkirn before Rock pulled the SUV off the highway and parked in what seemed a lonely, secluded spot.

"What are we doing here?" Deborah asked feeling nothing but contentment and maybe a little anticipation.

So far, her sex without commitment *pseudo* boyfriend had managed a Golden Globe nomination worthy date. Ninilchik had turned out to be a completely charming town that did its own bit of catering to tourists even if it didn't get quite the influx of cruise passengers Cailkirn did.

"Having our picnic."

She looked around for a parking sign, or picnic tables. Neither of which was in evidence. "Is it a park?"

"Not exactly." He smiled at her, the rare curve of his lips that reflected a genuine warmth in his eyes making her melt inside. "But it's a beautiful area all the same. I used to come hiking here with Tack MacKenna. He knows all the best off-the-trail spots. Don't worry, it's not much of a walk to where we'll be eating."

"Okay." She wasn't concerned about the walk. She was more worried about what it was doing to her heart to have Rock bring her to someplace special to him. "Why don't you hike here with him anymore?"

"He's gotten pretty busy with his business. We were never best friends, but he was a good guide and he's a decent guy. Committed to Cailkirn and building the town, not leaving it for greener pastures in the Lower 48."

"That's important to you."

He climbed out of the SUV and grabbed the picnic basket from the back. "A small town like Cailkirn is only going to survive if its people are focused on keeping it alive."

She followed him, carrying the blanket. "That makes sense." And explained a little of why he was so protective of the town. "But if someone's life isn't here, that doesn't make them a bad person."

"You mean like my brother and sister."

"Yes." She wasn't sure why she even brought Carey and Marilyn up. She was having such a good day.

But she wanted Rock to understand better why the younger Jepsoms had felt the need to leave Cailkirn. They hadn't abandoned their brother and still needed him. Deborah hoped he could see that. For his sake as much as that of his younger siblings. They might not be her family, but they were a family. A real one.

And it was important to her that he saw that, saw how much they all meant to each other still.

She didn't examine why.

Deborah only knew that she needed Rock, Carey and Marilyn to be on better terms, and for Rock, especially, to understand how much his younger siblings still loved and cared for him.

"Don't worry, beauty. I know my siblings have a life outside of Alaska. They've made sure of that."

"But they still love you." She caught up with him, grabbing his wrist, needing the connection. "That hasn't changed, Rock. It's not about where they live."

"So, they say."

"Do you doubt it?"

"Does it matter to you?"

She slipped her hand into his. "Yes."

"I don't see how." But he didn't break the connection of their hands.

"I care about all of you." Could he hear the truth in her tone? The emotion that shouldn't be there? The need she couldn't hide?

He gave her a sidelong glance before shaking his head. "You've got a soft heart."

"You say that like it's a bad thing." She meant the words to come out teasing, but they sounded just a little sad to her own ears.

She wondered what he heard.

His frown wasn't giving much away. "In your business, it's a definite liability."

"Says you." She'd survived so far. Maybe she wasn't where she wanted to be, but if getting there meant stabbing friends in the back or taking advantage of others like she'd been taken advantage of before she'd gotten smart...

Well, she'd rather be where she was.

Stardom wasn't worth the cost of her soul and she believed if it was meant to be, she wouldn't have to pay that price either.

"Tell me I'm wrong."

She couldn't. Not and mean it. She didn't want to talk about her suitability for the business anymore. Deborah had a feeling she wouldn't make any better of a corporate shark than she would a cutthroat actor.

Maybe for all her inner drive she wasn't driven enough to step over others to climb to the top of any profession. If her talent wasn't enough, maybe she would have to settle for something less than stardom, less than mega success on either side of the camera.

Done with her thoughts and the discussion, she said, "You were right that this walk is a beautiful one, anyway."

His laugh was cynical, but still so darn sexy and masculine. It really wasn't fair. They stopped at a small clearing that had a breathtaking view of the inlet.

Awed, Deborah sucked in her breath. "It's amazing."

"It is." Rock put the food hamper down and took the blanket from her, snapping it out over the grass.

"I'm surprised no one else is here."

"No trail." Rock shrugged, like that explained it all.

They ate a lazy lunch, the food everything Rock said it would be.

Afterward, she leaned against him, looking out over the water, content in a way she could never remember being. "This has been a wonderful day, Rock. Thank you."

"I've enjoyed myself, beauty. No thanks necessary." His arms wrapped around her, a barely-there kiss brushing against her temple.

She turned her face up to kiss the bottom of his chin, the moment so perfect she never wanted to forget it.

"Now, isn't that sweet, Virgil?" The sneering male voice was so out of place with her idyll, it made Deborah jump.

Rock tensed against her. They both turned to see two men dressed in flannel shirts, one was older with a graying beard and dark hair streaked the same. The younger man was a dirty blond and leering at Deborah in a way that made her glad they hadn't come up on her alone.

"Don't know about sweet, Amos, but she sure is pretty," the dirty blond replied.

Amos smiled, showing off a silver front tooth. "That she is, Virg. Think she's real attached to that guy she's with?"

Who wrote these guys' dialogue? It rang too genuine not to be real, but were they serious? If it weren't for the air of unsparked violence that they carried around them like a cloud, she would have found their ignorance darkly amusing.

Rock stood in one fluid motion, making Deborah gasp with surprise. He moved in front of her. "She is more attached to me than you'll be to your remaining teeth if you don't move along, *Amos*."

Deborah shivered at that chill in Rock's tone. The two men who thought they were clever talking about her like she was a new toy they might be interested in weren't smart enough to look worried.

But while they had a sense of potential violence about them, the underlying menace in Rock's tone was unmistakable. He was a grizzly to a couple of packless wolves.

Only by their expressions, they clearly didn't realize they were facing an apex predator.

"You think so, city-boy?" Virgil asked stepping forward all swagger.

Rock relaxed his body into a stance she recognized from classes she'd taken in self-defense. It wasn't exactly what her instructors had taught, but it was close enough for her to know he'd taken some kind of martial arts training.

"I know so, Virgil." Again Rock's voice was cold enough to stand in for an Alaskan winter.

"The way I see it, there's two of us and one of you," Amos said, completely dismissing Deborah.

She stood up and glared at the rude men. "Excuse me if you

think I'll stand quietly by while you attempt to hurt either of us. I'll kick your sorry butts into the ground." And she would. She'd learned enough self-defense for safety on the LA streets, these two backwoods thugs weren't going to scare her.

Amos and Virgil laughed, the sound ugly and loud, but not frightening. Not until Virgil pulled a gun from his waistband. Cold, black metal, he pointed the deadly end at Rock. "Now, I don't think you'll be doing anything but what we tell you."

Terror poured through Deborah. Images of the damage the gun could do to the man she'd come to love flashed through her brain.

Before she had a chance to shout, move or do more than imagine what could happen, Rock was in motion. Fast, efficient, violent motion. The sound of a crack preceded Amos screaming. The gun dropped one direction as Amos' body went flying in another. Virgil was headed for the action, but Rock was ready for him, his hand connecting with the older man's throat in a chop that sent Virgil to his knees gasping and grabbing at his throat.

Deborah dove to retrieve the gun, not wanting either of the miscreants to get their hands on it again. She didn't particularly know what to do with it when she got it, but she knew she didn't want them having it. She held it away from her body as she backed away from the physical violence.

Rock kicked Virgil in the side of the knee when he tried to come at him with one arm dangling uselessly, and then the dirty blond was down and not getting up any time soon. Deborah yelled a warning when Amos came at Rock from behind and Rock spun, laying Amos out cold with a punch combination that looked more like trained hand-to-hand combat than two men fighting.

He turned to her then, his sherry eyes dark with a fury she'd never seen in them before. "Are you okay?"

"I think I should be asking you that." Why was her voice so shaky?

He crossed the distance between them in a few long strides, and then wrapped his hands around her upper arms. "You did great, hot stuff. You got the gun."

"I've never touched one before."

"Not even for a role?" he asked, rubbing up and down her arms. Like she was cold.

She wasn't cold. Was she? Why was she shaking? "Not a real one."

"That isn't a prop."

She looked down at the gun in her trembling hand between them, part of her wondering why she still held it. "No. It's heavy. I don't like it."

"You want to give it to me?"

"I'm not weak."

"No, hot stuff, you are not weak."

"Guns are not my thing though." Why was her voice so quiet? Like she was whispering?

"That's okay. You want to put it on the blanket?"

"Yes." She didn't want him touching it. It was bad.

She didn't care if the thought made sense.

"Okay, let's do that then." He led her over to the blanket, where she carefully laid the gun on the edge of the blanket.

"We need to call 911."

"I'll call Benji Sutherland. We're close enough to Cailkirn, he'll get here sooner than State Police would."

Sooner was good. "Who is Benji Sutherland?"

"Cailkirn's sheriff. He's a vet."

"Doesn't that keep him really busy?" Were there a lot of animals in Cailkirn?

"A veteran, sweetheart, not an animal doctor."

"Oh, of course. My brain is not working."

"You're in shock, I think."

Maybe she was. "He knows what to do with guns, I guess."

"Yes."

"Good. And miscreants like those." They'd ruined her perfect moment. She wanted to kick them in the kneecaps, only maybe Rock had already done that.

"Yes, that too."

"Call him."

Rock kept one arm around her while he pulled out his phone to do just that. Deborah listened while he explained what had happened to the sheriff.

"Yes, I disarmed the idiot. I don't know. Virgil and Amos. You can check their wallets when they get here for last names."

Deborah shivered.

"Look, I've got to go. Just get out here and you'll have all your answers then."

Rock put his phone away and the pulled Deborah tightly into his body. "It's going to be fine. Benji will be here in about thirty minutes."

"What about them?" She indicated Amos and Virgil with her head.

"I need to secure them for Benji."

Deborah took a deep breath and let it out. "I'll help."

"You sure?"

"Yes."

Rock nodded. "Okay."

He went over to Virgil and said, "Give me your shirt."

"Suck my dick," the other man sneered.

Rock shrugged and grabbed the arm that was cradled protectively in front of the man sitting awkwardly on the ground, his knee cocked at a strange angle. Virgil yelled and started swearing.

CHAPTER FOURTEEN

"I need ties and I'm not cutting up my Grant plaid blanket for assholes like you." Rock sounded imminently reasonable as he yanked the man's vest off none to gently.

Virgil yelled, "Amos has got some of them zip ties in his back pocket."

Rock went still, his features going stone-like. Deborah felt sick to her stomach at the implication of Virgil's words. The last fifteen minutes reframed quickly in her thoughts to something a lot more sinister.

Amos chose that moment to stir.

Something came over Deborah, rage and the need to do something. Before she knew it, she was rushing toward the big, bearded man. Without thought or hesitation, she swung her foot. It connected with a satisfying thud and his head snapped back. He fell backward, going limp again.

Rock came up beside her. "Damn, hot stuff, remind me not to piss you off."

"He has zip ties in his pocket, Rock." Just saying it made her sick.

Rock nodded grimly, then knelt down and retrieved the restraints and used them to make sure that the next time Amos woke up he wouldn't be doing anything but a centipede style crawl. He went back over to Virgil and did the same thing to the other man, though Virgil begged him not to, promising he wasn't going anywhere with his knee and arm out of commission.

Rock stared down at the man and asked in a deadly voice. "Just how much mercy did you show the people you used those zip ties on?"

"They was for our game, that's all."

Rock secured the man's ankles amidst a lot of loud cursing and yelling. "You've got to be a better liar than that if you expect me to believe you, Virgil."

Deborah didn't know about Rock, but Deborah preferred to think about the two men hunting game rather than people and said so.

Rock's gorgeous mouth twisted in a grimace. "Baby, men don't hunt game with a Glock."

"There is that." Deborah sighed. "So, Sheriff Sutherland should be here soon, huh?"

"He will be."

"You're not going to get in trouble for breaking his arm and whatever it is you did to his knee?" She didn't know how much a force a civilian was allowed to extend to protect himself.

"It's his wrist I broke and I hyper extended his knee. He'll survive. And no, I won't get in trouble."

She hugged herself. "I can't believe you went after a man holding a gun."

"I wasn't going to let them hurt you." He cupped her face, as if emphasizing his point, but didn't let go right away, just kept their gazes locked.

She swallowed, her eyes burning, though she didn't know why. "He could have shot you."

"He didn't."

"But he could have."

"It wasn't likely. Men like that. They don't expect you to fight back."

Deborah spun away from Rock, immediately missing the warmth of his hands on her face. She turned back to face him and glared. She glared up at him. "But he could have, Rock. He could have shot you. You know he could have."

Rock didn't answer. He just grabbed her and pulled her close, wrapping his arms tight around her, like he knew that was exactly what she needed so she wouldn't feel like she was shaking apart.

That's how Sheriff Benji Sutherland and two of his deputies found them fifteen minutes later. Rock was still holding her tight against him, promising her it was alright, it was always going to be alright, telling her he was fine, that she was fine, that the bad guys were trussed up like turkeys for the authorities.

Something about his methods worked, because when the sheriff arrived, she was able to step away from Rock without feeling bereft. She was able to talk without her voice shaking and her shivers had stopped.

The officers made quick work of searching Virgil and Amos. They found one wallet between the two men which identified Virgil as one Virgil A. Jerome, two Bowie knives, a package of six condoms and a set of truck keys.

"We'll need your statements," Sheriff Sutherland said to Rock, his gaze shifting to encompass Deborah.

Rock nodded once. "We'll follow you into Cailkirn."

Deborah would have protested but they couldn't put it off to tomorrow. She had to work.

The statements took much less time than she expected.

"The benefits of small town sheriff's department," Rock replied when she brought it up on the way back to his place. "Benji wasn't going to make us wait until he'd processed Virgil and Amos to take our statements."

"He's a nice man, but kind of quiet." Intense too, but she didn't need to mention that.

"He's young for a sheriff, but he gets the job done."

"You said he's a vet."

"He served two tours in the Middle East."

"And he came back to Cailkirn."

"It's home."

"He's related to the man who owns the Northern Lights Lodge?"

"His grandson. He's cousins with the mayor too."

"Small town connections."

"Not like LaLa Land."

"You'd be surprised at the unexpected connections you find in LA politics, police and other public service agencies." Her lips twisted cynically. Sometimes it was downright incestuous.

"I suppose."

Her fingers drummed a random pattern against her thigh. "That was crazy."

"It was." He flicked her a sidelong glance, but she couldn't tell if there was concern in it or not.

"Are you going to tell Carey and Marilyn about it?" Carey would make a meal of it for sure. Marilyn...well, Deborah wasn't sure how Rock's sister would react to news of her brother facing down gunmen.

Rock let out a bark of laughter that didn't sound so much amused as cynical. "If I don't, I imagine you will."

"You imagine right." And it wasn't because she was a gossip. "Their brother is a hero."

"I'm just a man, beauty. I've never been a hero." Was that a blush showing through Rock's blond stubble?

"Oh, I think both your brother and sister would disagree with that statement before I ever tell them about what happened today."

Rock was the kind of man who saved people without ever standing in the limelight to take the credit. He'd raised his sister and brother, saving their family, saving their childhoods. He'd stepped up to the plate even more when their parents died, and then after. Who knew what all he did behind the scenes even now for others?

She'd bet he was on the board of a bunch of charities no one knew about. And the stuff he did for his small town? Deborah had no doubts it was as numerous as it was unacknowledged.

Rock was that guy. The larger than life hero who pretended to be normal, who acted like making a fortune out of a small insurance policy and a lot of hard work was nothing special. A man who considered using that fortune to take care of his siblings as well as a tiny dot of a town in Alaska to be nothing anyone should consider special.

Rock made a disbelieving sound. "You're nuts, beauty, but you turn me on."

"You can't be thinking about sex."

"Can't I?" he asked in that tone that never failed to send her mind in that direction too.

"Aren't you exhausted?"

"No."

She laughed. Well, that was definitive. Come to think of it. She wasn't as tired as she'd first thought when leaving the Sheriff's Office either. What was it about this man that made her think about making love even after the kind of afternoon they'd just had?

She smiled over at him. "Well, you just might be able to convince me."

Rock listened to Deborah recount their afternoon, making him sound like some kind of damn Kung Fu expert with a heavy dose of action adventure hero thrown in.

"I disarmed a couple of idiots who crashed our picnic. Story over." Rock glared at his siblings, daring them to keep making a meal of it.

Neither seemed impressed with his ire.

Marilyn's eyes filled with tears. "You took on a man with a gun? Was it loaded?"

"Damned if I know if it was loaded. I didn't check."

"I bet it was loaded," Carey said, his voice filled with awe.

Well, shit. Now his brother had that hero worship thing going on. It wouldn't keep him safe in Cailkirn though, would it? No, Carey would be headed back to the bright lights of Los Angeles just as soon as this movie was done filming.

"It was loaded," Deborah said, her voice quiet and serious. "I asked."

"So, he held it on me for about three seconds."

"Long enough to pull the trigger." Marilyn was definitely crying now.

Rock gave Deborah a look that let her know who he blamed for this situation. "We couldn't have waited until tomorrow to tell them about today's adventures?"

Like when he'd be working and the sister's tears could fall on Deborah's shoulders without his knowledge?

"You would not have put off telling us!" Marilyn smacked him on the arm. Hard.

"Damn, girl. Are you trying leave the bruises they didn't get a chance to?"

Marilyn's eyes went wide and then she burst out with a sob and threw herself and him. Feeling that panic that always hit when his sister went all emotional, he caught Carey's gaze. His brother looked back with the same panic Rock felt.

No help there.

Rock patted Marilyn's back. "Come on, sis. It's fine." He looked at Deborah with appeal. She was a woman, damn it.

She'd initiated this meltdown; she could do something to mitigate it.

But her eyes were bright too, her face filled with emotion he didn't understand.

"Shit. Carey, do something," Rock demanded.

"Well, did you have to take on armed gunmen?" Carey asked with annoyance.

"You think I should have let them hurt Deborah?"

"No, of course not."

"Besides, *armed gunmen* is redundant. If he's a gunman, he's armed."

"That's really beside the point here, big brother."

Marilyn sniffled and hugged Rock tighter. Deborah's breath hitched alarmingly and a stray tear spilled over. Rock let a word slip that he rarely said.

His sister reared back and stared up at him. "Rock!"

"What?" he asked, feeling a hell of a lot more stressed than he had staring down the business end of a gun earlier.

"You said *fuck*. You never say *fuck*."

"And if you think you're too old to have your mouth washed out for saying it, you're sadly mistaken Marilyn Kathryn Jepsom."

She gave a watery laugh.

Which had not been his intention, but he would totally take the win. He handed her off to Carey. "Take her into the media room and put on *The Quiet Man*. Watching that always makes her feel better."

"I don't know why. She spends half the time yelling at John Wayne and the other half at the long dead producers and directors."

"It's still a good romance," Marilyn declared staunchly.

She and Carey argued as they walked away toward the media room.

Rock turned to Deborah, who still looked on the verge of emotional melt down. Damn it. He did the only thing he could think of. He walked forward, swept the woman up into his arms and started up the stairs.

She caught her breath in shock, then demanded, "What are you doing?"

"Showing you just how okay we both are."

"I know I'm fine, Rock."

"Sure you do, hot stuff. You know I'm fine too. You can see it, but I guess you need some more proof and I know just the kind to give you."

"Just like a man to think sex is the solution."

"I'm a man, so that works for me."

She frowned up at him. "I wasn't giving you a compliment."

"I wasn't worried about it."

"You're so damn confident." She crossed her arms, but the gesture lost its intended effect as it pushed her breasts into prominence and had another impact on him altogether.

After taking a leisurely look at the beauty on display, he winked. "You swore."

"Are you going to threaten to wash my mouth out with soap?" she asked, all snippy.

"I have better things to do with your mouth."

He pushed the door open to his bedroom with his shoulder.

She pressed her hand against his chest her fingers clutching his shirt. "I don't know what I would have done if Virgil had shot you."

"Don't think about that. It didn't happen."

"It's not that easy."

"Let me make it that easy." He laid her on the bed and came down on top of her, letting his bigger body cover her smaller, feminine one completely. "Let me make you forget everything but how much we enjoyed being together today."

Damned if she didn't look at him with a combination of hope and trust he found irresistible.

He kissed her, soft and slow. There would be time for the powerful passion that always rose up between them, but right now she was so darn fragile. She needed gentleness.

So, that was what he'd give her.

Deborah wanted to tell Rock he didn't have to be so careful with her, that he didn't have to lay her on the bed with gentle movements. Only the words would not come.

She watched in silence as he turned and shut the door, locking them into seclusion where no one could intrude without her or Rock's permission. A press of his finger against the remote control and heavy drapes that covered the floor to ceiling windows whisked into place, but the still bright sky shone through the sky lights. The sense of expansive privacy grew.

"You're all mine until seven thirty tomorrow morning, beauty."

She'd had earlier casting calls, but right now she didn't want to think about how early that could come. "Okay."

"And I'm all yours."

"It was a good day until..."

"Yes, it was." Rock pulled his shirt off over his head, revealing defined muscles only she got to touch.

For now.

His dark blond hair glinted in the light coming in through the skylights, his gaze dark with desire and emotions she wasn't foolish enough to try to name. "You like what you're looking at, hot stuff?"

"You know I do."

"And look, not a mark on me." He turned in a circle before flipping the button on his jeans and then lowering the zipper with deliberate, slow movements.

"What are you? A tease now?" Her voice had gone husky, but she'd take it over the shaky whispers of earlier.

"You know what they say." He pushed his jeans down his thighs, revealing an erection already pressing against his underwear. "It's only teasing if I don't follow through."

She licked her lips, her mouth suddenly dry, her brain going foggy. "I don't know about that."

He kicked his jeans away before coming toward her. His expression was so intense, his jaw rigid, his eyes dark with blown pupils, his body sinuous as he made his way onto the bed, each move fluid and gorgeous and calling to her on a primal level she had no hope of denying.

"What if we'd been making love when they came up on us?" she asked, voicing one of her worst fears, hating the sound of tears in her voice, the ones she absolutely refused to shed.

He leaned down and kissed first the corner of her left eye and then her right. "They didn't. Focus on that truth, beauty."

Then he began undressing her. Slowly. Oh, so slowly. Excruciatingly slowly. Every inch of her skin revealed got kissed. Soft, sipping kisses, some followed by gentle bites, some followed by licks, others the simple press of his lips against her skin before he moved another inch of cloth.

By the time he'd removed everything but her panties, she was no longer thinking about what could have happened earlier. She wasn't thinking about anything but how she felt right that second.

Her body was on fire, her nipples tight and aching though he'd left them surprisingly untouched when he'd removed her bra, the only stimulation they'd gotten the feel of the fabric sliding away from them and then the sensation of air against them.

He'd sensitized her entire body to his touch. She ached for more; she couldn't get enough air.

She gasped as he kissed the valley between her breasts, his stubble brushing against the inner swell of her sensitive curves. "What are you trying to do to me?"

If her words came out in disjointed, breathy bits, who could blame her?

"It's all pleasure here, beauty."

"I want you, Rock." Just in case he'd missed it somehow.

His laughter was low and wicked as he rubbed his stubble right over her nipple, sending so much sensation zinging through her that she cried out. "You've got me, beauty. All night long."

"Don't want to take all night." Her legs moved restlessly, her body shifting against his in needy urgency.

He didn't speed up his oh so gentle movements but blanketed her body with his, adjusting so he could kiss her mouth. Not deep, voracious kisses like she was used to. Oh, no.

Soft, tender kisses. Kisses that could not be denied, slow, burning kisses, that stoked the fire inside her to impossible heights without taking her over.

Her hips cradled his, both their groins still covered, the fabric no barrier to the feel of his hard flesh pressing against her clitoris. In fact, somehow, it enhanced it.

But still, she didn't climax.

She felt tension which had become familiar since becoming his lover building inside, her muscles contracting and relaxing in haphazard spasms she didn't understand.

"Rock! Please..."

"Do you feel alive, beauty?" he asked, his tone as serious as she'd ever heard it.

"Yes. I always feel alive with you." Didn't he know that."

"Do you feel me? Feel how alive I am?"

A glimmer of understanding pierced the fog of her arousal. "Yes."

"No one that you care about got hurt today, Deborah." His kiss was an affirmation of that fact. "We are both better than fine."

Before she could reply in any way to his words, he pressed his sex against hers, rubbing his hard flesh up and down, sending more and more pleasure through her clitoris. Words were impossible. Any kind of real movement was just as impossible because of the way his heavy body pinned hers to the bed. It felt good, but she wanted more.

He licked against her lips. Finally.

She opened her mouth and met his tongue with hers, tasting, touching, affirming, pleasing.

His body continued to move against hers, giving pleasure, stimulating, but not taking her over into the realm of orgasm.

While it was frustrating and sweat gathered at her temples and trickled down between her shoulder blades, part of her was glad. She wanted him inside, wanted their bodies reaching that pinnacle together as close as two people could possibly be.

The kiss continued, her hands somehow twined with his against the bed above her head, his strength and control both a turn on and a comfort.

How long they went on like that, she didn't know, she only knew that the pleasure felt never ending, like it could get bigger and bigger with no end in sight. But finally, he broke away from her, pulling off his briefs before removing her panties with deliberate movements.

She put her hand out and grabbed his wrist. "No condom." They'd shared their test results with each other, but they hadn't taken the step of not using that final barrier of protection yet.

He didn't ask if she was sure. He just lifted her knees, making room between her legs for himself.

As the head of his sex pressed against her opening, she looked deep into his sherry eyes.

"We're safe," she whispered.

"We're safe," he promised. "You'll always be safe with me."

He pressed inside, the words giving her as much delight as the zings along her nerve endings while his hard-on stretched her vaginal walls.

"I've never done this before." She wrapped her fingers around his biceps, everything in her attuned to him.

Her breath gasping out in the same rate as his panting exhalations, invisible arcs of electricity connecting them where they didn't touch, the sensation of being almost one body where they did.

"Me neither."

She was glad he didn't make the joke about her not being a virgin. He got the importance of the moment, no matter how temporary their relationship.

He pressed forward, filling her, connecting to her, no barriers between them, nothing but the most intimate slide of skin against skin.

"You're so hot, so tight, beauty." He groaned as his pelvis settled against her. "So damn wet."

"You spent long enough making me that way."

"You complaining?" he asked, his expression not quite making it to mocking.

"No." There was no room for pretense with this new intimacy between them.

"I didn't think so." He pulled back and thrust forward again, the movement so delicious it drew a moan from her. "You're so responsive."

"With you."

"We're perfectly matched."

"You think?" she asked, her breath hitching and drawing the two words out to four syllables.

"I know."

She should ask why he thought they should end when the movie did then, but she already had one perfect moment ruined that day. She wasn't ruining a second one on purpose.

Letting her mind shut down and feeling take over, Deborah submerged herself in the lovemaking, reveling in the slow but driving pace he set, wringing every drop of ecstasy from her body's response to the excruciating copulation she could.

No matter how many times they made love, there would never again be a first time without the barrier of a condom between them. There would never be a moment like this in the silence of the room with Alaska's twilight coming in the through the skylights, the sensation of being the only two people in the universe.

The knowledge that right then as far as Rock was concerned, even his siblings weren't registering. Deborah Banes was the only person who mattered to him in this precise second. Her body, her pleasure, her responses.

It was heady knowledge she accepted it as the true gift it was.

Her orgasm came up on her without warning, like she'd been on the edge of coming for too long and her body would no longer be denied. It started with a contraction of her vaginal walls but radiated out until every muscle in her body went rigid, a scream tearing from her throat as her head went back of its own volition, her neck arch impossibly tight.

He drove forward, twisting his pelvis against her swollen clitoris and she screamed again, her voice giving out as the pleasure became too much. She'd never come so strongly, never experienced ecstasy so profound, never felt her body convulse so tightly.

Rock growled her name in a deep, primal tone and heat flooded her insides as he came as well, his body rigid above hers. He jerked his pelvis a couple of times, both their pleasure jolting with aftershocks that made their bodies convulse against each other. But finally, she went limp, her climax and its aftershocks finished.

He was still semi-hard inside her and she was glad. She knew it couldn't last, but for now, they were still connected.

CHAPTER FIFTEEN

His forehead dropped against hers. "You're lethal, hot stuff."

She made a semi-intelligent sound. At least she hoped it passed for intelligent. She wasn't sure what his answering chuckle meant in that regard.

"We're not done."

"What?"

But he meant what he said. He started kissing her and because he wasn't wearing a condom, he didn't have to even move from where he was before he started new small thrusts that brought his sex back to full hardness.

The harder he got, the better it felt for her. He never broke the kiss, never moved his body away from hers. She didn't know how he got a full erection so quickly again. She didn't really care. She only knew that once he was fully erect, he turned them so she was on top. His penis pushed up into her in their new position.

She threw her head back. "Oh, that feels good."

"Yeah, beauty, it does. I like the view too." His expression said he liked it a lot, his gaze paused significantly on her breasts and how they jiggled with her every forward and backward thrust.

"You going to bring us to another climax, hot stuff?" he asked.

He might say she was the one bringing them to the climax, but the way he was swiveling his hips? And now his hands were cuppings her breasts, his fingers manipulating her nipples, sending electric jolts straight to her core.

She kneaded his chest as she rode him, loving the freedom to touch, to be touched, to be able to continue making love without having to worry about the condom.

Which is what they did for hours. If Rock's goal was to

convince Deborah that she was okay, he more than succeeded. If his intention was to convince her that he was fine, he did that too. She fell asleep wrapped in his arms, replete and convinced he was some kind of super-stud.

That worked for her.

"You know, our brother and your girlfriend are the real deal." Marilyn's voice interrupted Rock's focus on his computer screen.

He looked up from his email.

"What?"

Marilyn pushed away from where she leaned on the doorjamb to his office. "Carey and Deborah. They're doing their scenes without a hitch today."

"Shouldn't they be?"

"After yesterday?" Marilyn made it sound like the actors were accomplishing some amazing feat rather than simply doing their jobs.

"If they didn't, I'm pretty sure Art Gamble would have a coronary." The director's schedule could not tolerate losing both his principles for an entire day's filming.

"But yesterday was so stressful." Marilyn leaned against his desk, her eyes so like their mothers filled with concern in a way Georgia Howell's never would have been.

Rock shook his head. "Don't be a drama queen, sis. Yesterday had its moment of unpleasantness." But it had ended just fine. "End of story."

"Only you would put it that way, brother dear." Marilyn flounced across the room and plopped into a chair. "You are such a businessman."

"Guilty as charged."

Marilyn gave an exasperated huff. "Don't be so, so, so..."

"What?" he asked, making no effort to mask his humor at her expense.

"Unemotional! You nearly died."

"Not even close."

"You faced down a gun."

"That was never even discharged." No one would question who in their family had the dramatic flair.

"You were still at risk." The look she gave him said just how unreasonable she thought Rock was being. "Were they escaped convicts? Did Benji say?"

Marilyn's assumption wasn't ridiculous. Not even all that

sensational. Alaska drew more than its fair share of people running from their past. "No. Home grown idiots with disgusting recreational interests."

Marilyn's shiver appeared involuntary rather than one of her exaggerated, dramatic movements.

"Nothing happened," he reiterated.

She frowned. "No, I know, but everyone is acting like *nothing* happened. And something did. Something really awful could have happened to both you and Deborah, but you didn't let it. You were a *hero*, Rock."

He was as uncomfortable with the claim as when Deborah made it.

"I did what had to be done."

"That's what you said when I was seven and you used the money you'd saved for a new computer game to buy me an outfit for school picture retakes when I cried over picture day until I made myself sick."

"You were a little kid. You were humiliated. Mom didn't understand how important it was."

Their mom had sent Marilyn to school in one of Rock's hand-me-down t-shirts on picture day, her hair unbrushed, jam from her toast still smeared on her upper lip. When the pictures came in, Marilyn had sobbed until she'd thrown up, utterly devastated by the visual record of their mother's neglect.

Rock had been determined to make it better for her, and he had. "But you did."

Rock rolled his eyes. "That doesn't make me special. Believe it, or not, most people understand that kind of thing."

"Just not people like Mom and Dad."

"No."

Marilyn looked at him with sadness. "You know you got it wrong, Rock."

He turned away from the computer, giving up on getting any work done until his sister said whatever she needed to say. "What did I get wrong?"

"You think they were the way the way they were because of the industry they were in, but it went the other way." Her blue eyes glowed with sincerity, her body leaning forward like she wanted to reach out to him.

"That's convoluted, even for you."

"Mom and Dad were drawn to the film industry because of their narcissism. It magnified their flaws for sure, but it didn't create them."

"Be careful what you say, Carey will have your head. He worships the memory of our parents."

Marilyn's mouth twisted in a grimace of acknowledgment. "He ignores the fact that the only family we ever had was because you made it for us, but deep inside? Rock, he knows. Just as much as I do. Why do you think I'm so upset about yesterday?"

"Well, don't be. Nothing happened." Rock sighed. "Amos and Virgil are locked up and will stay that way for a very long time. Benji figures DNA evidence is going to link them to a string of tourist assaults and robberies."

"Not rapes?"

"We'll see." Rock wasn't speculating when so far, the evidence pointed to thuggery, not depravity.

The tourists had been left incapacitated with zip-ties while their assailants made their getaways. The situation yesterday might have been a new deviation for them.

One that had clearly not worked out well for the pair. The fact that they hadn't been wearing the ski masks they'd worn during their previous robberies didn't bode well for the plans they'd had for Rock and Deborah either.

Although, according to Benji, they were claiming they'd only been joking around. Supposedly Virgil and Amos hadn't been planning to do anything at all. Hard to believe that when Amos had pulled a loaded gun on Rock, but no matter their intention the day before, the miscreants were facing hard time with multiple counts of robbery and assault.

"Well, at least I know how to get you to stop denying Deborah is your girlfriend," Marilyn teased.

"How's that?" Rock asked, exasperated.

"Call you a hero."

"You are a pest."

"You've said that before."

"Maybe you should have listened."

"It's an endearing quality."

"Pretty sure neither Carey nor I buy that."

"Did you know about Carey's ex taking him for all his money?"

"I didn't know the man was his ex."

"But you did know about the money."

"Yes."

"So."

"What?"

"What did you do?" Marilyn asked, maybe as stubborn as Rock.

"Let's just say that whatever career benefits he hoped to gain by taking advantage of our brother that way were not realized."

"You have connections in Hollywood." Marilyn said it like she was just making a realization.

"Yes."

"Does Carey know?" Marilyn demanded.

"No."

"Would you use them to help him if he asked?"

"I don't know."

"Would you use them to help me?" she asked, her tone hard to read.

"I don't know." Before this movie thing, before meeting Deborah, his answer would have been a resounding *no*. He met her questioning gaze. "It would depend on the circumstances."

"That's honest." Marilyn shifted in her seat. "So, his ex, is he working?"

"As an actor? No. And the likelihood of him doing so in anything but the adult entertainment arm of the industry is very slim. If he was wildly talented, it would be different, but he's not. Besides, he's an asshole."

"And he hurt your baby brother, so you made sure he didn't profit by doing so."

"Yes."

"People think you're laid back."

"What people?"

His sister laughed. "Okay, maybe that's the wrong term. They think you are civilized."

"Maybe." He made no claims in that direction. He knew that when it came to his family, the veneer of civilization fell away.

Rock was not that guy that trusted things to even out in the long run. He hadn't been able to trust his parents to take care of his family. He hadn't been able to trust in the world being a balanced place since he was a tiny boy. He never would.

He'd learned early on: men were predators or they were prey. He would be a predator.

"Does Deborah know what kind of man she's fallen for?"

"What Deborah and I have is temporary. There's no reason for her to learn my secrets." Though she knew more of them than some people he'd known for years.

"You keep telling yourself that, big brother."

Deborah finished her takes for the day and wasn't surprised to find Rock on the outskirts of the set. He'd been waiting for her the last two days since their trip into Ninilchik.

She liked it.

But she was smart enough not to make a big deal out of the practice.

For a strong alpha male who could run a billion-dollar company and take down armed criminals, Rock was as skittish as a newborn foal when it came to relationships.

They were in one though. A real live relationship.

Whether he admitted it out loud, or not. Deborah was of the school that if it walked like a duck and quacked like a duck, then it most likely was a duck.

He'd risked his life for her. He wanted to spend all their free time together...and it wasn't always for sex. Not every waking moment anyway.

Not that the sex wasn't amazing. It was incredible. Since Amos and Virgil's attack on them, Rock had been insatiable and inventive.

Taking pains to leave his mark on Deborah's body that makeup and wardrobe often grumbled about having to conceal.

Deborah didn't care. She'd never been so happy.

She ate breakfast each morning with Lydia, Rock and his siblings and dinner each night with him, Carey and Marilyn, the siblings always making sure that Deborah was drawn into the banter as they ate their meals. Marilyn treated her like a sister and Carey, like a friend rather than just a colleague.

Rock treated Deborah like she mattered.

He never spoke of the future, but maybe that was something she would just have to show him. She'd have to come back to Cailkirn and show him that sometimes, people came back from LA. Sometimes, people found reasons important enough to make a home away from the bright lights of the big city.

Her career didn't need her to be in Los Angeles full time.

She could compromise.

Would Rock?

She had to hope the answer was yes, because she wasn't sure she could give him up. She'd fallen and fallen hard.

As much for the feeling of being part of a family again as for the man she was rapidly realizing she'd fallen head over heels in love with.

Everything about Rock was right. He was so strong. So solid. So certain of his course without shoving that course on others. How could she not want this man in her life?

"What are you thinking?" Rock asked as she reached him.

"About you."

He gave her a lazy grin. "Whatever it is, keep thinking it. I like that look."

If only he knew. If any man were less ready to hear the L-word, she didn't know who it would be. She just smiled up at him. "Don't worry, I will."

"Now, you're starting to worry me."

"Why?"

Putting a proprietary arm around her waist, he pulled her close with a sexy look that made her shiver with want. "Because *that* look was all provocation and secrets."

"A woman without any would bore you to death."

"It all depends on what those secrets are, hot stuff."

A loud expletive from Art, interrupted her reply. "He can't do that, Elena!"

The blue language that followed shocked Deborah and caused a shiver of dread. Art wasn't one of those directors that used foul language as adjectives and cursed at his actors and tech crew as a matter of course.

He saw it a sign of a lazy brain and anyone who hoped to work their way up or gain a glowing recommendation remembered that.

"You ready to change back to twenty-eight-year-old Deborah and head into town for some dinner?" Rock asked, seemingly impervious to Art's vocal agitation.

Another date? Promising. Even if it meant missing a family dinner. "What about Marilyn and Carey?"

"They've both got plans this evening."

"Oh." So, more circumstance than design.

"What's the matter? Isn't my company enough for you."

"It's just…I like family dinners," she admitted, not without some embarrassment. They weren't her family after all. And the fact their *date* wasn't planned so much as happenstance shouldn't be disappointing either.

Thankfully, Rock gave her an indulgent look rather than a pitying or annoyed one. "I do, too, but sometimes I like you all to myself."

"That's nice to hear."

"We have little enough time left."

Deborah refused to let comments like that hurt her. She just had to prove to Rock that she was different. That she was coming back after the filming was wrapped up. She'd made a decision.

She wasn't sure how she was going to make it happen, especially without his cooperation, but whatever it took. She was moving back to Cailkirn and building a life with Rock.

Maybe a discussion with Lydia would help. The housekeeper was über resourceful. She'd know options for part-time jobs Deborah could hold between acting or production gigs. That is if Deborah stayed in the film industry after this movie.

The more time she spent considering her motives for doing what she did, the less she was sure of them. She was nearly thirty; and while she knew she was a good actor, she wasn't sure anymore it was worth the sacrifice. She wasn't sure what she wanted out of life except to have the one thing that had always eluded her, even when she'd lived with her parents.

A family that loved her for being herself. Full stop.

"Are we going?" Rock prompted. "You seem lost in your thoughts there, hot stuff."

"I am a little." She sighed and looked around for Art.

He was texting on his phone, his expression thunderous, his fingers stabbing the poor electronic device with cruel and unusual force.

"I think I should check on him." She nodded toward her director.

But Rock shook his head. "No. If he has a problem, he has a whole production team to take care of it, not to mention Ms. Morganstein. She's still in town."

"She is. Technically, I'm part of the production team." They'd been together for weeks, but she'd never talked to Rock about her specific role in the movie besides that of co-lead with his brother.

"Whatever that means, you aren't high enough in the food chain to be listed on the paperwork I signed, so whatever his problem is now is not your responsibility and there's no way you've got the clout to fix it either."

"Gosh, thanks!"

"I'm not putting you down, but whatever has your director that pissed off, you're not going to be able to fix it." Rock took her hand and gently tugged her toward the house. "Now let's get rid of your coming of age persona and find my gorgeous Deborah Banes again, shall we?"

"So, you're not interested in dating a much younger woman?"

"No."

"Are you telling me you don't hook up with young things on

your business trips?"

Rock stopped and yanked Deborah to him, giving her a searing kiss. When he released her lips, he kept her body trapped against his and her eyes locked by his own. "I have never been interested in screwing someone who reminded me of my responsibilities at home. That included choosing bed partners anywhere near or younger than my sister's age."

He shivered like the idea revolted him and Deborah laughed.

"Wow, I've got to pity all the younger women."

"Don't. No matter how worldly wise they think they are, I'm not risking some baby looking at me with stars in her eyes, thinking I'm looking for a fairytale when all I want is some good old-fashioned exercise and stress relief, no matter if she is old enough to drink."

What about a twenty-eight-year-old actor with a mostly cynical viewpoint? "I've met teenagers that make piranhas seem tame."

Rock shrugged and then kissed her again, long and slow.

"What was that for?" Deborah asked, more than a little breathless.

"No reason. Other than holding you against me makes me want to kiss."

"I like that."

"Me too."

The trip back to the house took about five times as long as it should have because he kept her body close to his on the walk and apparently that meant stopping to kiss every few feet. Deborah wasn't sure exactly how she was supposed to wash the stars out of her eyes.

Rock took her back to the diner for dinner and this time, made sure they didn't end up sharing their tiny table for two with anyone. Though the diner was as busy as it had been on their last visit.

The food was just as good, as well, but Deborah probably enjoyed it even more because Rock shared his with her and insisted on tasting hers.

He wasn't the least embarrassed to let his small-town brethren know he was dating her. No matter what he said, he had to be open to something of a real relationship. His actions spoke louder than his words and with a lot more meaning.

Just like they did with his siblings.

The revelation sent her head spinning.

"What?" Rock demanded, looking around, his body going taut, like he was preparing to protect her.

Again.

"I just realized something."

"You looked like you'd seen the start of the Zombiepocolypse."

She couldn't help laughing, releasing tension she didn't even realize she'd been holding. "Nope, just one of those inner revelations."

"Don't start taking scene notes in the middle of dinner and I won't have to hide the body." Rock gave her a mock glare.

She shook her head. "Believe it, or not, not all of my thoughts revolve around the movie. Especially when I'm with you."

Let him make of that what he would.

Rock's expression turned wary. "You and Carey don't talk much about the movie at the dinner table."

"Do you expect us to?" she asked in a tone that made it clear her question was rhetorical.

Rock gave her an odd look. "Yes."

"You're kidding. You've made your disapproval clear."

"I'm letting you film the damn thing in my home and on my land." And obviously, he expected his actions to carry sway over his expressed disapproval.

"So, it wouldn't bother you if we discussed how our day's filming went?"

"Marilyn is probably dying to hear the nitty-gritty."

"I'm sure she pesters Carey plenty."

"Not you?"

Deborah shrugged. "We talk some."

"I bet."

"She's smart. I think Elaine is considering interning Marilyn."

"They could both do worse."

"I'm surprised to hear you say so."

"Me too."

If he could change his opinion about the evils of the film industry this far, the man could definitely change his outlook on relationships. "So, you want me and Carey to talk about work at dinner?"

"Not exclusively." The horror that idea produced was clear in every line of Rock's face and depths of his tone.

Deborah couldn't hold back her laugh, but she managed to assure him. "Duly noted."

"You're not serious? We must have some kind of contract with him." Deborah could not believe what Ms. Morganstein had just told her.

Art looked at Deborah, frustration written all over the director's face. "You'll find that contracts with financial backers on indie projects like this are written with the majority of the concessions in their direction."

"But we're more than half done with the filming. He can't pull out now."

"He can. And he has."

"Because of the overages on the schedule?" she asked with disbelief. "That makes no sense."

"To him it does."

"And you can't change his mind."

"Believe me when I say I tried."

"I've spoken with Mr. Barston, as well," her movie's executive producer offered, her face tighter than usual with stress. "He's already cut off access to funds and has no interest in changing his mind."

"But even with the accidents and scheduling problems, we're barely going over budget. Every movie goes overtime and budget." At least every one she'd worked on.

Art rubbed his temples, the lines around his eyes and bracketing his mouth tight with unhappiness. "I think there's something else going on, but I don't know what it is."

"You think maybe he's run out of money?" Deborah asked.

"No. That would make more sense, but we checked his solvency when he came onboard as our primary financial backer. He'd just gone through a divorce, but he had a good prenup and she got nothing. The man has plenty of money."

"Then why?" Deborah just didn't understand.

It was a good movie, great scenery, solid acting, and writing that impressed her every day.

"I don't know." Art looked both frustrated and dejected.

"Okay, so we go to other backers. It was great to have a single producer with deep pockets, but he's not the only game in town."

Ms. Morganstein's smile was approving. "I like your attitude. I've already started putting out feelers to my contacts."

"Yeah, I might have a lead on some funds, not enough to finish the film, but maybe enough to keep us going for a few more days while we look for more support." Art sighed. "But one of Nevin Barston's requirements for coming on board was that he was the only financial backer. He wasn't even happy about the money Elaine and I brought to the project. I had to turn down people who were expecting to be part of my next project. That money has already gone into other ventures, or simply isn't available any longer."

Deborah understood what was unsaid. In order to get the generous funding of a single angel investor, Art had turned down people that wouldn't fund the project now on principle.

"You'll need to do your part as well, Deborah." Ms. Morganstein's expression was stern.

Deborah squared her shoulders, determined to do just that. "I'll do my best, but I don't have anything like the connections you two do."

"On the contrary, you have a connection even Carey would be hard pressed convincing to invest." Ms. Morganstein's expression was calculating.

Confused, Deborah looked at first the executive producer and then the director. "Who are you talking about?" Then the penny dropped. *"You want me to ask Rock?"*

CHAPTER SIXTEEN

Art nodded.

Ms. Morganstein gave Deborah a droll look. "Who else?"

"But you know how he feels about the film industry." Rock's recent softening did not mean the man was ready to invest in a movie production.

A single, thin, shaped brow rose on Ms. Morganstein's face. "We *know* that if we don't get an influx of some serious cash soon, not only are we going to have quit filming, but we're going to have a hell of a time making payroll at any level, much less fly our people home."

"It's that serious? You said you got some money lined up," Deborah reminded Art helplessly.

The director's lips twisted in a grimace. "Enough to juggle so we can keep going, but if we don't shore up our finances fast, this whole house of cards is going to come crashing down."

Deborah bit back what she wanted to say about signing a contract with a single backer who could pull funds without notice and less consequences. Art had his reasons, she was sure, as did Ms. Morganstein, but that didn't help what was happening now.

"Rock isn't going to invest," she said instead.

"Carey thinks he might. If you ask him."

"You already spoke to Carey?" Deborah wasn't happy.

Carey was lead actor, yes, but he didn't have production credits like she did.

"We wanted him to ask Rock, but he didn't think his brother would be as receptive to him as he would be to you."

"Because we're sleeping together? We don't even have plans to see each other once the movie wraps." Deborah ignored the twinge of pain that truth caused.

"Never underestimate how influenced by his libido a man can be," Art said with conviction.

Deborah scoffed, "Rock isn't the type."

"Every man is the type." Ms. Morganstein's shark's grin was not comforting.

"You want me to trade on our sexual chemistry?" Deborah asked with disbelief. "I'm not a whore."

"We're not asking you to sell yourself to him," Ms. Morganstein said, managing to sound offended. "You're already sleeping together. We're asking, no...telling you, to do your job."

"How is asking Rock for money *my* job?" Deborah demanded. "I'm getting a minor production and directing credit on this film. I'm not on any of the legal paperwork, other than my own contract."

Rock didn't even know she had other roles because of that.

"Trust me, getting investors is part of even a minor production player's job." Ms. Morganstein crossed her legs, smoothing her pencil straight skirt. "When necessary."

"So, I'll ask producers on my past projects." Deborah didn't have many connections, but she had some.

Frowning, Art shook his head. "We don't need everyone in Hollywood to know we're begging for money. This film is too important for it to have negative rumors surrounding it before we even make it out of production."

Which possibly further explained why the other two, with all their connections, were having a hard time replacing their angel investor.

"I don't want to ask Rock." There, she'd said it.

She wanted a chance at the future they never discussed. She didn't think asking him for money for the movie would help with that.

"Do you believe in this project?" Art asked, his voice intense with his own passionate support of the film.

"You know I do."

"Do you believe it is a movie that should be made?" he pushed further.

"Of course, I do." She'd taken lead female role, for Heaven's sake.

"Do you think it's going to fail at the box office and at the film festivals?" Ms. Morganstein asked coldly.

"No! I really believe this movie is going to do well. The production quality, the writing, the actors, all of it are top notch.

Which is why I don't think we'll have any trouble finding funding from usual sources."

Ms. Morganstein sighed, her gaze filled with mockery. "Then you are very naïve and I'm not sure how well you'll do on the other side of the camera."

That hurt, and scared Deborah just a little. "What are you saying?"

"That you learn to leverage the relationships you have to make a project work." There was no compromise in Ms. Morganstein's tone or expression.

She expected compliance from Deborah and she meant to get it.

Deborah looked at Art. "You're saying you'd ask your wife for the money?"

Not that she and Rock had nearly that serious of a relationship, but still.

"You don't think she's played major investor in more than one of my movies?" Art asked with a laugh. "What kind of marriage would we have if she didn't believe in me, in what I do?"

And just like that, an epiphany washed through Deborah's brain and heart.

If Rock couldn't respect her choice of careers, the single thing that had dominated her life for the past ten years, then they had very little chance at a future. She didn't need him to invest in the movie, but she did need to be able to ask the venture capitalist if he was willing to do it.

If doing so made him mad, or want to break off their sexual relationship, then they had less of a connection than she believed they did. They had no hope for the future.

"Okay, I'll ask him, but I don't think he'll do it," she felt compelled to point out.

"It's your job to convince him," Art replied implacably.

Deborah frowned. "I'll do my best, but I'm not making this about him and me and what we've found together."

"Nor should you," Ms. Morganstein said.

Deborah couldn't quite buy into the other woman's sincerity after the earlier part of their conversation. She believed neither executive expected her to prostitute herself, but they clearly expected her to trade on Rock's attraction to her.

Deborah ran into Carey and Marilyn in the hall when she returned to Rock's home. Both appeared stressed and worried.

The way Carey surged toward her the minute she walked through the door said he'd been waiting for her to show up. "Hey, Deborah."

"Hi, Carey."

"Did you meet with Ms. Morganstein and Art?"

"I did."

"They asked you to go to Rock for the money for the movie, didn't they?" The younger man didn't sound happy by the prospect.

Deborah nodded. "They made some good points."

Marilyn winced, her hands clasped in front of her tightly. "There are no good points about our industry as far as my brother is concerned."

"I think you'd be surprised." Deborah remembered the gallery wall of their parents' accomplishments. "He just told me last night that he wants us to talk about the movie at dinner."

"He did?" Carey asked with shock.

But Marilyn didn't look hopeful. "I think it's a big leap from there to asking him to fund a movie."

"I'm not asking him to replace Mr. Barston as a single investor." No matter what her bosses might want. "But I'm confident that he'll make a profit on whatever he does invest. That can't be a bad thing. He's a venture capitalist. It's what he does."

"Not in Hollywood," Marilyn said with certainty. "And you can never be sure about breaking even, much less making a profit, on a movie."

Carey nodded emphatically in agreement with his sister's words. "Look, Deborah, when I told Art and Ms. Morganstein that I thought you'd have a better chance talking Rock into it, I wasn't saying I thought it was possible at all."

"Did you tell *them* that?" Deborah asked.

"Yes," Carey replied, all earnest and still worried. "But they wouldn't listen. They're convinced that since he agreed to let us film and he's made compromises on the schedule because of the bad luck we've had and Marilyn's visit, that means he's more open to the benefits of making a movie than we think."

"They believe they know your brother better than you do?" Deborah asked, not too surprised.

Art and Ms. Morganstein were good at what they did, but with that success had come a certain amount of arrogant assurance they knew best.

Yeah, well, not so much, if they'd trusted Nevin Barston to fund the film and he'd backed out.

Carey nodded, unhappiness all over his handsome young face.

"But they don't. If you ask Rock for the money he's going to be so pissed at you."

"You've lost your affected accent completely, did you know that?" Deborah asked with a smile, realizing how much she'd come to like her costar.

Carey ducked his head, blushing. "It didn't work for the film anyway."

"No, it didn't."

Marilyn made a sound of frustration, her youth obvious in her impatience for once. "Who cares about Carey's stupid attempts to pretend to be something he's not?" She glared at Deborah, like she couldn't believe Deborah was as dumb as she'd accused Carey of being. "You're going to destroy your relationship with Rock if you do this."

"I'm not stupid!" Carey was so not happy with his twin. "And it wasn't about hiding."

"Wasn't it?" Marilyn asked with a knowing look, only a close sibling could give.

Carey deflated. "Maybe a little."

"Just be yourself. That's good enough." Marilyn patted her brother's arm.

"That's what Rock always says," Carey said.

"Where do you think I got it, dork?"

"I'm not a dork!"

Deborah had enough of this digression. "If asking Rock something complete strangers are allowed to pitch to him destroys what we have then we don't have anything." And Deborah had to believe that wasn't the case.

Marilyn shook her head, clearly not convinced. "I don't think you understand how deeply my brother's antipathy for all things Hollywood runs."

"Even me?" Deborah asked, pain twinging again. Because, really, that was what this was all about.

"Not you," Marilyn assured Deborah. "You're the one exception, I think."

"Your brother loves you and Carey. He's always on your side." That made them pretty big exceptions.

"But he hates that we followed our parents into their industry," Carey said morosely.

Deborah smiled at the younger actor. "He's made concessions for both of your dreams no one would have expected." Certainly not her.

At least not when she'd first met Rock. She'd come to see that his concern for his siblings outweighed Rock's dislike of the industry they were in.

Carey rubbed the back of his neck. "That doesn't mean he's going to be okay with you asking him to financially support the industry he hates so much."

"What is letting us use the property for filming if not supporting that industry?" Deborah asked, not sure she bought the young man's reasoning.

"That's different."

Deborah didn't see how and said so.

"I'd already made a promise, signed a contract. If Rock refused, then that was me breaking my word." Carey looked ashamed of what he was admitting. "He wouldn't make me do that if he had a choice."

"And you knew it when you signed that stupid contract," Marilyn said with some heat.

Carey scowled at his sister. "Let up on the *stupid* word, would you? I know I made a mistake." He sighed, then brightened. "But it turned out."

"You hurt him." Marilyn looked at her twin with reproach.

Carey winced. "I told him I was sorry."

"And were you?" Marilyn demanded, as if she was the older sibling instead of Rock.

"Yes, damn it, Mare; you know I was!"

"Okay, we're digressing here again, guys," Deborah interjected.

The siblings looked at her.

"The fact is, if asking Rock to invest in this movie causes a major chasm between us, then we've got no chance at making our relationship work." Because that would indicate they didn't really have a *relationship* to begin with, that he truly despised a big part of who Deborah was. "He doesn't have to say yes, but this is my industry and working in it is who I am. If he can't accept that, what kind of future could we have together?"

"But you're so good for him," Marilyn lamented, like a break-up was a foregone conclusion.

"He's really happy with you around," Carey added, looking like he was already grieving their lost relationship too.

"You two don't need to be so gloom and doom. As much as I didn't want to do this when Art and Ms. Morganstein first told me it's what they wanted, I honestly believe investing in the movie will be good for your brother. I wouldn't ask him otherwise."

"I'm not sure that's going to matter to him," Carey said woefully.

Frowning, Rock put the phone down. Benji had called because there was news about the attack on Rock and Deborah. Apparently, another criminal overheard them talking in the holding cell Amos and Virgil had been moved to after getting medical treatment for the wounds Rock had inflicted. The guy facing drunk and disorderly charges was looking for a deal in exchange for information.

He'd overheard the two miscreants talking about not going down alone if their employer didn't come up with a good lawyer for them. They'd complained bitterly about charging too little for all the pain they'd suffered.

Rock had almost smiled at that, but now he shook his head, disbelief warring with fury. From their conversation, it sounded like the two men had been hired to harass Deborah. The sheriff thought that might be why they'd threatened actions they hadn't perpetrated on their other robbery victims. Benji had surmised that no one had expected Rock's reaction and ability to overpower them, which had ended up with them being arrested.

What Rock couldn't figure out was why someone would hire those two losers to harass Deborah. Whatever the motive, he didn't like knowing she was at risk in some way. That some nameless person wanted to hurt her.

Rock considered all the bad luck the film had suffered since the crew and actors had arrived in Alaska and he didn't like the string of coincidences. Though none of them had been directly targeted at Deborah, it still felt off.

Like maybe somehow all of this was connected.

But why? Rock didn't like not knowing the answers.

"Hey, do you have a minute?" Deborah's sexy contralto interrupted his frustrated musings.

She stood in the door, her killer legs encased in skinny jeans the color of wheat, her blue tank top's scoop neck revealing the upper swell of her breasts, but their curves only hinted at by the long vest she wore over it. She'd put some chunky jewelry on, but it was her espresso dark eyes that really sparkled for him.

Letting go of his frustration over the call with Benji, Rock stood up from his desk. "For you? I've got several minutes."

He came around to stand near the beautiful woman, the warmth in her gaze going straight to his dick. He pulled her into his body without thought, smiling down at her. "I thought you were filming today, but the house is suspiciously silent."

Her smile dimming a little, Deborah sighed and nodded. "Art and Ms. Morganstein had something come up."

"Another accident?" he asked, his suspicions aroused all over again.

"No, nothing like that." She frowned, but settled in against him, her hands landing on his chest. "Not this time anyway."

"So, you have the day off?" he asked, intent heavy in his voice.

She looked up at him flirtatiously through her lashes. "I do. I'd like to talk to you about something later, but first let's take care of this." She reached down between them and squeezed his erection through his jeans.

Rock groaned. "I've got something I need to talk to you about too, hot stuff, but right now all I can think about is being inside you." It was always like that when she was around. His libido was in overdrive with no indication of burning out.

She gave a husky laugh. "Sounds about right."

Yeah, talking could definitely come later.

He leaned down and kissed her, the feel of her soft lips against his sending his pulse skyrocketing. She tasted so good and opened her mouth for him without hesitation when he traced the seam between her lips with the tip of his tongue.

This ache he had for her never went away and right now it was thrumming through his blood like an electric current. She kissed him back without hesitation, her arms coming up and her hands locking behind his neck, her body pressing provocatively against his.

Blood filled his cock, his own arms locking around her of their own volition. Rock grabbed Deborah's ass with both hands, so turned on by the feel of her curves in his grasp, he could hammer nails with his dick.

Rock's brain played technicolor images of her splayed out on his desk, naked and ready for him. Damn. He wanted her. Now. Just like that.

To hell with work. To hell with anything else.

He pulled her closer even as he started moving toward the desk, bringing her with him. Deborah moaned, trying to climb him like a jungle gym. Her reaction to him was more open and intense than any other woman he'd touched.

Rock cleared the desk with a swipe of his hand, not caring about the clunking of detritus hitting the floor. All he cared about was getting her clothes off and Deborah up on a flat surface.

He lifted her and placed her on the cleared desk, immediately going for the hem on her tank top.

She broke her lips from his, panting. "Rock..."

"Let me take this off you."

She nodded, lifting her arms and he tugged the top and vest off in one movement.

"Oh, yes, that's so pretty." Her luscious breasts were barely covered in a lacy bra that pushed them up for his delectation.

She pressed against his chest. "Rock."

"What?" He didn't look away from what he was doing, and that was removing the clothing blocking his view of his lover.

"Stop!"

"Stop?" he asked, trying to process the word.

"Not...just...the door, Rock. It's open."

"Oh." He took a deep breath, forcing his hands to let go of her, making himself take a step back. "Right. We don't need anyone walking in."

Apparently, she hadn't come in here with the intention of getting mauled. She didn't seem to mind the outcome though.

"No, we don't." Her sensual smile about broke his determination to get to the door and lock it.

But no way did Rock want his brother, sister or God forbid, Mrs. Painter walking in and interrupting him and Deborah during a critical moment. And all of them were in the house right now. Having sex in his office, even with the door locked, didn't guarantee they wouldn't be interrupted. Just not walked in on.

And he wasn't waiting.

Rock crossed the room with long, fast strides before slamming the door shut and locking it with a definitive click. He was back in front of her a couple of seconds later.

"Happy now?" he asked, taking in her smooth, barely dressed body.

She nodded, her gaze haze with desire. For him. "Uh huh."

Such a damn turn on, to be wanted with the same kind of uncontrollable need as he felt toward her.

"Take off your jeans," he growled, tearing out of his own clothes, urgency riding him hard.

The fact that they'd made love that morning didn't matter to Rock's body. He was already hard, aching to be inside her wet heat.

"I will." Watching him, her expression infused with lust, Deborah reached behind her back and unclipped her bra with a soft snick. Then she was peeling it away from her body, revealing the lush curves of her breast to his gaze, nipples already peaked and flush with desire.

Had he ever had a lover as in tune with him as this woman?

Naked and impatient, he moved to help with her jeans and underwear after she'd let her shoes drop to the floor. Their hands got tangled, but he got the button open on her fly and then the zipper down. He yanked at her jeans, pulling them off her body, taking the little scrap of silk she called underwear with them.

Deborah lifted her hips to make it easier to get the denim off, her breath already coming out in short pants.

She settled back on the desk, her legs spread, opening herself to him, letting him look his fill before beckoning with her hand. "Come here, Rock."

"You are so damn sexy, woman." Her neatly defined dark patch of curls glistened with moisture he wanted to taste. Her sex beckoned him to be inside her. Her nipples tantalized like hard, ripe berries.

The come-and-get-it look in her eyes infused him with another layer of want.

There was not one damn thing about her that Rock didn't find a sexual turn on. But hell, if he didn't want to spend time with her outside the bedroom too.

Deborah Banes, actor, was one hell of a *woman*.

"Pot? Meet kettle." She winked at him, her smile one-hundred percent sensual woman. "You *are* all that, Rock."

He laughed, his chest warm. This woman!

She touched her own nipples, letting her head fall back, the look of pleasure on her face gorgeous.

He stepped between her spread thighs, reaching down to gently brush her hands away, taking over the stimulation, loving the weight of her curves in his hand, the sensation of her already hard nipples against his fingertips.

She moaned. "That feels so good. You know just how to touch me."

"Touching you is addictive." So, addictive he seriously didn't want to have to consider the time that was coming when he wouldn't be able to do it anymore.

"I'm glad to hear that."

He pulled her hips forward so his sex brushed against her glistening folds. Canting his hips so his head rubbed against her clitoris, he elicited more sexy and tempting pleasure noises from her.

He leaned forward, nuzzling that soft place where her neck met her shoulder, her skin so soft, her scent tantalizing. "I want you, sweetheart."

"Then have me, Rock."

But he wasn't taking her until Deborah was as aching for it as he was. He dropped to his knees, inhaling the scent of her arousal, his mouth watering for the taste of her. Rock flicked his tongue out, swiping along slick, swollen folds, eliciting a deep moan from her. He tasted her juices, reveling in the fragrance of her need.

Moving to the swollen bundle of nerves at the top of her labia, he tasted, teased and finally nibbled oh so gently with his teeth. She rocked her hips, making desperate little sounds that amped up his pleasure and his need to be inside her. He sucked on her clitoris, putting two fingers inside her and curling upward, searching for her G-spot.

Deborah tried to come up off the desk, her shout husky and demanding.

Got it.

"Oh...Rock...I'm going to come if you don't stop." She moved with unselfconscious pleasure against his mouth and fingers.

He lifted his head, her sound of protest exactly what he wanted to hear. He smiled up at her, loving the way she was totally abandoned to pleasure. "That's the plan, right?"

"Inside me," she demanded, her voice choppy with her panting breaths. "I want you inside me."

"You sure?" He sipped at her pleasure point again, pressing inside against her G-spot.

"Yes, darn it. I want!"

CHAPTER SEVENTEEN

Rock took one last taste of his lover's ambrosia before surging to his feet and pressing the head of his cock against the opening to her body, pushing forward just a little bit, stretching tender flesh around his cock.

"Yes, oh, gosh! Rock, you're so big." Deborah had her eyes squeezed tightly shut, her face drawn in pleasure.

His own chuckle was guttural as her intimate flesh squeezed around him. "You're good for my ego."

"Get your darn ego inside me!" she demanded, pressing her body forward.

"If you insist." He thrust forward, sliding into swollen, slick heat and had to focus on every not-sexy thought he could manage so he didn't come in that instant. "You are so damn tight."

She smiled a siren's smile, her eyes still closed, her body bowed toward him, and very deliberately tightened her inner muscles around his cock, jolting him with an overload of pleasure.

Unable to hold back any longer, he lunged forward until he bottomed out, hitting her cervix. A passionate groan came from deep inside his lover as she pushed toward him, trying to take more. He pulled back, each centimeter tortuous pleasure, until he was almost completely out of her. Then he thrust forward and pulled back again, driving both their pleasure higher and higher as he repeated the urgent movements with his pelvis.

"Don't you dare stop!" Her eyes were open now and practically black with emotion.

"Why would I?" He pistoned his hips, settling on a fast, powerful rhythm.

Deborah moaned and offered a litany of breathy encouragement. "That's right, Rock. Oh, my gosh. You are too good at this."

He said the only truth he could admit to in that moment. "We fit." Rock brought his arms up behind her and wrapped his hands over her shoulders to hold her in place as he increased both the pace and power of his thrusts.

"Oh..." She gasped as he surged forward. "Yes. We fit!"

Suddenly her brown eyes were locked on his with an intensity he couldn't ignore. "This is better than good, Rock." She gasped, went silent as he continued pleasuring her body with his. Then, she grabbed his arms, just to hold on. "This is *right*. Nothing has ever felt so perfect."

He was tempted to just let the words go unanswered, but her emotional generosity deserved honesty. "For me either."

She could have no idea how much it cost him to admit that, but this woman, she got to him in ways no one else ever had.

Her gaze turned liquid. "Kiss me, please."

He leaned down and pressed his mouth to hers, sweeping inside with his tongue, letting her feel the claim he was staking, no matter how temporary, and losing himself in the sensations that were so magnified with this woman.

His balls tightened and Rock knew he was close. "Touch yourself. Come with me," he demanded.

She let go of one of his arms and reached between them to touch her clitoris, her head dropping forward against his chest as a long moan snaked out of her throat. "Don't stop, Rock."

"Not going to," he promised, hammering into her body reveling in the involuntary tightening of her vaginal walls around him as she gave herself pleasure.

"I'm going to come!" She leaned forward, biting his chest and sending him over the edge with a hoarse shout.

She convulsed around him, her keening cry music to his ears.

His climax roared through his body, the ecstasy from coming inside her going on longer because of the way her vaginal muscles contracted around him. It was almost too good. Almost too much, but he was in no way ready to withdraw from her body.

It took long moments before he came down enough to move away from her. Electric shocks went from his sex throughout Rock's body as he pulled out of Deborah's slick heat. She reclined on his desk, leaning back on her forearms, her expression completely satiated, her breath still shallow, her beautiful breasts on display, rising and falling in a gorgeous show of feminine beauty. Deborah made no move to get dressed, much less shift off the desk.

She winked at him, even that movement languid. "I think there's a wet spot on your desk."

Rock barked out a laugh. "Yeah, I'll take care of that."

"You wouldn't want to leave it for Lydia to find."

"Agreed." Rock walked on rubber legs to the bathroom attached to his office.

He washed up before returning to his lover, a warm, wet washcloth in his hand. Deborah had not moved.

"You going to take up residence in my office?" he teased.

She yawned, her eyes heavy lidded. "I'm half tempted."

Rock felt a smile crease his face as he tended to his lover, washing his spend from between her legs with careful movements.

"You're a considerate lover, superman."

He liked that she called him that. "I enjoy this and the fact you aren't embarrassed to let me."

"It's intimate," Deborah said. "Just between us."

He nodded. It was. As intimate as anything else they'd done.

She gave him a considering look. "I wouldn't have said intimacy was your thing."

"Unless it's sexual intimacy, it usually isn't."

Her espresso gaze warmed. "But I'm special."

"You are." Two admissions so close together.

Rock waited for the sense of dismay to hit, but it never came. Deborah Banes had found her way behind his walls and for the first time in his life, he didn't panic at the thought.

She let out a sound of pleasure as his fingers caressed the tender flesh he'd just cleaned.

He didn't ask her if she wanted another round, he didn't comment on the fact neither of them were teenagers and this kind of marathon sex should be in their past. Rock just picked Deborah up and carried her to the sofa on the far wall. He sat down and pulled her into his lap, her back to him, sliding his thick cock, which had never gone completely soft, back into her welcoming heat.

She rode him slow and easy, undulating her body, getting him fully stiff. He caressed her breasts, her stomach, her cheeks, her thighs, before concentrating on her clitoris, his other hand continuing its journey of mapping her body. This time, he brought her to a climax before lifting her and laying her on the sofa cushions, coming down on top of her again, and going back to making love.

Rock held back from coming until she'd had her third orgasm. Then he let himself go, releasing his seed inside her, wondering for the first time with a woman what it would be like if she wasn't on birth control.

What would having a child with this woman be like?

She wasn't his mother. Deborah Banes would love her child and give it the attention every kid deserved.

"You've got a strange look on your face," she said, her voice all lazy satisfaction.

"I was thinking you'd make a good mom." It was the day for unprecedented honesty, he guessed.

Her eyes focused on him, searching his face for something. "Even though I'm an actor?"

"You're not my mom."

"No, I'm not. I know what it's like to live without your parents' love. I'd never subject my child to the worry they weren't loved."

He kissed her with all the emotion he might never give voice to.

Still reeling from the amazing level of intimacy she and Rock had shared, Deborah finished dressing. "Rock?"

"Hmm?" he asked as he did up his belt, his shirt still hanging open to reveal his yummy muscles. He'd already cleaned all evidence of their lovemaking from the desk *and* the leather couch.

"I didn't actually come in here to get busy on your desk."

Humor sparkled in his sherry brown eyes. "I never would have guessed."

She grinned up at him. "Yes, well, I'm not complaining, that's for sure."

"Glad to hear it." Oh, he did smug, satisfied male *very* well.

She patted his chest, letting her hand linger for just a moment against hot skin. "Don't be arrogant."

"I think it's integral to my nature." He captured her hand and brought it to his lips, kissing her palm.

"I think maybe you're right." She laughed. "I like you anyway." Like wasn't the word she wanted to use, but this man? Would run a mile if she admitted the deeper feelings she had for him.

No matter how fast they'd come. No matter how improbable. Her emotions were *all in* with the Alaskan businessman. She loved him.

And as scary as that was, it was also really, truly wonderful.

He reached down and caressed her butt, like he couldn't help touching her, squeezing a little before moving away to tug his pants on. "Good to know."

She smiled at him, forgetting why she *had* come into the office for a second. Then she remembered and had to bite back a sigh. Who wanted to talk business, especially depressing business, after *three* mind-numbing climaxes?

But seeing as how the man had a real habit of sending her body into the stratosphere with pleasure, putting it off wasn't going to work either.

She settled into one of the chairs in front of his still empty workspace. "Our financial backer pulled funds from the movie."

Rock's expression turned serious as he leaned his hip against the front of the heavy wood desk. "I'm sorry to hear that. Maybe Art and Elaine can convince the other backers to pick up the slack."

"There aren't any," she lamented. "Mr. Barston agreed to fund the movie entirely, but only if no other investors were brought on board."

"*Nevin Barston* is your angel investor?" Rock asked with disbelief.

"Yes." Deborah frowned in confusion. "Do you know him?"

"I know of him." And from the tone of his voice, what Rock knew, he didn't like.

"What? How?" Barston might be obscenely wealthy, but he wasn't a big name in Hollywood, not famous enough to be known in Cailkirn, Alaska.

"He was married to Kitty Grant. Well her name was Barston when they were married. She's dating Tack MacKinnon, though I'm pretty sure no one else is supposed to know that."

"Then, how do you?"

"Sloan. He knows everything going on in this town."

"Kitty Grant is a local?"

"Yes, you've met her aunt. When we were in Cailkirn and her other aunt when we got our cookies."

Deborah remembered the charming elderly ladies who believed she'd fit into the town, one of them still on chatting terms with her dead husband. "Okay. And this Kitty, relations to Cailkirn's elder denizens, is Nevin Barston's ex-wife?"

"She is."

Weird. "That's odd."

"More than odd. I guarantee that piece of shit didn't invest in your movie with any kind of altruistic motives," Rock growled.

Deborah played with her vest, bundled into a ball on her lap, then shook it out and folded it neatly. "I'd have to say not, considering he pulled funds."

"For a movie that both Art and Elaine claim is so important to them, they've both made some unbelievable mistakes."

Despite agreeing with Rock, Deborah felt she had to defend her bosses, who really were no slouches when it came to film-making. "Accepting a single angel investor isn't unheard of."

"Trusting a bastard that beat his wife and had affairs shows poor judgement." Rock scowled. "He left her with nothing in the divorce."

"How do you know all that?"

"Slo—"

"Your friend, the mayor," Deborah interrupted, shaking her head. "That man is a gossip."

Rock shrugged. "He talks to *me*."

"If you say so. Anyway, I'm pretty sure neither Art or Ms. Morganstein would judge a person's business trustworthiness by their personal life."

"Then they're both fools." No doubt in Rock's voice, none at all.

"Isn't that a bit harsh?"

"Considering your movie isn't going to get made, I'd say not."

"Not everyone has your brilliant business acumen," Deborah chided.

"Both of them have too solid reputations for this kind of bad judgment to be the norm. I wonder what's different about this movie?"

Deborah thought she knew. Because she'd done her homework on the principle executives in the film. "Art's son was gay."

"Was? I didn't think that was something that changed."

"That's not what I meant." Sadness at the remembered tragedy she'd read about made Deborah's voice softer than normal. "Samuel committed suicide when he was fifteen."

"I'm very sorry to hear that. I can't imagine losing a child." Rock shook his head. "I guess I'm lucky all Carey did was take on a fake accent."

She thought he knew more about grief than he gave himself credit for. "You lost both your parents."

"Who were barely in my life. I had Marilyn and Carey to take care of."

Deborah nodded. "And you did a really great job of it."

"Thank you."

"What about Elaine?" Rock asked. "Do you know why she let her common sense take a walk when planning for this movie?"

"It's not as bad as all that." Both the director and producer had made a couple of bad choices, but they weren't stupid by any means.

Rock just gave her a look.

Deborah sighed. "Honestly? I don't know why the movie is so important to Ms. Morganstein, but I do know that it is. They're both emotionally invested in the story on a level you don't often see, even in Hollywood's indie industry."

"With that kind of commitment, I'm sure they'll find other investors."

"I think Art, especially, alienated some potential money people when he accepted the deal with Barston."

Rock nodded with understanding. "His usual investors wouldn't have liked being locked out of an important production like this."

"No. I don't think they did."

"Well, if they don't do something, the movie is dead in the water."

This is where things got complicated. "They wanted me to talk to you."

"Me?" Rock's expression went from confused to thoughtful. "I've got some connections in Hollywood, but I've never recommended a film production to investors. You know why."

"I do. And that's not what I meant either."

Rock's expression went blank at that admission. "Maybe you better explain exactly what you do mean, Deborah."

"The movie is good. You know that. We've talked about it, what this movie means both to Carey and to me, but more importantly, how good it's going to be. It's a good, solid investment."

"You're asking me to take over as angel investor?" Rock's entire demeanor closed up, his jaw as firm as granite.

"As an investor, yes, but not the only one." Deborah swallowed against her suddenly dry throat. "Think about it, Rock. I don't know what ROI you usually demand, but this movie is going to hit audiences in the heart. We're releasing over the holidays, it's already got slots at important film festivals. The video release alone is projected to bring in twice the investment in profit."

Rock moved, stepping away from her and the desk. Only a couple of feet, but the distance between them felt like a chasm. Cold chills went up Deborah's spine, though she wasn't sure why.

"Is that what this was about?" he indicated the desk and the sofa with a swipe of his hand. "Was all that sexual openness and generosity supposed to make me amenable to laying out a chunk of money for your movie?"

"What?" she gasped out, unable to accept what he was accusing her of. Her heart felt like it was in a vice and he was squeezing it tighter with every second he looked at her like she was dog poo he'd stepped in. "No, you can't think that. You started it." She'd come in to the office intending to talk, but he'd waylaid her intentions with his passion.

Couldn't he see that? He *had* to see that.

Rock's mouth firmed into a flat line, his sherry gaze weighing her in a way he'd never done before this second. Not once had she felt *less than* in Rock's presence, but right now, she felt dirty. Like she *had* tried to manipulate him with sex.

He crossed his arms over his chest, his usually warm gaze chilled. "I can't believe I was beginning to think we might have a future."

"And you're saying now that we don't?" He'd been thinking about the future? She couldn't accept the way this conversation was going. It made no sense to her. "Because I asked a venture capitalist if he wanted to make an investment?" she added with heavy disbelief.

"You know how I feel about the film industry."

"I know how you feel about your parents, but they were not the whole industry. You love your brother. You love your sister. You're not rejecting them because they chose to go into an industry you say you have such antipathy for." Would he really reject Deborah the same way her parents had, for the same reason?

Because it was okay if the people he loved did something he didn't approve of, but not her?

"You just told me you wanted us to talk about our day on set at dinner," she reminded him.

"That's a helluva distance from funding the movie," he said impatiently. "And it's not Carey asking me to bankroll his latest project."

"I'm not asking you bankroll it! I asked if you would invest. *Invest*, Rock. That thing you've been successfully doing since your parents' deaths"

"Why isn't Carey here doing the asking?" Rock's expression said he didn't believe the reason for his brother's absence could be anything that put Deborah in a good light. "Did he expect you to seduce me into it, too?"

"No! No one expected that." At least Art and Ms. Morganstein had said they didn't and Deborah was going with that. "It's just, Carey didn't think there was even a remote chance you'd say *yes*."

"And you disagreed."

"Not entirely," she answered honestly. She'd thought the chances of Rock offering production funds would be extremely low. "I know you have an unreasonable prejudice against what I do."

"You think it's unreasonable to see the ugly side of an industry that isn't all shining stars and glamour?" he asked with heavy disdain.

"Of course not. I think it's horrifically unreasonable to assume we just had amazing sex so I could convince you to invest in that industry. I think it's unreasonable to ignore any of the positives in an industry that brings a lot of good into the world." Deborah paused for a second and then said what was causing her the most pain in the moment. "I think it's beyond unreasonable, it's demeaning to both of us, for you to look at me like I'm a whore simply for presenting an opportunity to you."

Something flared in his sherry gaze, his eyes widening fractionally. "I did not look at you like you are a whore."

"Then what?" It had sure seemed that way to her. "What else would you call it for me to use my body to get money out of you."

"I... That's not what I meant..." He shook his head. "Why did *you* ask? You've skirted around it, but you haven't answered that question."

"It wasn't my intention to skirt around anything. I asked because I believed there was a chance, however remote, that you'd see the possibilities and not get lost in your own dark prejudices. *I* asked because *I* needed to see that you didn't judge *me* by the career I've chosen. That this big part of my life wasn't a deal breaker between us."

He opened his mouth, but she wasn't ready to hear what he had to say. Not yet.

She put up her hand. "No. You asked. I'm answering. I came to you with this because of what we have and not the way you think. I don't believe for a minute you're a man who can be led around by his dick, no matter what my producer and editor might assume. But you and I are more than casual sex-buddies, we have been since the beginning, no matter what you are willing to admit. *Damn it*, Rock, I'm falling for you." Had fallen, but she wasn't ready to lay it all out there for him. "I needed to know that you weren't going to reject me for just asking. I guess I learned the answer to that question though, didn't I?"

She moved toward the door, looking back at him with her hand on the knob. "Last of all, I asked, because it's my job."

Rock opened and closed his mouth several times without anything coming out until he said finally, "You're not in charge of funding for the movie."

"I'm on the production and directorial team. This movie was supposed to be my chance to establish my credentials for going to the other side of the camera."

Shock washed over his handsome face. "You never said anything."

"Yeah, it never came up. Until you told me you wouldn't mind us chatting about the day's work at dinner, I was still under the impression you barely tolerated talking about the movie at all."

"And you still asked me to invest." His tone said he found that incomprehensible.

"I needed to know. I guess I do now." No matter how much it hurt.

"That I'm not about to bankroll my brother's, or your career?"

He was not hearing her. Rock simply was not listening. "You really don't get it. You could have just said no, but instead you instantly assumed I was trying to use sex to manipulate you, and you keep talking like I'm asking for a heck of a lot more than that what I actually did. That right there tells me you're never going to deal with my career in a rational manner." She opened the door to leave.

"Wait a minute, Deborah. We're not done here."

"I think we are." She didn't wait for him to say anything else but headed to the room they'd been sharing since the beginning, her things having migrated from the guest room she'd been given to his room over the weeks.

CHAPTER EIGHTEEN

Tamping down the almost impossible to ignore compulsion to follow her, Rock stared after Deborah. He still couldn't quite believe she'd asked him to finance her movie. After one of the most amazing session of lovemaking they'd had to date. After he'd admitted unprecedented vulnerability.

He wasn't a cash cow.

He hit his chest with his fist, trying to dislodge the knot of pain there. Had he eaten something bad this morning?

Oh, to hell with it. He stormed out of his office, shouting his brother's name.

Carey and Marilyn came rushing toward him, together. No doubt they'd been lurking close by to see the results of his disastrous conversation with Deborah. Which meant they were probably aware of what Rock and Deborah had been doing before that.

And he could not care less.

Both looked wary as they stopped in front of Rock. "What?" Carey asked.

"Where's Deborah?" Marilyn demanded at the same time.

"What in the hell did you think you were doing?" Rock blasted his younger brother, ignoring his sister's question entirely.

"What?" Carey asked, rocking the deer in the headlights look. "What did I do?"

Rock wasn't buying it. "Getting Deborah to do your dirty work for you. Ring any bells?"

"That's not what happened."

Marilyn shook her head, like she was agreeing with her twin, but savvy enough not to say anything.

"Oh, really?" Rock asked, frustration riding him hard. "Then how is it that Deborah asked me for money to finish your movie and you didn't?"

Cary's hands fisted at his sides. "Because I thought there wasn't a single chance you'd say yes."

"We told her not to ask," Marilyn offered.

Rock rubbed the back of his neck. "She didn't listen."

"She said she needed to know she could ask." Carey was looking at Rock like *he* had done something wrong.

"I'm not bankrolling your career in Hollywood, Carey. You'll make it, or not, based on your own talent and ability."

"I never asked you to." Carey sounded stung, his gaze was wounded. "I don't believe Deborah asked you to do that either. "

"She's not the type," Marilyn agreed. "You overreacted, didn't you?"

"What type? The type to ask me for money? She did that."

"She asked you to invest in a movie that already has theater and video distribution contracts." Carey's eyes lit like they did when he really believed in something. "You might not double your money, but then again, you might triple it. You'll definitely make *something* back." Carey sighed, his enthusiasm dimming just a little. "Not like me when I got talked into investing in a poorly produced pile of crap without a single guaranteed distribution outlet."

"I earned my place in the world," Rock said, feeling a little like maybe he *had* over-reacted, but not yet ready to admit it. "Is it unreasonable of me to expect you two to do the same thing?"

"This isn't about us, Rock. Not even a little." Marilyn frowned. "What did you say to Deborah?"

"Besides accusing her of wanting me to bankroll her future?" Or as good as.

Carey shook his head, disgust on his younger face. "You didn't!"

Marilyn gasped. "Darn it, Rock, that was stupid! She didn't even ask you to be the only investor. Did she?"

"Oh, now you're the *stupid* one," Carey drawled.

Rock didn't bother to respond to his brother's sally, looking to Marilyn when he said, "No." Deborah *hadn't* asked him to be the new angel investor.

She'd asked him to consider putting some funding in the movie.

He had overreacted. Damn, if she had waited to ask until a time they hadn't just made love, maybe he wouldn't have felt so used.

"She told you it was okay if you said no," Marilyn guessed. "I'm sure she did. Deborah said it didn't matter if you wanted to invest, she just needed to know she could ask."

"We didn't get to that point." They'd gotten just far enough for him to torpedo himself with her.

"You did overreact." Marilyn groaned, like the long suffering sister she wasn't. "I knew it. You have to fix this."

"Why?" He blurted out the first thing that came to mind. Rock didn't work on relationships. "She'll be gone in a matter of weeks anyway."

What would be the point of opening himself up to her when she was just going to leave him anyway?

"Because, you big dope, you want her to come back." Marilyn smacked his bicep. "We all do. She's good for you. She fits with us."

Carey was nodding like a bobblehead doll. "You gotta fix this, Rock."

"How do you expect me to do that?" Rock demanded, wondering if his younger siblings were right.

"Apologize!" Marilyn's tone said she thought he was a couple eggs shy of an omelet right then.

"Tell her you're sorry and you didn't mean it," Carey elaborated, his expression stern. "You owe her that, Rock, even if you don't want to keep her in your life. You can't treat people poorly because our parents let you down every day of your life until they died."

Rock knew the look of shock on their sister's face was reflected in his own. Carey never criticized their parents.

"That's not what this is about." Though Rock wasn't sure if he was lying to his siblings, or himself.

He was pretty sure the whole damn debacle was about their mom and dad and the way Rock had learned not to trust from them.

"Isn't it?" Carey demanded. "They sucked as parents. And maybe I got into drama because I was looking for a way to understand who they were. But now, I'm an actor because that's *who* and *what* I am. Having you as my big brother, a better dad than he ever was, that gave me the freedom to be this person. The freedom for everything."

Marilyn's eyes filled with moisture as she smiled at Carey. Then she looked at Rock. "That goes ditto for me, but I don't think Deborah's ever had anyone that mattered to her be okay with her being herself and nothing else."

"We're not in a relationship," Rock said, a little desperately.

"Stop lying to yourself, big brother. You wouldn't tolerate that from one of us." Her gaze softened, like she got that this feeling of vulnerability scared the shit out of Rock. "Not only are you two in a relationship, but it's the most important one you've ever had with any woman. Probably the most important one you'll ever have."

"Yeah, I think she's the one, Rock," Carey added.

Not helpfully.

"Glad you two think you've got my life figured out."

His sarcasm was lost on both of them, as Carey and Marilyn stood giving him identical significant looks.

He wished he could deny their claims. But he couldn't. Not without lying.

And Marilyn was right, Rock expected honesty from his siblings, even when it hurt. He didn't know what the future held for him and Deborah Banes, actor, but they had more than sex right now.

A hell of lot more, or it wouldn't have hurt him so much to think she was using him. And it wouldn't have bothered her so much that he'd thought she was using him if there weren't more feelings involved than sexual ones.

Damn it all to hell.

Refusing to let the tears burning behind her eyes fall, Deborah finished packing her case and zipped it up.

"What are you doing?" The sound of the guestroom door snicking shut accompanied Rock's voice.

Deborah turned and came face to face with the man himself. He'd crossed the room and stood a lot closer than she expected. She backed up quickly, needing distance between them.

Her legs hit the bed, so she sat down, scooting to the end, as far from him as she could get. "Don't be obtuse. What does it look like I'm doing?"

"Leaving."

"Give the man a dollar for his insight." Deborah made no attempt to hide her sarcasm. It was better than revealing her hurt.

Rock shook his head, his chiseled jaw set. "You can't leave."

"I'm pretty sure I can."

"No, it's not safe."

"What in the world are you talking about?" Not safe? What was that supposed to mean?

"Benji called earlier."

"They let Amos and Virgil go?" she asked with shock.

"No. They're still being held for the string of robberies."

Her brows drew together in confusion. "Then, why not safe?"

"He said they were hired by someone."

"Someone hired them to rob people?" She wouldn't have

thought the men made enough with their sordid business to be part of some organized enterprise

"That's not the working theory." Rock shifted closer, his hands curling and uncurling at his sides. "Benji thinks, from things that were said in the overhearing of the police informant, that you were the target."

"That's ridiculous. If anyone was a target, it would make more sense it was you. I'm nobody, you're a multi-millionaire businessman."

"That's not what Benji thinks."

"Well, your friend, the sheriff, is wrong. There is no reason for someone to go after me. There just isn't."

"There's evidence to the contrary."

Why was he pushing this? He couldn't want her around on the daily. Not now. "You mean the overheard conversation between two cretins that probably couldn't tell their own asses from a hole in the ground? I'm not buying it."

Rock's eyes flared, like Deborah's comment surprised him. So, she swore. Big deal. The man couldn't expect perfection from a woman he thought would sell her body for her career.

And she wasn't feeling particularly tactful right now. In fact, she felt like her heart was splintering in her chest.

She just wanted him to leave, then she could finish gathering her stuff and go.

His sherry gaze bored into hers, speaking messages she knew she couldn't fool herself with any longer. "You agreed to stay here while making the movie, hot stuff."

"Don't call me that!" She took a couple of deep breaths, reining in her emotions. "Why would you want me to stay?"

He blew out a breath, dry-washed his face and let his head drop down, staying like that for several long seconds. Then he looked back up at her, his expression as vulnerable as she'd ever seen it.

If she could let herself believe the evidence of her eyes.

He reached toward her, then let his arm fall again. "I'm sorry, okay? I shouldn't have made it seem like I thought you were using sex to get what you wanted from me."

"I'd rather know the truth." He *had* thought that.

He appealed to her with his eyes, his body rigid with tension. "It was a mistake. I know that now."

"Why now? Why not thirty minutes ago?" She shook her head. "No. Never mind. It doesn't matter. That's where your brain went first. We both know it, now. And that, more than anything, told me where I really stood with you. I kept thinking we were building something, no matter what you said. I thought your actions said something else. Now, I know I was fooling myself."

And that hurt. Hurt so badly she just wanted to curl into a ball and grieve.

He dropped down to his knees in front of her, reaching for her hands. "You weren't being stupid."

"Oh, yes, I was." She put her hands behind her back so he couldn't hold them. It felt childish and completely necessary.

"No. We had…we *have* something." He ran his fingers through his dirty blond hair. "Something I've never had with another woman."

A couple of hours ago those words would have melted her. Now, she didn't trust them. She couldn't. She knew too well how easy it was for important people in her life to reject her for simply being who she was. "Amazing sex isn't what I'm talking about."

"More than sex."

"Don't!" She had to take a hold of her emotions again. "Don't," she said in a more modulated tone. "You were honest with me from the beginning. No matter what you think, I don't blame you for my own self-deception. But I'm not lying to myself anymore."

"Damn it, beauty, I'm trying to tell you. You weren't lying to yourself." He reached around her and pulled her hands forward until he held them trapped against his chest. "I don't know what happens after you wrap the movie, but what we have right now? It's more than sex. A helluva lot more."

Part of her wanted to smack him for saying something like that *now* when it was too late. When she knew that whatever they had, it *didn't* have a future. The other part of her marveled at how fast his heart was beating under her hand. He was nervous.

This conversation was important to him.

Because he liked the sex, she reminded herself. Hadn't he said that from the beginning. He'd agreed to let them film so he could have access to her. She hadn't believed that was why, but now? Now she knew how he really saw her.

But which of them was the whore when she would give herself to him for nothing and she'd told him so?

"Look, chances are we aren't even going to finish filming—"

"You don't know that," Rock interrupted her. "Art Gamble and Elaine Morganstein have access to more money than they're willing to admit. Those two have successfully funded over a dozen indie projects. They're not going to let this one fail."

She didn't ask how Rock knew that. He'd told her he had contacts in LA. He'd obviously used them to do some deep digging on the suits for this project. "I hope you're right. I really do, but new backers mean different production terms."

It could mean her name being taken off the production and editorial credits.

Rock inclined his head, acknowledging her point. "Maybe."

"Right. We've already lost a day of filming, what scenes do you think are going to get cut because of it?" she asked with all the cynicism she'd been trained to have in her decade following her hopes and dreams in Hollywood. "Not the big scenes Art is directing."

"You were supposed to direct a scene?"

"Two, but even if they're kept in, he probably won't let me direct them. Art will be focused on sticking with the schedule and production time is always longer with a new director."

"You really want to get on the other side of the camera," Rock said wonderingly.

What did he think she'd lied about that? She wasn't the one who pretended feelings she didn't have. "I'm not setting the world on fire in front of it."

"You're talented." He lifted one hand to his lips and kissed her palm. "You're beautiful." He did the same with the other hand. "You've got presence. You've got everything that makes a great actor."

She refused to let herself feel the warmth his words wanted to engender in her heart. If he believed that, he never would have accused her of using sex to convince him to invest. He would have believed she didn't need to.

"And I've been in the business since I went to university at the age of eighteen." She sighed, reminding herself that it wasn't Rock's fault if she lost her chance at production and directorial credits. This was her life and she had to make it work. "Ten years is a long time to work for a break that may never come."

"Some actors don't find their niche for twice that time in the industry." He released her hands and rubbed her thighs in a comforting way that she wished *didn't* comfort her.

And darned if she didn't leave her hands where they were, though she curled her fingers into the slick cotton of his dress shirt. "And some find success on their first movie or television program."

"Any industry based on artistic expression is fickle."

"At best."

"So, you don't give up."

She felt her own eyes widening at his pronouncement. That's not the advice she expected, but it didn't matter. "I'm not giving up. I'm redefining what I want out of life. I'm done seeking success as an actor just to prove to my parents and sister that my choice to go to a performing art school over university and then law school was justified."

He let his head fall forward, their foreheads touching. "You don't have to prove yourself to anyone."

Like she didn't have to prove herself to him? He'd shown how untrue that was not a half an hour past.

She let her hands fall away from him, crossing her arms around her stomach. "That's easy for you to say," she said in a low tone between them. "I doubt there's a single person in the world you want approval from that you don't have it."

He looked up then, his sherry eyes dark with remembered pain. "My parents were always disappointed in me."

"Because you didn't want to follow in their footsteps?" How could any parent not see Rock for the amazing son he had been?

Even a couple as self-involved as his?

"They accused me of having a pedantic view of life more than once." And that attitude had hurt Rock, it was in his voice.

Despite their failure to provide safety and security for their children, Rock had loved his mom and dad. The gallery dedicated to their accomplishments showed just how much.

She couldn't stop herself from reaching out and cupping his face. "Even if it wasn't true, it makes sense. If they acknowledged the role you played in your family, they would have to admit how badly they messed up fulfilling the ones they were supposed to."

Rock looked away, hiding his vulnerability. Or maybe just trying to keep the pain inside. "You're probably right."

"Rock, you were an incredible son, who cared about everyone in his family. You're a larger than life man." There was a reason she called him Superman.

"But you want to leave me."

Oh, crap. She couldn't let herself fall into the abyss of emotion those words elicited. She sighed. "Listen, Rock, I'm sure I'll be just as safe as I need to be at the Lodge." Her heart couldn't handle living in this man's house and knowing they had no future.

It definitely wouldn't survive another bout of hope and love dashed into smithereens beneath his mistrust.

For the second time that day, Rock gave her a look she'd never received from him. All at once, he was all cold, corporate shark, no compromise in his sherry gaze. "You agreed to stay here for the duration of the filming."

"That was when we were sharing a bed. There's no reason for me to stay here now." She wasn't having sex with a man who thought so little of her, no matter how he claimed *that* had been a mistake.

The only mistake had been him giving voice to thoughts he now realized he should have kept hidden if he wanted to keep her in his bed until she left Alaska.

Her heart told her she was being too cynical, that Rock was genuinely sorry. But she'd given that organ enough leeway in the past weeks. Right now, her brain was in control and her brain knew that her soul had been wounded enough by this man.

She should have listened when he said all they had was sex, and temporary at that.

"I don't agree," he answered implacably.

She wanted to stand up and move away from him but doing so would press her body against his and that was not going to happen. "Oh, come on, Rock."

"If you want to keep filming, you'll stay."

"You can't do that." Sex, no matter how good, wasn't worth the fight he'd have on his hands if he followed through on that threat.

"You'd be surprised what I can and will do."

Maybe she shouldn't be though. A man didn't get where he was and build the life he had for his siblings when he had still been a child himself without having a strength of purpose that outdid normal mortals.

She brought up a knee, crossing her arms over and creating a barrier between them. "You're being ridiculous. I'm sure Benji misunderstood whatever was said in the holding cell."

"He's not the one that overheard it and the state police detective who got the information from his informant didn't have any doubts about what was said."

"No." She shook her head. "There is absolutely no reason for someone to come after me." He had to believe her.

"Not even your family? Maybe your parents are done waiting for you to fall back in line."

"No. They wouldn't. They don't think..." But maybe they did. The last time she'd talked to her sister, Alicia had said their parents had made comments about that very thing.

That they might need to take things in hand. Ten years

following a wild hare was long enough.

"I can see from the look on your face, you aren't even sure of that yourself."

"They're not going to fly to Alaska and hire some petty criminals to harass me." That wasn't her parents' style.

"Maybe. Maybe not. Someone hired Amos and Virgil."

"According to some criminal who is probably getting a deal for information, that may, or may not, be true."

"You don't think our detectives can tell the difference between bogus and good intel?" Rock asked, sounding offended. "You think that just because they're not big city cops, they're not good at their jobs."

"That's not the point."

"That's exactly the point. Either you trust our law enforcement, or you don't."

"You're being really frustrating right now."

"Because I'm concerned about your safety?" he asked with patent disbelief.

Like he couldn't imagine her not appreciating his concern on her behalf.

But she was a big girl and she'd been entirely on her own for a very long time. "I'm an adult. I can watch out for myself."

He surged to his feet, stepping back, spinning away from her like he had to get a handle on his emotions. Then he turned back. "Look, hot stuff, we have a deal. And backing out has consequences."

Oh, she wanted to scream. "I never thought you meant that."

"You agreed to stay here."

"You can't want me to." What was the point?

"You are wrong. I very much want you to."

"You're being a bully."

"For expecting you to keep your word?" he asked, clearly unimpressed with her reasoning.

"You know I didn't believe you were letting us film here in exchange for me sharing your bed."

"Be that as it may, you agreed to stay here during the duration of the filming."

"Why does it matter to you?"

"I told you why."

"Because you're worried about my safety." That wasn't a bad thing, no matter how her independent nature chafed against it.

"Among other things."

"Name them."

"I already did."

"Tell me again." Maybe she'd believe him this time. Probably not, but maybe.

CHAPTER NINETEEN

"Because we have something bigger than sex, something more than either of us has ever had with someone else."

"You don't know that." She'd been in a relationship before.

The fact it had ended with her being betrayed and learning once again she could only rely on herself was beside the point.

Rock just looked at her, his expression calling her on her honesty.

She stood up too, moving to the window and looking out at the beautiful landscape. Leaving here was going to be hard, for so many reasons. "Fine. I'll stay here, but I'm not having sex with you, Rock. That is over."

"Let's take one thing at a time, beauty."

She turned her head to look at him, his tone implying things that scared the heck out of her heart. The look he gave her indicated he wasn't convinced about the no sex rule.

He'd learn she could be stubborn too. When her own emotional survival was at stake, she could be positively intransigent. "Yes, let's. Look, I need to call Ms. Morganstein."

Rock nodded. "What are you going to tell her?"

"That you refused to invest. What else?"

"I never actually said no."

No, he'd just made her feel like she'd committed a grave sin by asking. "Do you need to say it to feel better?"

"I need to spend some time looking at all the details before I decide."

"Are you kidding me?" she demanded, in no mood for games.

"I never joke about money."

Now, that she could believe. "Look, you and I both know you're not going to invest. There's no point getting their hopes up." Art and Ms. Morganstein needed to be looking at other financing alternatives.

The sooner, the better.

"Carey pointed out how likely it is that the movie will not only break even, but make a substantial profit." Rock's mouth twisted with something like remorse, like maybe he realized he should have listened to Deborah to begin with. "I'd need to see the actual numbers, projections, project budget and marketing plan before I could decide, but I'm not saying no out of hand."

Knowing he'd listened to his brother when he'd been so dismissive and hurtful, with her, caused another slashing wound across Deborah's heart. She didn't care if that was a professional, or even rational response. Her feelings were hers and she'd spent years denying the pain of her family's rejection. She just didn't have that in her anymore.

At least not where Rock was concerned.

"I'm glad you were able to see past your prejudices to listen to your brother anyway," she offered with honesty, if some pain as well.

With a sigh, Rock moved to stand beside her, laying his hand on her shoulder. "I'm sorry I hurt you."

She shrugged, not prepared to accept his apology and honest enough to admit that to herself. She was still hurting too much. "It's not your fault you didn't feel what I did."

"Who says I didn't?"

"You did." If nothing else, that message had come through loud and clear.

He rubbed up and down her arms. "I felt used," he admitted, his tone not cold anymore, but mirroring the hurt she couldn't deny he'd felt as well. "I didn't like it."

And he'd lashed out in his pain. For the first time, she realized her heart wasn't the only one wounded by their latest discussion. Though maybe not his heart so much as his pride. Either way, Rock *had* been wounded.

She turned to face him, needing to look into his eyes when she said what needed saying. "I haven't used you in any way." He would either believe her, or he wouldn't, but it needed to be said. "And I had no desire to do so when I asked you about investing."

His eyes scanned her face and then he sighed. "I believe you."

"Honestly, if you weren't a venture capitalist, I don't think I would have asked you to invest, no matter how rich you are."

He sighed, his expression saying he was reorganizing some things in his mind. "You sure you belong on the business side of things?"

"I thought I did, but I'm not so sure now," she admitted. She'd hated the idea of using the people in her life to fund the project, no matter how much she believed in it.

He squeezed her shoulders. "You're a strong woman, Deborah, but you don't have that instinct that allows you to leverage any relationship to make your business work."

"You didn't think that back in your office."

"I did think it. That's why you asking for the money was such a shock."

"But it's what you do," she said painfully, not understanding how he couldn't see that.

"It is. But that's not why I'm going to seriously consider an investment in a project I would reject out of hand if anyone else had asked me."

Anyone but his brother, he meant. Because he sure hadn't been willing to consider it when she'd brought it up.

Deborah's phone rang, the ringtone telling her it was either Art or Ms. Morganstein. Grateful for the interruption, she pulled away from him and went to get the phone from where she'd set it on her nightstand. "That'll be one of them. What do you want me to tell them?"

"Why don't you let me talk to them?"

She wasn't going to argue. Weak, it might be, she'd rather Rock dealt with the suits about his own willingness, or lack thereof, to invest.

Swiping to connect, Deborah gave a short greeting to Ms. Morganstein before telling her she was going to pass the phone over.

Rock told the other woman what information he needed in order to make his decision about whether to put money into the project, or not. His face took on a stony expression and Deborah guessed Ms. Morganstein was trying to push for some kind of commitment before providing anything.

Rock's words confirmed her guess. "No, I will not tell you what ballpark I'm considering for the investment without that information." He listened for a second, his lips tightening. "A soft copy would be fine, but I expect hard copies of all contracts involved before I make a final decision."

Rock listened again, his silence growing, his expression not softening one iota. Finally, he said, "Yes, I'm still here. Are you finished trying to talk around my requirements?" Ms. Morganstein said something else.

Rock walked back over to Deborah, touching her face gently before speaking again. "Let's be very clear, Elaine, your current situation is neither my fault, nor is it my responsibility. I have been more than generous with this production." Ms. Morganstein spoke again.

Rock sighed, looking directly into Deborah's eyes when he answered. "No, I will not give a week, but I will agree to a two-day extension to filming while I look over the information and you seek investors elsewhere. And I do not think it is the least I can do. In fact, I think if you want me on this project, you had better learn to show some respect and appreciation for what I've given already."

His scowl turned dark as he listened to Ms. Morganstein. "Deborah is an adult, as is my brother. Neither needs this movie as impetus to have whatever relationship they plan to have with me in the future." His entire body went rigid with obvious fury and Deborah couldn't help herself. She laid one hand on his chest, right over his heart while grabbing for the phone.

He let her have it without issue.

"Ms. Morganstein?"

"Deborah? That man is terribly arrogant."

Seriously? Said the woman arrogant enough to tell Rock, who hadn't wanted them filming on his property in the first place, that the least he could do was to extend access for a week.

Deborah took hold of her irritation. "You do realize you are asking him for money?"

"I do not think there is anything wrong with pointing out that if he refuses to invest, he's probably going to do irreparable harm to his relationship with his brother, not to mention his access to your bed."

Deborah felt cold chills run all down her back. "Excuse me, but not only are you wrong on both counts, I think making a statement like that is a lot more likely to turn Rock right off from even considering this investment."

"Why should it? He'll make a lot of money on this movie."

"Why don't *you* concentrate on getting the documentation that will convince him of that?" Deborah asked, rather than saying the ugly words that really wanted to come out of her mouth.

It was bad enough Rock had thought that of her, she didn't need her executive producer confirming suspicions he'd just given up.

"Don't forget who you're talking to, Deborah," Ms. Morganstein said coldly.

"I haven't forgotten, but maybe you have. I am a lead actor on your project with production and editorial credit. You are not my pimp."

Ms. Morganstein gasped. "That's entirely uncalled for—"

"My personal life is my *own*," Deborah went on, interrupting the other woman. "It doesn't have a darn thing to do with the movie. You've said you understood that."

"Well, of course I do, but it is entirely natural for me to assume that you would have issue with a lover who didn't support your career."

"On the contrary. I trust *myself* to make my own way and hope I never turn into one of those women who expects a man to make her hopes and dreams come true."

Ms. Morganstein was silent for several seconds. Then finally, "Just how committed are you to this project, Ms. Banes?"

"As committed as I ever was, but I have never put my body on the line to get ahead." No matter how, or when, she'd been encouraged to do so. "And I'm not going to start now."

"Well, naturally not!" Ms. Morganstein's tone was full-on scandalized.

Just what the heck did she think she'd been trying to push Deborah into doing?

Tired of the whole mess, Deborah said, "It sound like you've got stuff to do. I'll let you go."

"You do realize we expect you to help Rock interpret the projections and other things we send him. He's not in the industry, after all."

Try to strong-arm him into their point-of-view more like. Deborah wasn't going there.

"Rock won't need any help, but I will be on hand to answer whatever questions he might have." He sure wasn't okay with her going anywhere else.

"That will have to be good enough, I suppose."

"I suppose it will." Deborah was done playing nice.

They ended the call and she turned to Rock who looked even angrier than he had when he'd been talking to Ms. Morganstein.

"Whatever has that look on your face, could you save it?" Deborah asked, truly done with this whole topic and what it had cost her already.

"She expected you to withhold sex in exchange for getting me to invest in the movie." And apparently, he no longer thought that was the way Deborah was leaning. "She told me my brother would never forgive me if I didn't. That his career was on the line."

"She's under a lot of pressure." And not thinking straight if Ms. Morganstein thought she could threaten a man like Rock into doing what she wanted.

"That's no excuse."

"No, it's not. But, Rock, I think being told I should do that was a little more demoralizing."

"Why the hell do you think I'm so pissed?"

Oh. "Because she said it to me?" Deborah hadn't considered that possibility.

"You are not a whore!"

"No, really, I'm not. I don't think she believes I am one either. She just couldn't imagine not cutting off a relationship with a lover who didn't offer wholesale support of what she does."

"That's bullshit."

"You think?"

"I do." He got a strange look on his face. "Don't you?"

"Oh, yes. My career is my own. It's not anyone else's responsibility."

"You said you didn't want to be one of *those* women."

"My sister has a master's degree in chemistry. She's really smart, but after she got married, both her husband and my parents expected her to quit her job in the research laboratory. She wasn't a doctor, or *anything important* in their eyes, so she could stay home and take care of the children, his home, *his* schedule. Everything they have, he provides."

"If it makes her happy."

"Maybe it does. I don't know. I do know she's told me more than once how much she misses her job, how much she wishes she was back in the lab."

"Some women, and men, like being the at home parent."

"Yes. And honestly? Alicia loves being a mom. But what happens when the kids grow up?"

"Midlife crisis?"

Deborah's laugh was harsh, even to her own ears. "Yeah, maybe. It's just it should have been *her* decision. Not her husband's. Not my parents."

"Agreed."

"But they've got her convinced she needs *him* to make her dreams come true. As long as she's happy, content, that's great. I worry about her future, but at least I understand it's not *my* decision."

"You'd never be happy subsuming your own goals for someone

else."

"No. And honestly? I don't want anyone else taking credit for my successes either." It was a double-edged sword she'd never be willing to be pilloried on.

"You're very independent."

"It's the only way I know how to be." She'd spent too long on her own, with no back up, no supportive family, or even loyal friends, she'd learned one time too many, to be any other way.

He smiled, his sherry eyes warm. "I like it."

He would. He'd raised both Carey and Marilyn to be independent in their thoughts and actions. "Your sister is really independent too, but she knows she's got a safety net if she fails. I spent too long without it to trust in one now."

Another strange expression came over Rock's chiseled features. Like he'd had some kind of epiphany, but she couldn't imagine what it would be.

She was probably just seeing things.

The next day, Carey had set up a formal excursion with MacKinnon Brothers Tours for everyone in the production. It had been planned a couple of weeks before, but only for those that weren't supposed to be working today. Now the whole cast and crew had the day off and Deborah decided to go.

Hanging out in the house alone with Rock would be dangerous to her commitment to staying out of his bed, or off his office desk, or away from being pressed between his sexy body and the wall. Darn it. She needed to focus on something else.

"You're going on the tour?" Rock asked her at breakfast.

"I am."

"Oh, I want to go too," Marilyn said.

"I'll call Kitty and see if there's room for one more."

Marilyn grinned. "Great. I hope Egan's running the tour. He's hot."

"I didn't need to know you thought that," Rock said as Carey gave an exaggerated groan.

Deborah's heart did a little skip when Rock slid into the driver's side of the SUV she, Marilyn and Carey were taking to the tour. What was he doing here?

"I can't believe you're coming on this tour," Carey said from the backseat. "I'd think you and Tack get enough trekking into the wild without adding a scheduled tour. Egan was glad we were driving to the trailhead on our own though. He said there wasn't enough room in the van for everyone, now."

Deborah bit back a protest at the idea of the enforced intimacy of the car. Even if Carey and Marilyn were there, they had taken the backseat. Deborah now realized that had been on purpose, to put her in the front with Rock. If her brain had been firing on all synapses and not exhausted from a sleepless night alone in the guest room, she would have realized he was probably the driver.

Since his siblings obviously weren't.

"Tack has been busy this summer," Rock said as he put the SUV into gear.

Marilyn made a scoffing noise. "He's always busy in the summer. He's a tour guide in a town that caters to cruise ships. That's never stopped you before from spending time hiking the remote wilderness with him."

"Kitty Grant is back in town."

"She is?" Carey asked with shock. "I didn't think she'd ever come back to Alaska. She wanted to live in the Lower 48 pretty bad."

"How would you know?" Marilyn asked with the kind of affectionate sarcasm reserved for close siblings. "She was years ahead of us in school."

"Everyone knew she wanted out of Cailkirn. She was one of Rock's friends, or don't you remember that?" Carey asked with his own dose of friendly disparagement.

"I'm not feeble minded, of course I remember."

"Did either of you know that her ex-husband was the angel investor for Carey's movie?" Rock asked, his tone saying clearly what he thought of that state of events.

And it wasn't good.

Something twinged in the region of Deborah's heart at the way Rock referred to the movie. If she'd needed confirmation of the way he saw her, it was right there. She was adjunct to his life. Carey was primary.

"You're kidding me." Disgust laced Marilyn's voice. "No wonder he pulled funding. He probably did the whole thing on purpose to get back at the town."

"For what? Being her hometown?" Carey actually did sarcasm better than his sister when he got going. "That doesn't make any sense. Divorce happens all the time, especially among the glitterati of LaLa Land."

"Her grandmother had to go down to the Lower 48 when she was in the hospital. Ms. Moira thinks her ex put her there," Rock said, his tone hard.

The sound of pure disgust and anger Marilyn made echoed in Deborah's heart.

"I bet Tack is beside himself," Marilyn said.

"Oh, he's probably pissed as hell at Nevin Barston, if he knows about the abuse," Carey agreed.

"Why wouldn't he know about that?" Marilyn demanded.

"Did you know?" Carey asked.

"I've been out of town most of the year since we turned eighteen."

"You know Rock finds stuff out no one else knows," Carey said, admiration saturating his tone. "Everybody talks to him."

"Because they know I don't gossip."

"Yeah, you only tell us," Marilyn said, her own voice filled with approval.

Rock had revealed plenty in front of Deborah. What did that mean?

"Still, I bet Tack's thrilled to have the love of his life back in town," Carey surmised.

"I think he's taking things a day at a time." But Rock had told Deborah he knew Tack and Kitty were dating.

She looked at the handsome man, trying to read something in his chiseled features and firm jaw. Were there things he didn't tell his siblings?

Rock frowned, his focus on the road ahead of them. "I don't know if she's shared her past with him."

"But Tack always thought Kitty was the one," Marilyn said. "She adored him. Everyone knew. It was so romantic. They were like the perfect couple."

"That broke up when they went to college in the Lower 48," Rock said.

"It seems like you blame where they went to university for their breakup," Deborah said.

"I do."

"Don't you think that's a little irrational?" Deborah chided.

"Don't bother arguing with him, Deborah. Rock thinks leaving Cailkirn is close to a mortal sin."

"Bullshit. If I did, I would have fought you and Carey leaving."

"You didn't argue with them?" Deborah couldn't imagine it.

"No. He was like the rock he's named after, all solid and we could come home if we needed to, but he knew we needed to pursue our own dreams." The admiration in Marilyn's voice was nearly in the stratosphere.

"Yeah, Rock is the best," Carey added.

Marilyn gave Deborah and earnest look from the backseat. "It's like him and Sloan."

"The gossiping mayor that knows everything that happens in Cailkirn?" Deborah asked with a smidge of humor.

"Sloan's not a gossip," Marilyn assured Deborah. "He doesn't tell anyone anything."

Carey offered, "Except Rock. They brainstorm ways to fix stuff."

"Did you fix Kitty's life?" Deborah asked, hoping he had.

"If I'd known what was going on earlier, I would have flown to LA and brought her home where she'd be safe. But by the time Ms. Moira confided in me, Kitty was in the process of getting a divorce."

"Does Kitty know that?" Deborah asked. "That you would have helped her?"

"No, I don't imagine she does."

"Maybe you should tell her. Believing you're alone dealing with the worst life has to throw at you is scary stuff." Really kind of terrifying, if Deborah were honest with herself.

CHAPTER TWENTY

Rock cast her a probing sidelong glance before focusing back on the road. "She has her grandmother and great aunts."

"Did her grandmother bring her home?" It didn't sound like it to Deborah.

"No, she didn't."

"So, Kitty was alone dealing with a psychopath husband."

Rock gave her a look. "Have you been alone dealing with psychopaths?"

"There are still plenty of directors and producers who believe offering a beautiful woman a part in a movie includes fringe benefits." And not just power players in the film industry.

She'd dealt with her share of predators in her jobs on waitstaff.

"Hell," Rock cursed.

"I was on my own, but I knew what I was willing to do and what I wasn't. It came close a couple of times, but I never gave into pressure."

"It came close?" Marilyn asked, her tone timid in a way Deborah hadn't heard before.

Maybe she was worried about offending Deborah, but the younger woman didn't need to. "They didn't always ask nicely."

"Someone tried to rape you?" Carey demanded, fury making his voice deeper than usual.

"He wouldn't have seen it that way, I'm pretty sure."

"But you said 'no' and he kept pushing." Marilyn paused and then offered tentatively, "Physically?"

"Yes. You learn early on to research the principles in suits on a project and just to be on the safe side, you're never alone with them if you can help it."

"That's insane. You should be safe." Marilyn sounded like her cherished beliefs were shaking apart.

Deborah was sorry to break the rose-colored glasses the younger women had been wearing, but the world wasn't always a kind place. Being beautiful could paint a target on a woman that was neither fair, nor okay, but it landed there all the same.

She turned so she could look more squarely at Marilyn. "And with most execs, you are, but do you want to risk letting your guard down for the few that aren't?"

Marilyn shook her head. Carey was looking at his sister like he wanted to wrap her in cotton-wool. Rock, on the other hand looked neither shocked nor worried. He knew the world was a scary place and he'd protected his brother and sister to the best of his ability.

He flicked a glance at Deborah. "There's a reason both Carey and Marilyn were in Judo from the time they were six."

"Judo? Since you were six?" Rock had only been sixteen then. How had he managed it for them?

"I did janitorial for the dojo and whatever else the sensei wanted me to in order to pay for their classes."

"Are you still practicing?" Deborah asked the other two.

"Rock would have a hissy fit if I let my training lapse," Deborah said with more seriousness than her usual sarcastic demeanor held.

Carey snorted a laugh. "Are you kidding? It's worth more than what I'd have to deal with from big brother if I didn't."

"He takes good care of you both."

"We're lucky," Carey agreed.

"And you, did you learn Judo?" Deborah asked Rock.

That kind of training would help explain his muscles on top of muscles. The fact he worked the horses and cared for them did too.

"He's a *rokudan*. That's sixth level black belt," Marilyn said proudly. "He's been the one training us at the dojo since we hit our teens."

"You teach Judo?" When did the multi-millionaire businessman have the time?

Rock shrugged. "I did, when the twins lived here. Now, the only training I do is when I spar with lower level black belts."

"So, you've kept up your training?" She had an overwhelming desire to see him inaction at the dojo.

"He still competes," Carey said enthusiastically. "He's going to get his *shichidan* soon."

"From competing in Judo tournaments?" she asked, finding that way too much of a turn on.

The image of Rock in hand-to-hand combat with another man trained in Judo sent heat right through her body.

"That's one way, yes," Marilyn said.

"Rock's favorite," Carey teased. "Big brother is really competitive. He's the challenger to beat in the summer Highland Games."

That didn't bother Deborah one little bit. "I don't imagine he would have been nearly as successful financially if he didn't."

Rock cast a quick look, his expression surprised. "You're right."

That competitive nature showed itself when they started their hike. Egan did turn out to be their guide and while that thrilled Marilyn, and Carey actually didn't seem to mind either, Rock insisted on being in the front of the group and keeping Deborah with him.

"Come on, hot stuff. This is an easy trail. You can keep up."

"It's not a race," she huffed as they rounded a curve in the trail, putting the others out of sight. "Besides I'm missing Egan's description of the flora and fauna."

It was a legitimate complaint. Egan MacKinnon had a way with words that brought out the beauty of their surroundings. He explained how some plants were native, some were imports, just like the people. He sprinkled Alaskan history in with his narrative, along with the history of the peninsula.

"I can tell you everything he is telling the others."

"So, start talking," she challenged.

He grinned down at her and spoke quietly, "How about we just stop and watch the bear foraging?"

"A bear? No, that's…they don't really come out on the trails." She looked around them, turning her head side to side, disbelief warring with the hope he wasn't teasing.

Sure enough, a small black bear was indeed foraging for food amongst the bushes near the trail. Deborah had stopped beside Rock, her heart beating so hard now, she thought she might give right in and faint for the first time in her life.

Rock stepped closer, continuing to speak quietly. "He'll move on as soon as he hears the others approaching. Enjoy the moment."

"I'm going to hyperventilate."

"No. You're fine." Rock rubbed her back.

Deborah found herself relaxing under the comforting touch. "He's beautiful," she whispered.

"Alaskan wildlife is." Rock nodded toward a clearing in the trees in the opposite direction. "Look over there."

It was a group of deer, unconcernedly eating leaves from the many bushes.

"Why aren't they running?"

"The bear isn't a threat to them. He's far enough away, they'd outrun him if he gave chase."

"They can't know that."

"Their instincts tell them a lot."

"But we're here."

"People on the trails have become commonplace. It actually makes it too easy for the hunters in season."

"Because the deer don't know to run."

"Or they smell the gun oil too late."

"Hunting is a big thing in Alaska."

"It is. Being self-sufficient is part of the Alaskan way."

"Do you hunt?" Deborah asked, not sure how she'd feel about it if he said yes.

"I tried a couple of times, but I'd rather shoot the animals with my camera. I'm no vegetarian though."

"I think I would have noticed if you were."

"Smart Alec."

"That's smart Deborah to you, bub."

"Bub?"

"You prefer buddy?" she asked archly.

"I prefer being your lover."

She gasped, her mind going totally blank for a second. She didn't know why, but she'd sort of assumed he wouldn't bring that up now. Not while they were out on an excursion with his younger siblings.

She'd tried to convince herself that he would just let their physical relationship go, considering the fact it wasn't an actual *relationship*. Just sex.

Even if her aching heart hoped for something different.

"That cannot be a surprise to you."

"You'd think."

The bear's head came up and then he turned his furry body around and disappeared in the brush, the sound of clumping hooves telling her that the deer were also taking off.

The rest of their group must have caught up, but Rock didn't look like he was interested in anyone else. His sherry gaze holding her own.

"We aren't done, hot stuff," he vowed.

"I thought we were."

"Not by a long shot."

"But what difference does it make? I'll be leaving in a matter of weeks and you've made it clear you don't want me back."

He pulled her into his arms. "I never said that."

"Didn't you?" Not all communication was verbal. "And anyway, you all but said you don't expect to see me again."

"I don't."

She tried to step back. "Exactly."

Steel bands around her stopped Deborah from gaining any distance.

Rock looked down at her like she was the only person on the peninsula, despite the sounds of the others coming closer. "That doesn't mean I don't *want* to."

She pressed on his chest. "You're not making any sense."

He let his forehead fall against hers like he had yesterday and created a haven of intimacy that should have been impossible under the circumstances. "You really think that once you get back to tinsel town, you're not going to forget all about your Alaskan interlude?"

"*You* really think I could forget you that easily?" They were both speaking even more quietly than when the bear had been close by.

"My parents did."

Unable to help herself, she nuzzled her head against his. "I thought we agreed I'm not like them."

He made a soft, primal sound of approval, pulling her closer. "It's not just them. Do you know how many people leave Cailkirn to *visit* the Lower 48, or go to school down there and never come back?"

"But Kitty came back," Carey said from behind Deborah.

Suddenly she understood the benefit to being so far ahead of the group. She looked at Carey over her shoulder, speaking from within the circle of Rock's arms. "We saw a bear."

She should be moving away, embarrassed to be caught in such an intimate moment with Rock, but she just wanted this moment to last a little longer.

"No way! Rock has all the luck," Carey said with disgust and no small dose of envy. "Him and Tack get the best pictures of wildlife."

Rock shifted Deborah to his side but kept one arm around her. "It's not luck."

"It's skill, hasn't he told you, Deborah?" Marilyn asked with a smile.

"How did he *skillfully* arrange for a black bear to be foraging on the trail?" Deborah asked, her heart lighter than it had been since their fight the day before.

"*He* was quiet and didn't spook the bear," Rock said with his own dose of sarcasm.

"Darn it, Rock, you saw a bear?" Egan demanded, clearly chagrined. "You and Tack have all the luck."

"Maybe Tack doesn't talk the whole hike, you think?" Rock mocked.

"The bear is going to hear us coming if I'm talking, or not."

"But the animals around here are used to humans. He wouldn't spook right away, maybe." Rock's raised brow clearly mocked the other man.

Deborah added her two cents, "We saw some deer too."

"Of course, you did." Egan's mouth twisted in a grimace. "Tack is not going to let me live this down. He maintains he trained you for the outdoors, Rock."

Rock shrugged. "I won't deny it."

Egan shook his head. "Aw, hell. I'm really never going to hear the end of it."

"Does it really matter?" Marilyn asked, her tone confused. "You're doing a great job and I'd rather hear what you have to say than see a bear, or some deer."

Oh, Rock's little sister *did* think the tour guide was hot. She had a little crush on the auburn-haired tour guide, if Deborah was not mistaken.

The look Egan was giving her said the appreciation might be mutual.

Rock cleared his throat, scowling at Egan. "Don't you have a tour to conduct?"

Egan looked between Rock and Marilyn, not concerned in the least, but with an expression that said Rock's reaction had confirmed something for him.

"You're right. Time to get back on the move, people. We're headed to a small lake, where, if we are lucky, we'll see some of our own wildlife. We'll want to get as quiet as possible once we round the next bend in the trail."

"I don't want to see a bear," the director's second assistant said, her face pulled into a frown.

"Then close your eyes, Jana," the first assistant said, his youthful unconcern something Deborah sort of envied.

Because her first reaction was always to try to make things right.

The look Rock gave the middle-aged woman wasn't super friendly either. "Why did you come on a nature hike if you didn't want to see nature?"

"Bears are not normal nature."

"Um..." Deborah wasn't sure what to say to that.

"I'm pretty sure they are," Carey said, his snark full force.

"You know what I mean. Deer won't eat you."

"You're not going to get eaten by a bear," the first assistant dismissed.

"And the chances are pretty low we'll see one anyway," Egan offered, clearly ready to make peace. "Rock and Deborah were really lucky to get a sighting so close to the trail."

They were heading back to Jepsom Acres when there was a sound like a gunshot outside the car, startling Deborah. Rock swore. Marilyn screamed and Carey yelled. The car swerved wildly, but Deborah wasn't scared.

Rock was too darn controlling and competent to let them crash.

He did something with the gear column and then got the car back in their lane a second later. She was grateful for the lack of traffic going both directions. In LA, they would have already been in a multi-car fender bender, if not worse.

"Shit, the brakes are gone." Rock sounded more annoyed than worried. His foot pumped against a brake pedal that was clearly not working, because they were not slowing down.

Not until he shifted the automatic gear shift down to second, the engine whining as the car began to slow somewhat.

"What's going on, Rock? Are we going to crash?" Marilyn's high-pitched voice filled the tense silence of the SUV.

"Stay calm. I've got it under control."

It was telling that none of them questioned that statement, not Deborah, not Carey, not Marilyn.

He shifted the gear down again, the grinding whine of the engine louder this time as the car continued to slow, but not stop. He banked the car to the left, the muscles in his forearms straining as he fought the wheel. Metal screeched against pavement from the front passenger side as he pulled the emergency brake and managed to guide the now wobbling car toward a low embankment on the opposite side of the road.

"Let your bodies go lax. We're gonna hit," Rock barked, his hands tight on the now shuddering wheel.

Deborah tried to obey, forcing her muscles to relax. She was glad she did when she barely felt the impact as they came to a stop against the embankment. Rock had managed to use the SUV's front driver's side quarter panel as the point of impact, minimizing the risk of damage to any of his passengers.

He turned off the car with a jerk of his wrist. "Get your seatbelts off and get down. I don't know what blew that tire."

The sound of four seatbelts releasing almost simultaneously was overlaid with the heavy breathing of stress.

"What's going on, Rock?" Marilyn asked again, her voice shaky.

"Get down," Carey told her, yanking his twin down to the backseat floor board before turning and opening his own door to follow Rock out of the SUV.

"Oh, no they don't," Deborah muttered to herself as she too exited the car. She hunched down and moved to where Rock was examining the front right tire. "What happened?"

Expression grim, he looked up at her. "The tire blew."

"Is that why the brakes failed?" She didn't know anything about cars, but that sounded wrong to her.

"No. I'm not sure why they went. The SUV was just serviced before you all arrived in Cailkirn. The brakes were fine."

"It sounded like a gunshot."

"That was the tire blowing. A gunshot sounds a little different."

"How would you know?" she asked, thinking the man just might be a little too knowledgeable.

"Calm down, hot stuff. I may not hunt, but that doesn't mean I've spent more than two decades in Alaska without learning to shoot, both a pistol and rifle."

"Oh. Okay." She rubbed her arms. "Why did you tell us to get down then?"

"Yeah, what was up with you and Carey getting out of the SUV like action heroes and leaving me and Deborah behind? We aren't anyone's definition of damsels in distress." Marilyn sounded peeved.

"So, you made yourself a target?" Carey demanded of his sister, his expression every bit as grim as his brothers.

For the first time, Deborah saw the family resemblance in a big way.

"Like you didn't?" Marilyn snarked. "Besides, a target for what? A blown tire."

"We didn't know what caused the tire to blow," Carey snarked right back.

"Rock just said it wasn't a gunshot."

Rock sighed, giving his siblings a look that Deborah interpreted as *settle down and stop sniping at each other*. "Not all gunshots are loud enough to be heard through a closed car window."

"You think somebody used a silencer?" Deborah asked, horrified.

That would not be a stray bullet shot by some poor marksman.

"Before we got out of the car, I didn't know."

"Now you do?" Deborah asked and then, "Why would you even think that was a possibility?"

Rock frowned at her like she'd lost her mind. "You know why."

"Because those two miscreants claimed someone hired them to harass me? It's a big stretch from harassment to shooting out a tire." Wasn't it?

"They pulled a gun on us, if you remember. Their plans for you weren't benevolent."

Man, the eldest siblings put the others to shame when it came to his mocking tone.

"What?" Marilyn demanded. "Someone wants to hurt Deborah? I thought those guys were a couple of local troublemakers."

"That's not cool." Carey scowled at Deborah. "Why didn't you tell us?"

"Rock just told me yesterday." She sighed. "And I didn't believe it."

"Well, I'd say this is proof." Sarcasm dripped from Carey's voice, once again reminding Deborah how very much alike the brothers were at their core.

"We don't know what made the tire go." Deborah looked around them and then back at the damaged vehicle. "It could have been a nail in the road, or something."

Only he'd said he didn't know before he got out of the car if the tire had been shot out, implying that now he did. Which meant he knew what caused it to blow and if it had been innocuous, she didn't think his expression would be nearly so dark.

"And the brakes?" Rock asked, his brows raised, ignoring the issue of the tire.

Temporarily, she was sure.

"I don't know," Deborah answered testily. "I'm not a mechanic."

"Neither am I, but I know they shouldn't have gone out like that." Rock wasn't giving any quarter. "Carey, call Benji."

Carey didn't question his brother's direction, pulled his phone out of his pocket and made the call, his conversation with the sheriff short. The younger actor tucked his phone back into pocket. "Benji said he'd be here in a few."

"Why did you tell him to call the sheriff?" Deborah asked Rock. "We need a tow truck, not the cops." Maybe.

"If the SUV's been tampered with, Benji needs to know about it." Carey answered implacably before Rock could even open his mouth.

"You have a lot of your brother in you, did you know that?"

But maybe they were both right.

Carey flashed his winning grin at her. "Thanks."

"It wasn't a compliment." But maybe it was.

"Oh, I think it was."

Deborah growled and then blushed when she realized what she'd done. Seriously? They were driving her to primitive woman.

"I'm bringing in security for the remainder of the movie." Rock didn't look like he was open to argument.

Deborah tried anyway. "That's not necessary. You know it isn't. Be reasonable."

"Like you, you mean?" Rock mocked. "What's reasonable about refusing to acknowledge you're at risk?"

"I'm not refusing. I really didn't think Amos and Virgil were telling the truth." It had just seemed so unlikely.

"And now?" he asked, his voice gentle.

Unexpected tears burned at the back of her eyes as Deborah accepted that someone *was* trying to hurt her. "You're sure the brakes couldn't have failed because of something just, I don't know, *car* related."

"I'm sure."

"You said you're not a mechanic."

"But I trust the one that did the SUV's service check." He pulled her toward him. "Come here, hot stuff. I'm not going to let anyone hurt you."

"This is crazy, Rock. Isn't it? Stuff like this happens in the movies we make, not the lives we live."

"It's happening right now, in your life, sweetheart. And I'm not taking any risks."

"You're right." Darn it. He was. Her refusal to acknowledge the risk had put Rock and his siblings in danger. "You, Carey or Marilyn could have been hurt too. If you weren't such a good driver..." Deborah's voice petered out, her brain short-circuiting at the image of what could have happened.

"Yeah, everybody is getting personal bodyguards along with the general security detail for the property."

"I don't want a bodyguard," Marilyn complained.

Rock shot her a quick look. "Hopefully Benji will figure out what's happening soon, but until then, it's not negotiable."

"If I leave—"

"Don't even think about it, Deborah." His focus was back on her. 100%. "You're not going anywhere while someone wants to hurt you."

"I can leave Alaska if I want to."

"Not according to your contract, you can't."

"Art and Ms. Morganstein would understand." Deborah wasn't actually sure of that, but she could hope.

"Bullshit. Those two sharks aren't giving you any free passes, but let's make something very clear here. If you go back to LA, you won't be going alone."

"What? Who would be going with me?" she asked, not getting his meaning at all.

"I would," Rock said, like it should be obvious.

"Who did you think?" Carey asked with a duh tone.

"He'll probably insist on bringing your bodyguard too," Marilyn pointed out.

Deborah shook her head, making no move to leave Rock's arms. "I'm not getting a bodyguard. I'm not part of the family."

"I didn't see you hit your head, but you're talking like the accident scrambled your brains." Rock placed one hand against the small of her back, rubbing a little. "Of course, you're getting a bodyguard."

CHAPTER TWENTY-ONE

"But I'm not family."

"You already said that," Carey snarked.

"What the hell does that have to do with anything?" Rock demanded, sounding pissed.

"Well, of course you're worried about Carey and Marilyn right now. They're like your own kids even if they are your brother and sister, but I'm just a woman you were sleeping with."

"Were?" Marilyn asked and then glared at her brother. "You were supposed to say you're sorry."

"I did." Rock said, without looking away from Deborah. "I screwed up. I said I was sorry. Deborah is thinking about forgiving me."

She was? Okay, she was, but wasn't that making a pretty big assumption.

"We're still sleeping together."

"I slept in the guest room last night."

"You needed time to get over being mad at me."

"You think?"

"Sure, but what we have is too unique, too intense and too damn good for either of us to just walk away like it never mattered."

"You said just sex."

"I was wrong and I told you that too."

She remembered that last time they'd made love, the way he'd admitted that what they had was special. "You thought I used my body to get you to invest in the movie."

"Rock!" Marilyn admonished. "Didn't you tell her that was a mistake? That you didn't mean it."

"You really are the stupid one," Carey added. "Deborah isn't like that."

"I know. I was feeling vulnerable, all right?" Rock asked, aggrieved. "And this is between me and Deborah. You two can put your oars back in the boat."

Marilyn crossed her arms and gave them both a chastising look. "We have a vested interest in Deborah and you working out."

"How do you figure that?" Rock asked, rubbing Deborah's back.

"Because we want you happy." Marilyn's expression said she thought her big brother was playing the stupid role very well.

Carey nodded his agreement. "Seriously, Rock. She's good for you."

"And you're good for her."

"This isn't permanent," Deborah said, even as she let herself settle more comfortably against Rock.

She really needed to get her body online with her brain. Later.

She needed comfort and for once there was someone there to give it.

"Like hell." Rock glared at them all, but he didn't let go of Deborah.

Sirens and flashing lights announced Benji's arrival, cutting off what was an obscenely overly personal conversation for the side of the road.

Benji did a quick look over the SUV after making sure everyone was okay. He wasn't smiling when he stood up after looking underneath.

"What is it?" Rock asked.

"The brake line was cut."

"I figured."

"And the tire looks like its sidewall was sliced, probably just enough to weaken it so that it would blow when you were driving."

Before Deborah could ask Benji if he was sure, Rock said, "That's what it looked like to me."

And that was how Rock had known the tire hadn't been shot.

"Who would know how to do something like that?" Deborah asked.

"Anyone with access to the Internet and halfway decent knife skills," Benji replied. "Let's get you folks home."

They rode back to Jepsom's Acres in the sheriff's Jeep, Deborah, Marilyn and Carey squeezed together in the back seat.

Rock climbed out of the car and turned to the rest of them. "I don't want any of you leaving the house until the security detail arrives.

"You're being darn bossy," Deborah said with a huff. "What if I want to go for a walk?"

"Stop being contrary. We just got back from a daylong hike. Don't you have lines, or something, to go over?"

"Ms. Morganstein probably has calls for me to make," Deborah admitted morosely.

She really didn't like this part of being listed on the production team.

"You can make them in my office if you like."

"Where will you be?"

"In my office."

"I wouldn't want to impose."

"It won't bother me."

"Still, I think I'll go somewhere I won't bother anyone else with my talking."

"You can't avoid my office forever, hot stuff."

"You think that's what I'm doing?"

"I'm pretty sure of it."

"Well, it's not. I just don't want to interrupt your work."

"I like when you interrupt my work."

"Don't you have calls of your own to make?" she asked, refusing to answer that salvo.

"Yes."

"Well then."

"I'll make them from the living room and then join you in my office."

"That's silly."

"I don't think so."

"Fine." Deborah wasn't in the mood for further argument, but she found herself reluctant to walk into Rock's office when she reached it. Memories of what they'd shared in there, both the amazing and the painful, assaulted her.

Taking a breath to calm down, she gave herself a pep talk about not letting a room intimidate her and walked inside. Rock had put his desk to rights again, the rest of the room pristine in its tidiness. No proof of the interlude they'd shared anywhere to be seen.

Deborah sat down on the sofa, making a conscious effort to ignore the memories of what they'd done on the leather cushions, and called Ms. Morganstein. The executive producer had a list of people for Deborah to call, but first she wanted to talk about Rock.

"Do you think he's going to invest?" Ms. Morganstein pressed for something like the third time.

"I don't know," Deborah repeated for an equal number of times. "He's researching the project and that's more than I thought he'd do, to be honest."

"Why wouldn't he? This movie is bankable. Besides he has personal reasons for saying yes."

"Throwing what you think are his personal reasons for investing in his face like you've done hasn't helped your cause."

"*Our* cause surely."

"I'm not sure I want Rock to invest at this point." Deborah had had a few epiphanies of her own since their argument.

One. Rock *was* sorry. Two. Rock *didn't* believe she was a whore. Three. No matter how important the movie was to Art Gamble and Elaine Morganstein, it was not okay that they *did*. Four. Deborah *wanted* a relationship with Rock. Five. The movie was important, but not more important that one through four.

"You don't mean that." Ms. Morganstein's tone was filled with shock.

"You suggested I should break up with him if he refused, Ms. Morganstein. I'm not feeling nearly as passionate about this project as I was before."

The executive producer made a dismissive sound. "I expressed what I thought was a natural outcome."

"And threatened me."

"I did no such thing."

"Not overtly, no."

"Well, then."

"So, tell me that my role in the movie is not in jeopardy if Rock refuses to invest."

"I can't," Ms. Morganstein said in a calculating tone. "The role may have to go to someone else who can bring in a capital infusion."

"How does that make sense? We're halfway through the movie."

"It wouldn't be the first, or even the fiftieth time a principle actor was replaced during production."

"What about Carey?"

"We still need Jepsom Acres for filming."

"Give me the list of people you want me to call."

Deborah was on her fifth phone call when Rock came into his office. She finished her pitch and hung up. "That's exhausting. I don't know how you do it every day."

"It has been a while since I had to cold call investors for a project, but I thrived on the pressure."

"I don't." Not any of the pressure. Not that Deborah had any intention of telling Rock about the threat of her losing her role if she couldn't bring in capital.

Deborah's career was not Rock's responsibility, whether or not Elaine Morganstein understood that. She'd done her best to encourage investment from the people Ms. Morganstein had instructed her to call.

"I'm beginning to wonder if my producer gave me the list of people least likely to invest. It seems every one of them has some kind of issue with either Ms. Morganstein or Art. One was a flaming homophobe that wouldn't invest in a coming of age and coming out story about a gay man if it would make him a million-to-one investment. And that's a quote."

Rock came around the desk and leaned next to where she was sitting in his chair, reaching out to touch her. "You're tough, hot stuff. You can handle it, but I'm sorry you have to."

She couldn't help leaning into his hand. "You're being awfully nice."

"You're easy to be nice to."

"Usually you're being nice to my body," she teased.

His expression turned serious. "I know I screwed up when you brought up investing in the movie, but I haven't treated you like I don't see anything but your body, have I?"

"No." In fact, he'd taken pains to treat her like she mattered, spending time with her that was nothing about sex.

Which was how she'd fooled herself into believing he valued her more than he was willing to admit.

Only now she was starting to wonder again, if she'd been fooling herself at all.

"You ready for a break?" he asked.

"I wish I could, but I really need to finish this list before I take one."

Rock's sherry gaze glowed with approval. "I can respect that. I'll take my laptop to the sofa and work."

"I can move away from your desk," she said with a shake of her head. "I don't need it to talk on the phone." She stood up before he could argue with her, grabbing the notepad she'd been jotting her thoughts down on.

He touched the notepad. "Do you mind if I look at it?"

"Not at all."

He scanned her notes, his expression thoughtful. "You've got a couple people here that are strong potential investors."

"I do?" She hadn't thought so. In fact, she'd thought the last hour of talking had been a total waste.

"You see this guy who asked you all the questions?"

"Yes. He was really dismissive of the potential for profit from the movie."

"He's setting himself up to make a more favorable deal for the money he wants to invest."

"He *wants* to invest. How do you get that from my notes?"

What followed was a fifteen-minute lesson in Venture Capitalism 101. Rock explained how to spy an eager investor behind a reluctant façade, how to answer certain types of questions and what to say to increase her chances of being listened to and sparking interest from the money people.

Her phone calls after that went a lot better and Deborah began to think she might not be such a wash on the production team.

She had two investors wanting more detailed specifics, though none as demanding as Rock had been. She wondered at that. Did they trust her producer and director's word more easily because they'd invested in Hollywood before, or was Rock just a very smart guy?

Considering how he'd built his fortune and the time it took him to do it, she was going with the latter option.

The two money people he'd said were actually interested had already emailed her with further questions too. Yep, Rock was a highly intelligent guy.

Deborah was at the door when Rock looked up from his work. "You taking off?"

"I'm getting my laptop so I can send and answer some emails. Those two you thought were interested both emailed me asking for more information and three of the final people I talked to want me to email them projections too.,."

"Good." He stood up and stretched. "I think I'll go down for a tray of coffee."

"I bet Lydia would be happy to bring it up." Deborah knew the older woman would. She'd said as much, lamenting how little Rock let her do for him.

"She doesn't need to make an extra trip up the stairs on my account."

"You really are a nice guy, Rock."

"Only to people who matter to me."

"Then a lot of people must matter to you."

"No. I'm tolerant and persuasive when I have to be, but nice?

No."

"You've been nice to me." With one painful exception and that argument really hadn't lasted long. She now wondered what would have happened if she'd stuck around to fight it out.

"And that doesn't tell you something?"

"What do you want it to tell me?" she pushed. She wasn't assuming anything with him again.

Deborah wasn't entirely convinced that Rock hadn't changed his tune simply because his younger siblings had convinced him to. And if that was the case, that was not okay.

She needed him to believe in her because of who *she* was, not what the important people in his life thought about her or the positive influence she had on his life.

"It means you matter to me, beauty. Don't ever doubt it."

"Not even when I go back to LA?"

"As things stand now, no way in hell are you going back without me."

"I'm sure it will all be resolved before I leave Alaska." Sheriff Benji Sutherland was another very smart man and Deborah didn't have any doubt he'd make the issue of someone wanting to hurt her a priority.

If no other reason than because the results had put the denizens of his town in harm's way, but she thought he would have anyway. He gave off the vibes of a lawman who really cared

Rock just gave her a look that said he thought her optimism was misplaced. "I got ahold of the security company I use. Their people will be here tonight."

"They got a flight that fast?"

"They're in Alaska. A group of vets who went into personal and corporate security when they came home. And they have their own plane."

"Swanky."

"There are plenty of places in Alaska that are only accessible via plane during the winter." He came closer to Deborah. "Besides, some of their accounts are in the Lower 48, it just makes sense."

"Oh, okay." Did Rock have his own plane too? She'd never thought to ask, but there were places on the property the film crew had been told to stay away from and she'd never ventured there herself.

He massaged the back of her neck with one hand, the other landing on her hip. "So, you think it's impressive to own your own plane?"

"Doesn't everybody?"

"I have a helicopter. What kind of cred does that get me with you?" he teased just before brushing his lips over hers.

Her lips parted just slightly, but he kept the kiss lips to lips, breath to breath, sending her ordered thoughts scattering to the four winds. After several seconds of one of the most romantic kisses she'd ever received, he backed away. "You're a temptation, Deborah."

"You're the one doing the tempting right now. I was on my way to get my laptop when you waylaid me."

His smile was pure primal male. "You didn't complain."

"Why would I? You're a very pleasant kisser."

His laugh was warm and joyous. "Oh, you do delight me, beauty."

Rock came back into his office, ridiculously relieved when he found Deborah already there, sitting on the sofa, feet propped up on the coffee table he'd had commissioned with the desk, and laptop open in her lap.

She'd been thawing since their argument the day before, but he wasn't dumb enough to assume she was fine with everything. He'd accused her of using something that had been incredibly powerful and special for *both* of them to try to manipulate him. He'd hurt her and now he was working on regaining her trust.

Because he'd finally accepted he *did not* want this thing between them to end with the movie.

She looked up. "You're back with your coffee. I miss coffee."

"When was the last time you drank it?"

"Five, maybe six years ago."

"That's a long time to go without the elixir of life." He placed the tray with both his coffee and a carafe of chilled water with lemons floating in it for her on the table a few inches from where her feet rested.

She laughed, the sound going straight to his dick. Damn did he like it.

"It's all part of keeping myself in perfection for the camera."

"Do you really need to be that strict with yourself?"

"Oh, I just practice clean eating. No hormones, no caffeine, no trans fats. I know actors that live strictly on raw foods or have gone entirely vegan to stay in top shape."

"I'm pretty sure your beauty isn't because you don't drink coffee."

"No, but looking years younger than my actual age? It's all part of it."

"Is that so important?"

"I used to think so."

"You're not so sure anymore?" he asked, not sure what he wanted to hear.

"I've enjoyed this movie, but I'd rather play older characters."

"So, why don't you?"

"You want the truth?"

"Yes. From you? Always."

"That goes both ways."

And that fast, their conversation was in deep water. Not bad water. Just deep. "Agreed."

She nodded. "I love acting. I've actually really enjoyed talking to investors, though mostly after you gave me that lesson in what they needed to know to be interested."

"I'm glad I could help." He hoped she knew he meant it.

"Like I said, you're a good guy."

"As long as you think so." Especially after yesterday.

"I do. Anyway, there's a lot about my industry that fascinates me, inspires me and gives me joy."

"I hear a but coming."

"Because there is one. *But* when I went to performing art school, it was because I enjoyed being on the stage and I was very, very, *very* good at it. Movie and television acting is not the same. It's not bad, but it *is* different."

"Different in a way you don't like."

"In a way I don't prefer."

"So, why LA instead of Broadway?"

"Because I believed my family would come to terms with my education and career choices if they saw me as a success."

"And that wouldn't happen on the stage?""

"You think it's unlikely to hit stardom on the screen? It's even less likely to have the kind of financial success and recognition my parents would approve of on the stage."

Maybe. Maybe she would have made it, but she'd pursued a whole different type of career looking for her family's approval. "What do you want now?"

"I've finally realized it's not their approval. If it takes becoming world famous and worth millions to gain their love, it's not really love, is it?"

"No." He didn't sugar coat it, or waffle his answer.

That wasn't love. That was conditional approval. And in his opinion, any parent that put those kinds of expectations on their children wasn't much of a parent at all.

"I want to be happy, Rock."

"You deserve to be happy, beauty."

"I do. Everyone does."

"What is going to make you happy?"

"I'm not sure. I think a return to the stage."

"In LA? In New York?" Wherever she wanted to go, he was going to support her.

Deborah Banes was not his mother, not his father. She was the woman he loved and he thought who might very well love him.

"Maybe in Anchorage." She looked at him like she was waiting for him to tell her what a terrible idea that was.

"You're not going to gain any recognition performing on stage in remote Alaska."

"I'm not looking for recognition, or even monetary success. I want to be happy."

That was the second time she'd said that. "Are you saying you're not happy now?"

"No. I haven't been happy for a very long time. I don't trust people. I don't open myself up to friendship. I spend a lot of time alone, even when I'm with other people. That changed when I came here. You, your brother, your sister…the other residents of Cailkirn. This is a good place, Rock."

"I've always thought so."

"I want children and I don't want to worry if that changes the shape of my perfectly proportioned figure."

Oh, hell. His whole body went *twang* at the idea of her having his child.

He settled down beside her, took her laptop from unresisting fingers and placed it on the coffee table with the tray, then pulled Deborah sideways into his lap, kissing the side of her neck. "Want to make a memory to erase the one of my stupidity after the last time we made love in here?"

"I thought you had to work."

"You're hell on my schedule, beauty." He smiled.

She didn't.

He kissed her, lingering until she kissed him back. Then he spoke against her lips. "But you're good for *me*."

"That's what Carey and Marilyn said."

"This time, they're right."

Neither of them spoke again for a long time.

CHAPTER TWENTY-TWO

Rock was livid when he got off the phone with Elaine Morganstein two days after reconnecting physically with Deborah. He'd been pissed before speaking to the director, after getting the report from the security agency he hired, but talking to the Hollywood barracuda had just made him angrier.

Didn't his hot stuff have a single person in her life besides him and his siblings who had her back?

He found her in the barn, talking to his Percheron mare, Amanda.

"Life just doesn't feel fair sometimes, you know?" she asked the horse, feeding her a carrot. "Then you probably *don't* know. I think life might be a lot easier as a horse."

"In a good home, you're probably right," he said, laying his hand on Deborah's shoulder.

She jumped. "I didn't know anyone else was in here."

"I just got here. I was looking for you."

"Well you found me."

"I did," he acknowledged. "Talking to my horses."

"Just to Amanda. Orion is a bit too intimidating, but I gave him a carrot too. I didn't want him to feel slighted."

Rock laughed. "He probably would have, too, and made me pay for it the next time I went to saddle him."

Deborah turned and looked up at Rock. "Why were you looking for me?" She moved closer. "Or can I guess?"

"If you guessed that, you'd be wrong. This time."

She went to step back. "Oh, well—"

He grabbed her, keeping her close. "That doesn't mean I'm not open to it."

"But you wanted something else."

Tension filled Rock as he remembered his conversation with her executive producer. "Why didn't you tell me Elaine threatened your role in the film if you didn't get me to invest in the movie?"

"So, you called her?"

"I did."

"What did you decide to do?"

"Invest, but that's not what I want to talk about right now."

She met his gaze, her eyes dark and serious. "I didn't tell you because my career isn't your responsibility. I did my best to bring in other investors."

"You did a damn fine job of it too."

Her lips twisted. "I don't think Art and Ms. Morganstein were as impressed."

"Those two can shove it up their assess and sit a while."

Deborah's eyes went wide, her mouth opening and then laughter spilled out. "I can't believe you said that."

He shook his head. "You're too independent for your own good. You know that?"

"Because I refused to use you the way you worried about? I don't think so."

"I was furious when Elaine told me the threat she'd made against you."

Rock loved the way Deborah's body just naturally relaxed into his. "I was pretty mad myself when she made it."

"She's probably regretting both making the threat and telling me about it right now," he surmised.

"Why? Did it change your mind about investing?" Deborah asked, sounding not so much worried as curious.

She really *didn't* expect him to fix her problems. Too bad for her, that was in his DNA when it came to the people he loved. And he did love her.

No point in denying the inevitable.

If nothing else, discovering what he had today made him realize just how deeply he cared about the woman who turned him on like no other, but more importantly managed to touch a part of his soul he'd thought dead.

"I told her that since she valued the investment that much, she could make a few concessions for getting it. You're being listed as producer right under her, and will have two more scenes to direct, making you a solid contributing director on the movie with acknowledgement in the credits and directorial credit on IMBD for the movie."

Deborah's eyes widened, her mouth opening, but nothing came out.

"Cat got your tongue, hot stuff?"

"You? Why? How?"

"Me. Yes. Why? Because somebody has to have your back. How? I'm a very good negotiator."

"I'd say so." She just stared up at him for several long, silent seconds.

Then she reached up and cupped his face, that single connection with her hand sending warmth through his whole body.

She licked her lips in unconscious provocation, her expression saying she wasn't thinking about sex right now. Or even kissing. But she was looking at him. Like he was some kind of hero.

Rock liked it. A lot.

"Thank you," she said on a soft sigh. "I didn't expect that."

"I get that, but you might as well get used to it. I'm not going anywhere, beauty."

She looked away, toward his mare. "I want to believe you."

"But it's hard after so many people have let you down?"

"So many?"

"Your family makes three, four if you count your stuck-up prig of a brother-in-law."

"How did you know he was a prig?"

"The security company did dossier on all your family members."

"Why? You really think my parents are behind someone cutting the brakes in your car?"

"Yes."

"But..." She clearly wanted to argue but was smart enough to realize they were as likely as anyone.

And because of what Rock now knew, they were at the top of his suspect list. "Your father is running for a city council position. It's not national politics, but it's big enough to make him care a lot about how his children appear."

"He's always cared."

"But not enough to act on it before now."

"You sure he has?"

"Your father's campaign fixer made a trip to Los Angeles two months ago."

"He has a campaign fixer? He didn't come to see me."

"No, he was in town learning about you, assessing your potential for benefit or damage to your father's political aspirations."

"How can you know that?"

"He met with people."

"Like who?"

"Like Art and Ms. Morganstein. Your father offered funding for the movie if they fired you from the cast. He has no idea this would be your production and directorial debut."

"They had to have said no. I'm still the female lead."

"That's one of the reasons I went easy on them when I found out that Elaine threatened your job to try to force you into pressuring me to invest."

"Getting me recognizable production and editorial credit was going easy on them?"

"Oh, yes." She needed to know he wasn't a very nice man, so she wouldn't be shocked by his ruthless nature later.

Deborah's lovely face showed no signs of disgust at his assurance. Instead, she smiled. "Thank you."

He wasn't sure what she was thanking him for, but he kissed her in response anyway. "You're welcome. For whatever."

Her melodious laugh filled the air around them. "I like having you on my side."

"I'll always be there."

"You keep making these grandiose promises."

"And you have a hard time believing anyone will stick with you no matter what."

"Would you? Even if I wanted to go back to Hollywood? Even if I wanted to make another movie, or try for a part on television?"

"Yes. We'd make it work." They wouldn't be able to live in Alaska year-round, but they'd figure something out because he wasn't letting her go and he wasn't ever going to allow anyone to make her give up her dreams.

Not even him.

"You really mean that, don't you?"

"I can see why you have a hard time accepting that, but yes, I do."

"You keep implying you know about the people who have let me down."

"Maybe not all, but enough." He didn't want to tell her about what he'd discovered before calling Elaine, but Rock wasn't going to lie to Deborah. "There's a new story in the tabloids."

"There's always a new story in those scandal sheets."

"It's about you. And me."

Deborah tried to pull away. "What? No. I didn't talk to any

reporters."

"Settle down, hot stuff. I never said you did, but someone did. A producer from one of your early projects."

Deborah paled. "I know who you're talking about."

"He claimed you offered your body in exchange for a bigger part on the film."

She didn't look surprised, heartbroken more like. "Everyone will believe it. Even if it's not true. He's a big name and I'm a nobody by Hollywood standards."

"He tried something on, didn't he? And you turned him down?"

"Yes, how did you know?" She sucked in a breath and let it out in stuttering gasps. "Why do you believe me?"

"Because you don't lie, hot stuff. You would never exchange your body for a part, or a location for your latest movie."

"Is that what they're saying? That I'm having sex with you so you'll let us use Jepsom Acres? Is everyone ignoring the fact your brother is in the film too?"

"Yes, to both. I've already instructed my lawyer to file a defamation suit against both the tabloid and the producer."

"But...you can't throw away money on something like that. Those papers are used to law suits."

"So is the law firm on retainer for me."

"You don't care what they say about you."

"No, I don't."

"But you're still spending tens of thousands of dollars to sue them."

"Yes."

"Because you care what they say about me?" she asked, her voice infused with wonder.

"I know you're used to the people who should have your back letting you down, but if it is within my power, and most things are, that is never going to be me."

"I'm beginning to appreciate your arrogance."

"Just beginning? I'd say you appreciate the hell out of me, hot stuff." Even if she was holding back on the trust.

He understood. He'd had his own demons to slay in that regard.

She offered a small chuckle then snuggled into him, her body showing the trust her mind hadn't yet accepted.

Deborah and Art blocked one of the scenes she was going to direct. She enjoyed having creative input and the behind-the-scenes preparations, but her mind was stuck on the conversations she and

Rock had had. First in the barn and then later at dinner with his siblings, where he'd shared his investigator's belief that Deborah's father's campaign fixer was the one to turn the tabloids onto the story about her and even dug up her former producer to spout his old bile.

Rock's investigators had found links between the two, which had shocked Deborah at first. It seemed counter intuitive if her father didn't want her embarrassing him for his fixer to hold her up for public vilification.

However, it was Marilyn who pointed out that a politician *graciously* accepting his wayward daughter back into the fold was probably going to gain more points with his conservative constituents than one with semi-successful Hollywood actor for a daughter. His attempt to buy her out of a job hadn't worked, now he was trying to make her such an embarrassment that the principles wouldn't want Deborah's name associated with their movie.

He hadn't counted on Rock though.

Not even a little bit.

And Deborah was beginning to accept she *could.* In every way.

"Deborah, do you have a minute?"

Looking up from the tape line she'd placed, Deborah found Ms. Morganstein standing near Art.

She'd done her best to avoid the producer the last few days, not anywhere near forgiving the older woman for the stunt she'd pulled.

"Art and I were going over the blocking for this scene," Deborah hedged.

"We're pretty much done here. You can take ten." Art gave Ms. Morganstein a reassuring pat on her shoulder that Deborah didn't understand.

The older woman tugged at her suit jacket, though it wasn't out of place. "Yes, well, let's take a walk."

Deborah followed the other woman silently, waiting to hear what she had to say without any sense of urgency. She no longer had the least inclination to follow in Elaine Morganstein's footsteps, not if meant treating people like crap when things got tough.

"I owe you a deep and sincere apology," Ms. Morganstein said as they got out of earshot of the others.

"I agree."

The producer nodded. "Yes, well, I expect you do. What I don't expect is for you to understand, but I'll explain anyway. It's the least I owe you."

"Okay."

"This movie is very personal and very important to Art and

myself."

"I knew that."

"What you may not know is why."

"I know about Art's son."

Suddenly, Ms. Morganstein looked about ten years older. "He was my son too. An indiscretion with Art Gamble early in my career, during a time when I wasn't prepared to be a parent. I had the baby but gave him to Art and his then wife to raise."

Shock coursed through Deborah. She'd never expected something like that. "No one even whispers that you've had a child."

"No one knows. I went abroad to give birth. It was all very Victorian, and necessary, I thought."

"Now you don't?"

"Now, I grieve every day for the life we lost twenty years ago to prejudice that has never been even remotely adequately eradicated. My son took his own life at the tender age of fifteen because he thought he could never be happy being gay. His so-called friends, teachers, so many, including myself, let him down."

"You told him you didn't approve?" Somehow Deborah couldn't see it.

"I never even told him I was his mother! I would have told him he was fine the way he was, if I'd had the chance. If I'd taken the chance. Me not being in William's life was always my choice, not Art's. He would have shared our son with me, but I thought my career was too important. That I was going to change the world with my movies."

"You have."

"I've also allowed something very precious to be destroyed because of my tunnel vision."

"So, you were going to make this movie, no matter what it took."

"Yes. Tunnel vision again. And I hurt you with it."

"You did."

"I am genuinely sorry. I can't tell you how much. Art and I both feel we let William down. This movie was to be our path to redemption."

"I think redemption in this case comes from forgiving yourselves." Deborah found it was easy to forgive the other woman, now she knew the story.

She still didn't want to be like her, but Deborah could accept that people made poor choices when motivated by grief and guilt.

"I let my son down. How do I forgive that?"

"By acknowledging you aren't perfect, by trying to be a better person now."

"I failed at that one."

"No. You hurt me. You said things that should never have been said between a producer and an actor, but you haven't failed at humanity. You also apologized. If you didn't mean it, I'd feel differently, but I can tell that you do."

"I do."

"So, the only thing left is to forgive yourself."

"My son would have been lucky to have a friend like you."

"Thank you."

"Carey is very lucky to have the family he does, to have made a friend of you. His life will be so different than the one my son lived in his short fifteen years."

Deborah wasn't going to confirm that Carey was gay until he chose to come out officially, but she said, "Carey's a lot more like his brother than you'd think."

"I've noticed. The longer we've been in Alaska, that boy has shown more of his true nature and it's making his acting even more brilliant."

"It has."

"You're amazing in female lead. You know that, don't you, Deborah? And I was wrong to say you might not be suited for the other side of the camera. You brought in investors I thought would never even consider the project. Art says your instincts for directing are strong too. You can take your career down whatever path you like from here."

"I'm going to take it to Anchorage and local theater." Saying the words to someone besides Rock, made them feel more real.

She wondered if they felt real to him. Deborah wasn't the only one with trust issues, but all at once she knew, deep inside where it counted, that she and Rock were going to find their way through to the other side.

What they had was too important not to fight for it.

She told Rock and his siblings about her conversation with Ms. Morganstein that evening over the dinner table.

"That poor woman," Marilyn said.

"She made her choices," Rock said implacably.

"But she's not responsible for what happened to William," Carey protested.

Rock surprised them all when he agreed. "No, she's not." He looked around at all their surprised faces and frowned. "I still think an apology doesn't begin to make up for the way she treated Deborah."

"But she and Art refused when my father tried to buy my dismissal from the movie," Deborah reminded him.

"When they had an angel investor who had already stipulated no other money people could get involved with the project."

Deborah hadn't thought about that.

"Still," Carey said. "I mean, they're not bad people."

"Would you feel that way if you were the one they threatened?" Rock asked.

Carey shrugged. "You don't think they tried?"

"Ms. Morganstein told me they needed this location, so your job was safe."

"That's not the story she tried to give me, but I wasn't raised by a pushover." He gave his brother a jaunty look. "I channeled big brother here and told her good luck getting rid of me."

Marilyn gave her brother an exaggerated look. "I'm impressed, Carey."

"Don't sound so shocked to be," he snarked back.

"You two." Rock shook his head. "Are you ever going to just get along?"

"We get along fine. We like teasing each other," Carey said as he dished up a second helping of roasted cauliflower.

Rock turned to Deborah to say something else when her phone rang. She didn't usually bring it to the table, but she'd wanted to be available to the last potential investor who had not yet made up his mind.

But this ringtone wasn't the generic one, it was her sister calling.

She looked at the others apologetically as she got up. "Sorry, I'll take this in the other room."

"No need," Rock said.

Carey nodded, spearing his vegetables with his fork. "Yeah, we're all family. Take it here."

Marilyn just made an *answer it already* motion with her hand toward the ringing phone.

Deborah swiped and put the phone to her ear. "Hello, Alicia."

"Deborah, I'm so sorry. If I'd found out earlier, I would have called. You've got to watch out."

"What? What am I watching out for?"

"Dad. He hired some fixer guy to help with his campaign for city council. He's got ideas about working his way into national politics."

"That sounds like him."

"Well, the fixer is going to try make trouble for you so you'll move back from Los Angeles and start *behaving the way a dutiful daughter should* and I'm quoting Dad on that."

"He's already tried, but I'm not letting a few tabloid articles make me tuck tail and run."

"It's worse than that, I overheard them talking. The fixer has someone on the inside of your movie production, someone who I guess already tried to make you have an accident. You're okay, right? You would have called if you'd been hurt, wouldn't you? Why didn't you call when you had the accident?"

"Wait a minute, Dad was behind that?"

"Him and this fixer guy, yes."

"And you called to warn me?"

"Of course. I would have called earlier, but I didn't know."

Alicia had said that already, now it was sinking in. Deborah's younger sister was standing up against their parents' wishes, for Deborah's sake.

"Tell me you're fine," Alicia demanded. "The fixer was mad about the accident."

"Why?"

"Because it didn't work."

"No, it didn't. I'm fine and so is everyone else who was in the car with me."

"There were other people in the car? Those bastards! It's not bad enough Dad would go after his own daughter, but not to care about collateral damage. Yes, he'll be a fine politician," Alicia said with more bitterness and sarcasm than Deborah had ever heard from her younger sister.

"Alicia, do you mind if I put you speaker phone. Rock's going to want to hear all this."

"Rock, that guy you told me about the last time we talked?"

"Yes."

"Is it serious then?"

"Yes."

"Good! You deserve somebody special who really loves you."

"I'm beginning to believe that."

"Well, you should. You're the only person in my life who loves me for me, you know that?"

"Considering I never thought I had anyone who loved me that way, yes I can believe that."

"I'm sorry." Alicia made a sound suspiciously like a sob.

"You're my big sister and I've always loved you, but I was terrified of losing Mom and Dad. I saw how they just cut you out of their life for making *one* decision they didn't agree with. I wasn't strong enough to face the same rejection. Not then anyway."

CHAPTER TWENTY-THREE

" That sounds like you want to do something you don't think they'll approve of."

"I'm going back to work. I already told Robert. He wasn't happy at first, but he came around."

"Wow, I'm impressed."

"Thanks. It's time I started making my own choices. Look, I didn't call to talk about me. Put me on speaker so I can tell Rock what I told you."

So, that was what Deborah did and her sister told Rock and the rest of them about a conversation she overheard between the fixer and their father. Not only did the fixer have someone who was working on the movie on his payroll, he had plans to do more tabloid damage to Deborah.

"He doesn't know about the lawsuit I already filed against them. He's not going to find such an eager audience the next time around," Rock said.

"No, I don't think he knows about it. Who are you suing?" Alicia asked.

Rock told her.

"Couldn't you include the fixer in the defamation suit? That would spike Dad's guns for sure."

"We need proof that he was part of the conspiracy to defame Deborah."

"Would a recording of the conversation he had with my dad be enough?"

"You recorded it?" Deborah asked with shock and some hope.

"Not right at the beginning, but I got enough there's no question what he's up to."

"Because the car accident would get him arrested for attempted murder."

"Oh, yes. I like that. I'll send you the file right now."

"Does Robert know you're calling me?" Deborah asked, concerned. Her brother-in-law lived her dad's pocket.

"No. He'll find out soon enough though."

"Will you be safe?" Rock asked.

"It doesn't matter," Alicia said, her voice only quavering a little. "I've spent enough time being silent on what matters to me. I'm not going to be any more."

"Listen, I want you and your children safe. It's not important to me that you tell Robert you're on my side," Deborah said, feeling desperation well inside.

If they would engineer an accident for her, what would they do to Alicia, who was right there? In their grasp?

"I'm going arrange for my security people to send a team to pick you and the children up. We won't turn the tape over to authorities here until you are safely on a plane headed for Alaska."

"You want me to come to Cailkirn?" she asked, hope sounding in her voice.

"If you'd like."

"I would. I really don't think either Dad or Robert is going to be okay with me standing up for Deborah. I don't know what they'll do."

"Better to be safe than in harm's way."

"Okay. I'll be looking for your security team."

Rock got up and went to speak to the head of the security team that were now living and working on Jepsom Acres.

Deborah finished the call with her sister and then stared down at the table, an inexplicable urge to cry assailing her.

"She loves you," Carey said perceptively. "That can be hard to take when you've spent a long time wondering."

"Like you ever had to wonder," Marilyn scoffed.

"I didn't know if you and Rock would accept me being gay."

"Then you don't know us very well."

"Don't be like that to your brother, Marilyn. He was scared. Give him a break."

Marilyn jumped up and went around the table to hug Carey. "I love you, you big idiot."

"Love you back, pest."

"And my sister loves me." Hot tears tracked down Deborah's cheeks and she did nothing to stop them.

"So does our brother, if you hadn't noticed," Carey said in that *duh* tone he'd perfected so well.

"I think that's something I need to hear from him."

"I'm not sure how many ways I can say it before you'll believe me," Rock said from the doorway to the dining room.

Deborah stood up from the table, drawn to him by an invisible and inexorable band. She stopped in front of him. "I wasn't aware of you saying it even one way?"

"If I didn't love you, would I be willing to live in Los Angeles?"

"You'd move for her?" Carey asked, awed. "You really do love her."

"That's enough from the peanut gallery. Let's go talk about this somewhere more private."

Deborah nodded, ignoring the protests of the younger siblings, who were clearly enjoying the exchange.

Rock took Deborah by the hand and led her outside and in the direction of the land the film crew had been told to stay off of. "Want to see my helicopter?"

"I want to hear how you told me you love me."

"Deborah, I'm letting a whole damn film crew invade my home and property for months. What else would you call it?"

"You're doing that for Carey."

"Am I?"

"Aren't you?"

"Not entirely, not even from the very beginning."

"Oh."

"Yes, oh."

She moved closer, hinting with her body and Rock read her intent, putting his arm around her shoulder, pulling her so near their hips brushed as they walked.

"I believed you when you said you weren't trying to use me for my money."

"You did."

"I did."

"And that was supposed to tell me you loved me?" she asked, a little awed by his masculine obtuseness.

Or was *she* the obtuse one?

"Yes. So was the fact that I couldn't keep my hands off you."

"You're a highly sexual guy."

"Not that virile. I've never had a lover I wanted as often and as much as I want you."

"Sex is not love."

"The way we do it is."

She couldn't disagree. Didn't want to.

"And you protected me, every way you could."

"Like I do with all the people I love, yes."

"You wouldn't let me walk away."

"How could I? You'd take my damn heart with you."

"I love you, too, Rock."

He stopped, grabbed her and pulled her around for a kiss that about melted her socks off. "Say it again, hot stuff."

She smiled up at him, happier than she'd ever been. "I love you, Rock, my Superman."

"I love you, Deborah." He kissed her, sealing his words inside her with his lips until they were both panting, her heart racing in her chest. He kissed along her jaw. "I didn't want to love anyone else, but I can't protect my heart from you."

She could barely believe he was saying these things. That he was making himself as vulnerable as she knew herself to be.

"It's hard to have faith in others when the people you should be able to trust the most betray you. I didn't want to fall for you either. It gave you the power to hurt me."

"And I did that."

She grabbed his shirt, pulling him close. "People hurt each other, Rock. Without meaning to, because life is imperfect. We're going to hurt each other again, but if we love each other, if we trust each other, we're going to find a way through it. And we'll never hurt each other on purpose."

"You're the other half of my soul, hot stuff. Hurting you hurts me. I thought the pain would never go away when we fought."

"But it did. Because we looked for a way to the other side of it."

"You forgave me."

"You admitted you were wrong. That's huge. Do you think my father has admitted he's wrong, even once in his life?"

"No?"

"No. He hurts people all the time and he *never* says he's sorry. When he gets in trouble for hiring the fixit man who arranged with someone to try to incapacitate me through an accident, he's not going to apologize. He's going to make it all my fault."

"Him being a selfish asshole that hurts instead of protecting his daughters is not your fault."

"Thank you. I know that. I do, but having you say it to me. It matters."

"I don't want you quitting Hollywood on my account, Deborah."

He kissed her again, like he couldn't help himself. "I don't."

"I'm not sure my dreams were ever in Hollywood. I love the stage; I think maybe someday I might even manage to start a small community theater here. I could see it being popular with the tourists."

"That couldn't be enough for you and your talent."

"Aren't I the best judge of what's enough for me? For my talent. I want joy, Rock, not fame. Not fortune. Joy."

"I've got enough fortune for the both of us."

She laughed. "Nice to know you see it that way, but I'm not going to be a kept woman."

"That's a pretty old-fashioned term for a modern woman, hot stuff. And when we get married, what's mine is yours. We belong to each other, body and soul and that's what really matters. Not money. Not business success."

"When we get married?"

He dropped to his knees, right there in the Alaskan summer evening, his blond hair glinting in the late sunlight, his sherry eyes shining with purpose and he dug something out of his pocket. It glittered, catching the light.

And Deborah wasn't sure she could breathe. "Is that?"

"A ring? Yes. The diamond is almost as flawless as your heart, beauty. But nothing could be that."

"Oh, man…you don't…that's…" Words would not come.

He lifted the ring toward her, the huge square cut diamond surrounded by a cluster of brown diamonds. "Will you marry me, Deborah? And fill my life with joy for as long as we both shall live?"

"Oh, Rock…" She fell to her knees in front of him, tears sliding wetly down her cheeks, her heart feeling like it wanted to burst out of her chest, it was so full of incandescent joy. "Yes, I'll marry you and we'll fill each other's lives with happiness, and everything else that comes with a true commitment that lasts a lifetime."

The kiss was incendiary after. He took her to a large air hangar about fifty yards from where they had stopped then made love to her on the seat in the back of the resting helicopter.

Afterward, she was snuggled in his lap, naked against him. "I love you, Rock."

"I adore you, my own."

Oh, she liked that. He was hers, too. And that worked. "We're signing a prenuptial agreement. I'm no gold digger."

"Whatever you say, hot stuff."

The prenup was unlike any business document Deborah had ever read. In it, they agreed to kiss each other every day, as often as they liked, to tell each other they loved each other at least every day, to be loving and present parents to their children, to be kind to one another's siblings, to protect one another and to *share* in all their worldly possessions without regard to who brought what to the marriage.

Her father ended up doing only a couple of months in jail and getting community service for his part in trying to hurt Deborah. The fixer gave up his cohort on the movie crew in exchange for a lesser sentence, but still went to prison for two years and the person who had sliced Rock's tires, deleted scenes shot from the hard drive, messed up the hotel reservations and engineered more small mishaps turned out to be the editorial intern.

He had been an easy sell for the fixer, believing a movie about a young man coming of age and coming out should never be made. His homophobia was going to cost him his freedom, for a long time, and his career in Hollywood forever.

Robert surprised everyone by supporting her sister's actions and coming forth with his own testimony about her father's involvement, among other things. The press had a field day. While Dr. Banes would not spend a lot of time in jail, his political aspirations were over.

Deborah's dreams were just beginning. Rock insisted on funding a small community theater right in Cailkirn when Deborah convinced him that was what she was honestly working toward for her own happiness. Marilyn and Carey were thrilled and had already committed to helping with the theater between school terms and their own projects.

Alicia and her family came to visit and returned to attend Deborah and Rock's wedding, as did practically the whole town of Cailkirn.

Rock had found the love of his life and Deborah had found her home and family in Cailkirn, Alaska.